THE SPARK
and other stories

Elspeth Davie's reputation as a short story writer has been growing steadily over the last ten years. Her work has appeared in the *London Magazine*, the *Transatlantic Review*, the *Cornhill Magazine* and many other publications, and short story enthusiasts are already familiar with her unique world of baffled people locked in combat with very ordinary objects that strangely refuse to remain inanimate. It is this sense of the continual dramatic interrelation of people and their 'things' that gives Elspeth Davie's writing its power and consistency, and her observation its humour and compassion.

The eighteen stories in this volume reflect a wide range of mood, from the chilly atmosphere of *Family House*, where five ageing brothers and sisters find their lives brought to a standstill by the accumulated possessions of generations of their ancestors, and break out in revolt, to the wry impudence of the pupil in *Sunday Class* who becomes incensed by the teacher's nagging questions about 'things God wants us to be grateful for', and gives a startling answer.

Elspeth Davie was born in Edinburgh, where she attended university and art college. Her first novel, *Providings*, was a considerable critical success, and she has just completed a second novel. Her husband teaches philosophy at Edinburgh University, and she has one daughter.

THE SPARK

and other stories

ELSPETH DAVIE

JOHN CALDER · LONDON
RIVERRUN PRESS · NEW YORK

Reissued in 1984 in Great Britain by
John Calder (Publishers) Limited
18 Brewer Street, London W1R 4AS

and in the United States of America by
Riverrun Press Inc
175 Fifth Avenue, New York NY 10010

First published 1968 by Calder and Boyars Limited

Copyright © Elspeth Davie 1968, 1984

ALL RIGHTS RESERVED

Some of the stories in this volume were originally published in magazines as
follows: A Private Room, *London Magazine*, 1963; The Spark, *London Magazine*,
1965; Removal, *London Magazine*, 1964; A Conversation on Feet, *Cornhill*, 1961;
Sunday Class, *Transatlantic Review*, 1964; Oven Gloves, *Cornhill*, 1964; The
Eyelash, *Lines* No. 18; A Visit to the Zoo, *New Saltire*, 1961; A Collection of
Bones, *Cornhill*, 1963; A Woman of Substance, *Cornhill*, 1959; Traveller,
Cornhill, 1967.

British Library Cataloguing in Publication Data
Davie, Elspeth
   The spark and other stories.
   I. Title
   823'.914[F]   PR6054.A873

ISBN 0-7145-0538-2

Printed in Great Britain by Unwin Brothers Ltd, Woking.

CONTENTS

A Room of Photos   7

A Private Room   17

Family House   26

The Spark   48

Removal   63

A Conversation on Feet   75

Sunday Class   82

The Siege   86

Oven Gloves   94

Promise   105

A Map of the World   126

Space   143

The Eyelash   153

A Visit to the Zoo   159

A Loaded Bag   168

A Collection of Bones   182

A Woman of Substance   190

Traveller   206

Camera   214

A ROOM OF PHOTOS

DURING the height of summer a couple of pavement photographers stood all day on either side of the main street of a northern town which called itself a holiday centre—a title laboriously built up on the strength of its long, grey strip of north-facing beach and a vast, streamlined bus-station from which people went day-trips to distant and more desirable parts of the coast. At first the two men had seemed to concentrate on spotting and snapping the holiday-makers, but after a bit they gave that up. Cold had levelled out distinctions between inhabitants and tourists except that women holiday-makers, though muffled to the neck, wore white shoes and carried new straw beach-bags, and the men, with a casually freezing air, wore their gabardines and raincoats slung over one shoulder or looped about their necks with their cameras. The photographers now snapped continuously and indiscriminately—one hand making the machine whir, the other dealing out white tickets to the passers-by. Amongst those inhabitants who did not duck or swerve were two young men who amiably accepted the tickets informing them that their photos would be ready late that afternoon if they called at a certain shop. They were not on holiday. The one a draughtsman, the other a research worker in the same laboratory—they had this Saturday morning free. Late in the day, having nothing better to do, they presented themselves at the counter of a small shop not far from the photographers' stance.

"No, not ready yet," said the girl. "Maybe twenty minutes—half-an-hour. Do you want to wait ?"

Behind her the whole of one wall was filled with a squared-off pattern of portrait heads, overlaid with a central fan-shaped arrangement in smaller, snapshot sizes. The girl was used to people shifting their eyes from hers to study this wall as though intent on finding a better face than her own. She had stopped competing with faces. Her nails were brilliant, and she wore two jingling bangles and a glittering green ring. The two young men sat down on a bench near the entrance. On either side of the doorway, and visible from a long distance down the street because of the great swirls of ectoplasmic whiteness which came from them, were long, luminous strips of wedding photos side by side with the darker shapes of young men and women in gowns holding degrees and diplomas in tubular boxes.

"I once saw a photographer's shop in a seaside town where every one of the wedding couples had been made to pose with their heads together," said the younger of the two men on the bench.

"What's odd about it?" said the other.

"You haven't got me. I don't mean just close together. I mean actually touching. The way you see two big melons side by side in a greengrocer's window."

"Cheek to cheek?"

"Not exactly. Temple to temple's more like it. I looked at every one and the window was full of them. They were all absolutely identical." The other was silent for a moment contemplating this. He said: "Then I suppose the man would demand that they did this. I suppose if anyone actually refused he would go across and place the heads together."

"I suppose so."

"What if they fell apart—rolled away from one another as the melons might?"

"He'd go over and knock the heads together most likely. Bang them together with his two bare hands."

His friend failed to smile, but after a pause said: "Do you think there's something cruel about the professional photographer?"

"That's going a bit far. There might be with some, of course."

"This particular one had a streak of it, don't you think?"

"Maybe he had. But where do you think the particular cruelty lay?"

"Well, he never considered the future. Or worse still, he did think of it. It was in his mind all the time he was clicking coldly away, but he ignored it. He laughed it off."

The other threw up his hands and stared around, exclaiming: "Well! Which would you say was the cynic? You or he? You with your talk of the future!"

"I don't agree. The man had a responsibility—asking, demanding they should pose in a certain way."

"A certain way? Aren't you making it sound indecent? This was not pornography, you know."

"No, but he insisted on the pose—and the smile too. I take it they were all smiling?"

"Every one of them."

"The point is he never looked at the past or the future or anything happening in the air around them. I'll bet he never actually looked at them either. All he thought of was just this bit of the forehead here. A gimmick for the window!"

"Yes, you may well tap your head. Aren't you beginning to rave?" His friend got up and started to roam around the walls where the larger framed portraits were hanging. The girl had retreated to a back office and was flipping through files of faces, her own slightly more scornful. And now the second man was on his feet, following the other in a scrutiny of each photo.

"What on earth are we looking for?" he exclaimed as be bent close to the wall. "Have you noticed this is how everyone looks at photos—this minute inspection that's seldom given to paintings or even to flesh and blood persons—a close study of the eyes, often as not a comparing of eyes and mouth, a glance at the set of the ears, a quick look to ascertain the shape of nose and probably a second or two's mental twisting to imagine the profile from all the rest? It's the same with albums. People lift the book right up to their eyes to study in silence the faces of absolute strangers. Well, look at them round the door!"

"A veil and bouquet can always draw crowds."

"Maybe. But in the end they come up close and stare right into the eyes. And what a desperate look it is! Are they hoping to get a message? To glean some information? Or just to make contact?" He disengaged himself from the wall and stood with his hands over his eyes for a moment.

"What are you doing?"

"Trying to think what it is I'm looking for. Because I'm looking *for*, not at. I'm trying to spot something. But I haven't a clue. Am I, for instance, trying to spot happiness or unhappiness? A quick look when they're off guard."

"Off guard? In front of a camera?"

"Off guard to me, though, and to the people at the shop window. We have time to stare right through the surface of these eyes, closer and closer, as though penetrating to the back of the skull. Would you dare to scrutinize a living eye like that? Who would? Only a specialist probing with his light in the dark room, eye to eye, knee to knee with the patient, would take such a look."

"Supposing, then, that we're all desperate to spot some emotion in these photos. To take it, as it were, by chance. Off guard. And what then? Supposing you think you spot something. What do you do with it?"

"You match it up with yourself, I should think. Have they got something you haven't got, for instance? Or do you spot a lack in them? Something you've got that they haven't."

The girl entered from the back room with an armful of white faces—faces in vertical strips, in horizontal strips, in rectangular mounts, in patterns of six and twelve. She let the faces drop on the counter where they splayed out—a great, irregular fan stamped with grey and white ovals. Amongst them she found a few street photos which she hung up around the counter. Theirs was not in the pile.

"If you two gentlemen would prefer to call again they should be here for you in about fifteen minutes." For answer the pair of them went back to their bench smiling, and the girl, impatiently back into the inner room.

"Did you notice the slightest pause before 'gentlemen' there?" said the older man. "And no wonder. Can you think of anything less gentle than going round gaping at these exposed faces— thrusting one's head in, prying, discarding, sniggering?"

"No, you exaggerate. The look was almost clinical, as you said yourself. A search simply. I've no more wish to laugh—staring into the human eye—than your specialist. Can you imagine the surgeon smiling at what he sees at the back of the eye?"

A middle-aged woman had entered from the street and now stood at the counter with her ticket, waiting to be noticed by the girl in the room beyond. At last her look was returned, her ticket matched with the strip of photos laid before her.

"Oh dear!" said the woman, bending her head. "But what can have happened there?"

10

"Sometimes it's like that if you happen to be in a slant of reflected sun," said the girl briskly. "You see, you must have been walking there beside that shop window just as the sun struck it."

"Sun? Was there really sun that day?" murmured the woman as though surprised, but glad to hear it.

"I shouldn't think so," called one of the young men from the bench. "But there would be light, of course. We still have light in this town. I would never think myself of calling it sunlight."

"Well, certainly, you'd think I'd have remembered the sun," said the woman politely, turning round. "I mean it's not like the continent here. Last time I was here for ten days and I had ten minutes sun. I suppose you could say I'm sort of trained up never to miss a moment. And particularly when you're by yourself you miss nothing."

"Where exactly were you when it happened, if you don't mind me asking?" said the young man.

"Well, actually I was in a bus going to another beach," said the woman apologetically. "But I didn't grudge it to the others. And after all I still got it through glass."

"Often warmer through glass," said the young man.

This word recalled her to the counter, and she turned back eagerly again to examine the photos as though in the interval they might have changed for the better. But the young men had to witness an even worse disappointment. It was different from staring at portraits on the wall, and they were surprised to feel themselves involved to such a degree with this plain woman. They had to turn their heads away in case the disappointment, spreading and deepening every minute, should swallow them up.

"But I thought that nowadays they had ways of getting over things like that," the woman was murmuring.

"I'm afraid not *always*," said the girl impatiently, tapping her fingers on the glass counter. She had endless arguments with people about their faces, and she had seen the faces fall.

"Well, I suppose I'd better just take them," said the woman, opening her handbag. "This last one is better, isn't it? I was almost out of the sun, reflected light, or whatever it was."

The girl said nothing. She was putting them into a long envelope. On her way out the woman nodded to the young men, glanced into a small mirror behind them, and left, pressing the envelope and the handbag flat against her stomach.

"Oh thank God!" exclaimed the draughtsman. "Thank God she's gone! The difference between the coming-in and the going-out! Is it quite fair to onlookers—letting your face drop to that extent? Did she have to see herself so clearly? Wouldn't a mirror do after all?"

"Oh, she knows her face all right. But this is different. Something—man or camera—had chosen her out. She was chosen, actually looked at. It makes the face something again—gives it a hope that it's utterly different from the mirror one."

"Well then, she must learn not to walk in patches of reflected sun, that's all."

They sat still, staring in front of them until the girl came from the inner room with an armful of street-photos and began to hook them up on the space behind them. They had to duck their heads while she did it, and finally screwed them round to stare at the finished wall.

"You notice there are no deformities amongst this lot," said the draughtsman, "and yet the street's full of them. At least half-a-dozen have gone past since we've been sitting here. Well, where are they? Is it just chance or design? Does the camera decide there's no money to be made with crutches—that one-legged holiday-makers don't want photos of themselves?"

"Well, would you?"

"Why not? Have you never heard of hunchbacks who were proud of their fine eyes, or cripples who were dandies? That's the cruelty of the camera for you."

"Or the tact."

"Tact! Would you care to hear the thing stop whirring as you went by?"

They sat, staring before them again at the wall of portraits. The elder man exclaimed: "But oh, the fantastic difference between these people here and the ones you find in albums at the back of old drawers!"

"Are they so different, though—apart from the clothes?"

"Haven't you noticed how even our grandparents managed to look tragic in photos—those great, dark eyes, pleading, under swishy hats, plump arms lying limp and melancholy across a lap all glistening with black jet tears. Even the men—sombrely stoical, arms crossed over a solid heart. Even our fathers and mothers could get away with a hint of this in their young days—

12

but not for long. And now it's all over. People feel ashamed to look tragic any more."

"What? You're not saying no one has reason to feel tragic nowadays?"

"Oh feel—yes! Besides, who's to gauge someone else's tragedy? Perhaps my plump grandmother had plenty. What about the deaths of children? But to stand alone and be snapped, muffled up in tragedy, feathered in it. No, it can't be done."

"At any rate I'm glad you mention plumpness and tragedy in the same breath. People can grow fat with grief. I suppose you know that?"

"Oh, people can eat their way out sometimes. If they've got the food. No, it's standing alone, as I say, and showing it that's over. Sorrow pasted into an album. All finished."

"For ever?"

"For as long as we're likely to remember."

They got up and stood at the open door for a while staring up and down the street. And now their eyes seemed suddenly drawn to all the exuberant heads and figures which were drawn slowly past on the sides of buses, gesticulated from huge, corner hoardings, or were pasted across shop windows—ecstatic girls holding up babies, smiling blondes brushing their teeth, soaping their backs, redheads showing off suspender belts, greyheads holding up pills and polish. The gleam of gargantuan smiles surrounded them.

"Rapturous women," said the young man. "They'll always be around, polishing up rocket windows without having to rub."

"But the photos—" said the other, going back into the room. "What became of the big, tragic eyes? What made them finally quit?"

Great buses trundling past cut off part of the answer.

"Did you say tragedy could be fat?"

His friend now shut the door of the shop, turned and came over to the bench again.

"I said this idea that tragedy could be fat went out suddenly, became unpopular. Even that it might conceivably be well turned out or handsome began to have a perverse sound to it."

"Yet why should a bit of extra padding in flesh or cloth mean anguish must be counted out? Unjust in a way, isn't it?"

"Maybe it is. But people's eyes changed focus suddenly. One

13

day newspapers, films, photos, still seemed fairly normal. Even the horrors were the expected ones, so to speak. Then suddenly, almost accidentally, at the cinema between the shot of a pair of beauty queens getting out of uniform and a Donald Duck cartoon, they're looking at this stretch of scabrous ground covered with slow-moving skeletons. Sexless people—hairless, no flesh, and showing those deep, shining muscles in their arms and legs that nobody'd ever seen outside an anatomy book. One or two seem actually to smile at the camera. And they are alive. Isn't it a relief, almost, at the next shot, to see the corpses? Only two shots—the living and the dead, and almost identical, except that the last are piled up on one another, and don't move. Well, that was it. A flash, like something gone momentarily wrong with the reel before it adjusts itself and clicks round from obscene to normal again. But in that time the eyes watching had gone through a change as though something in the lens had altered. After that all photos must be judged differently. The camera begins to stall at the tragedienne and the hero. Padded emotions go out. Some of the fat melted out of tragedy overnight."

"And the big, dark eyes, the loopy heads?"

"Can you imagine the neck gradually stiffening up when presented with those film shots—how the head would try to move back from what the eyes saw, and at the same time resist this movement? Your loopy photo heads stiffened up too . . ."

"Oh no, *please!*" The girl came racing through from the inner room and flung back the door of the shop. "Would you mind *please* keeping it open! If you have to wait here would you please not try to change *anything* around this place!" She went into a frenzy of activity, straightening photos on the walls, squaring up the piles on the counter, and taking quick short steps back and forth in front of the others to show up the laziness of their crossed legs and empty hands.

"Well, as the loopy-necked girl steps back out of the picture . . ." went on the young man.

"What's that?" The girl spun round towards them as though pivoted on a deadly insult.

"Not you . . . not you . . ." said the young man, waving his arms.

"Really!" exclaimed the girl, glaring over her shoulder as she clicked back into the inner room again.

"As the tragic-eyed girl and the hero-stoic make their exit from photo-frames, the camera goes searching on. As though making up for missing real tragedies, for all the sham sorrows set up decades ago against phoney backgrounds—now it closes in, licking up horrors with a vengeance. The distant scream isn't enough—it's got to show the teeth and tongue of that scream, and if it's a yawn —the larynx of that yawn. It misses nothing—slides between kisses and tracks the tears from eyes to chin. Every rib-bone of famine is counted, the black bullet-holes in heads pin-pointed."

"Well, there are no horrors here, no deformities even, as you said yourself. The faces round these walls look blank enough."

"Oh here! This little hole and corner shop! These are simply for private view. They're still catering for albums and piano-tops. The faces I'm talking about are hoarding faces—heads where it takes you minutes to walk past from one ear to the other, or the money-making faces that cover magazines and stretch across newspaper folds—crying faces, yelling, laughing, fainting—dead faces! The camera had to peer down into beds and graves for these."

"They're here now," said the girl, coming in from the back and putting a strip of four photos on the counter. The young men sauntered across and one of them bent down to study it.

"Well, what do you see?" said the other. "Have we walked through a shaft of sunlight? Don't tell me the heads are blurred."

"They're all right," said his friend, carrying them over to the door for closer inspection.

"Let's see." They studied their own faces together—each with a thumb on the strip. Standing very still, they stared close and long.

"Go on then," said the younger man at last. "You've commented on every other face around here. What would you say about these?"

"Would you mind very much paying me now," said the girl from the counter. "It's just that I haven't got all day. This isn't a holiday for me, you know."

"Just coming. Well then—one word to describe these. We're not allowed tragic faces, are we? You wouldn't call them that?"

The other stared intently. "No. Like it, though. Terribly like it."

"What then? Is it guilt?"

15

"More a sort of blankness. These faces have got something all the others have around here."

"Oh rot! What absolute rubbish! I'm not to ally myself with albums and piano-lids any more than you are. Look here—you're staring at your own face, man. Is that all you can say about it? A sort of blankness! Come on. One word. Is it curiosity? Bitterness? Restlessness? Is it fear?"

His friend looked again, long and hard. "No, it's boredom. Plain, common or garden boredom."

"Well, I'm sorry, I can't wait," said the girl. "If you want them you'd better come back Monday morning."

"Boredom? You're speaking for yourself?"

"No, you too. And all those round the walls. The prevailing look—blank and glassy. The wedding pairs have it, very thin-laid. But take a look at some of those behind you. Staring through a positive myopic lens of boredom. Impenetrable boredom! Encased in it."

He returned the strip to the counter, paid, and took the narrow envelope.

"Sorry if we kept you waiting," he said. "Do you never get tired of this job? You must get bored in that little room in there, shuffling faces. You said you didn't want anything changed around here, but I bet you could see those faces far enough!"

The girl gave him a look, turned without a word and went into the room at the back.

"Well, what do you intend to do about the boredom, if that's what it is?" said the young man who was still over at the door. "Starting with yourself—what will you do?"

"I'll smash through somehow," said his friend.

They stood for a moment longer looking out, and then barged through into the street. The door crashed shut behind them. "Idiot!" exclaimed the younger man. "Is *that* all you can do? You might have smashed that glass! And didn't she say she wanted it kept open?"

The girl had come running from the inner room and they looked back to see her staring after them through the long pane of the door. Still swinging under the impact, the white wedding-groups and the young men and women with their tight-rolled degrees formed a restless and dislocated frame for her face.

16

A PRIVATE ROOM

No MATTER how late it was the child lay awake every night waiting for her aunt to come upstairs to bed. She lay in a room labelled 'Private' to mark it off from the residential part of the hotel, her head under a windowsill on which the heavy black wedge of night sea lay, sparked now and then with slow-moving ships and spotlighted near the shore by the headlights of cars as they came down the steep road and swung slowly round the corner close to the harbour. Sometimes sleep overcame her for a few seconds and she would raise her head with a jerk out of the first crash or flicker of dream and stare across at the other bed. If it was still empty she let her head fall back heavy with relief, but if the woman was there—a great, soft, crimson-quilted mound— she would stealthily draw herself down deeper into bed to smother a stinging pang of disloyalty.

There had been nothing of this on either her first or her second visits. On the third visit, however, they met one hot afternoon in the corridor outside the bedroom marked 'Private'. The hotel was very silent. The aunt had a handkerchief in her hand and gave the white letters a flick as she let the child go by. "Would you believe," she said, "that when I go past that door there I'm so utterly different they wouldn't know me; not a soul would credit it—the way I am once I get myself through that door. It's shocking, isn't it, to think that of all the hundreds I've had through my hands not one of them has an inkling of what I'm really like? It's a thing that gives you a turn as you get older, I can tell you. And to think there's just nobody behind that door to share the shock or even to give one a second thought!" She gave

17

it another contemptuous flick and went on her way.

The girl looked at her aunt more curiously during the next few days as she moved around downstairs about the public rooms of the hotel. She had never seen much of this aunt who considered it enough that her brother's child should have the run of the place for ten days of the summer plus the company of any children who happened to come and go during that time. She was a large woman and she walked with a stately, corseted dignity down the long corridor which led from bar to lounge, turning her head slowly to left and right so that she could see through the glass doors into the dining-room, the television room and the writing-room. When she bent to remove anything from the small tables in the lounge the long string of amber beads slid and rattled recklessly on the polished surface, but her own movements were more cautious as though the powerful elastic in which she was contained might snap if she allowed herself to unbend too low or often to her guests. Her hair, yellowish-white at the parting, was dyed dark brown and set at the back of her head in rigid waves which she would finger as she talked.

"Have you been up the West Cliff road yet?" she would ask in her flat voice a dozen times a day or more in the high season. "It's magnificent. You get the view all round the coast from there. And on clear days, of course, you have the mountains behind as well." With eyes expressionless as glass she would smile as she said this, and walk on to prevent any discussion about landscapes. She had heard descriptions and comparisons of landscapes every summer day of her life for the last twenty years. Yet she smiled continually whether she was crushing her way between the tables in the dining-room, handing out keys at the counter or watering the huge brass pots of hydrangea which stood on either side of the door in the entrance hall. Even after a series of the wildest days she still smiled, looking out at the sea from a roomful of guests who were sullenly slipping lower and lower down in their chairs like people gradually giving up hope in the midst of a shipwreck. Above the set smile the irritable eyes, blue and slightly protuberant, dared anyone to complain. And in the last few days whenever she set eyes on her niece it seemed as though she dared her to remember the words she had spoken to her outside the bedroom door.

But the child remembered. She lay at night and thought about her unbending, smiling aunt and whenever her eyelids began to

18

droop she heard like a shout in a dream: "There's nobody behind that door to give one a second thought!" and she would force her eyes open and focus them through the half-light on the photo of her aunt's husband who had died four years ago. He was standing, eyes bright and gleeful, one foot placed high up on a rock. She knew exactly where the rock was on the shore, but all the same, this was no seaside snapshot. He looked like a man posing triumphantly on the summit of some mountain never climbed before. He was not one who would ever close his eyes once such a shout had gone up, and neither would she. They waited together supporting one another by the steadiness of their gaze as long as the light lasted.

The woman who kept the hotel came up to her room every night sometime between eleven o'clock and midnight. Those who were still awake could hear her moving about briskly down below circling the little tables in the bar. Sometimes a paper would rustle, there was a clinking of glass and finally the heavy curtains would be rattled back in the lounge and there was a long silence as she stared out. The wakeful ones in the private bedroom stared painfully with her—saw the dense blackness on her right slowly sharpen into the cruel profile of the western cliff and beneath her, leaning together, the great, rectangular, tombstone rocks from which the sea slowly withdrew, uncovering bits of wood and glass and unidentified objects which rolled and writhed each time the water touched them. On her left, seats were spaced out on the steps of the hotel and sometimes in the darkness great seabirds sat motionless, two on the back of each of the four benches—white-carved, fierce-beaked ornaments—until suddenly the frieze would break into wings and bitter cries and they would circle down one after the other to the rocks below.

At last when the silence became unbearable to the listeners overhead the woman would walk to the switchboard at the foot of the stairs and snap off the downstair lights one by one till all was black below. Then she would slowly mount the stairs pausing every night without fail halfway up. Having climbed these ten stairs to the landing there was nothing else she could be staring at but the huge oil painting which had hung there when the place was a private house and had remained through decades while the hotel changed hands three times. Against a black sky studded with stars stood a fleshy nymph in white gauze, pink-slit from

19

shoulder to waist, supporting her great, rose-tinted breasts on a platter upon which were also heaped apples, melons, peaches, grapes and in the centre a bristling, green-tufted pineapple. A heavy platter—but she held it in her hands with as little trouble as she would balance a saucer on her fingertips. Yet the fruits did not interest her. Her head was flung back towards the sky as though searching for new stars. It seemed likely that it was at this spot in front of this picture between eleven and twelve every night that the smile left the proprietress's face. Along the corridor to her bedroom her footsteps would come slowly, scuffing a little as though she had unfastened her shoes and was already unbending with the release of various buttons and clips in her dress, and the crack of light which appeared on her entrance would be cautiously shut out again as she closed the door silently and prepared for the night.

One night the aunt came up rather earlier than usual. It had been a lashing wet day and hot too so that by evening when at last the rain stopped a heavy steam was rising round the shore, and even from the distance of the hotel the sea was hidden from the visitors. Most of them had gone to bed early, dazed and dis-heartened by this new landscape that had grown up around them —a landscape of endless, grey plains from which the tops of the rocks jutted like standing-stones. It was not ten o'clock and the girl was wide awake when her aunt came in. The heavy breathing and the rustling began and the crunch of springs as the woman leant on the bed to kick off her shoes. One startling note rang out, clear as a bell, as the sharp point of her shoe struck the chamber under the bed—the only invisible ornament in the room, useless and elaborate as the garlanded basin and urn and the white enamel towel-rail, and all long ago made obsolete by the bathroom which had been built next door. The woman took her hands off the mattress and froze into stillness, her eyes moving in the direction of the other bed.

"It doesn't matter," said the child lifting her head, "because I'm never asleep. So it's not true, is it, to say there's nobody behind this door when we wait like this for you night after night?"

"We!" the whisper was frightful, like a gust of freezing wind blowing from one bed to the other. The aunt had subsided on to the mattress, only the tips of her toes on the ground, her hands rattling up the beads about her neck. "What did you say? We!"

20

There was a short silence. "In the photograph," said the child in a more subdued voice. "He looks as though he'd never known how to shut his eyes."

"I see." Her aunt cautiously placed her feet on the ground again and took her hand away from the rope of beads. She sat for some time staring ahead of her, preparing to make the final effort of the day. Then she stood up, and holding her breath, started to undo her stays. Each individual release in the long metal chain had to be preceded by a last fierce compression before the hook could be eased out, and every night the price of sleep was exacted from her body under the fearful pressure of fourteen hooks sliding from their slots. Tonight her niece was holding her own breath in sympathy until the seventh hook snapped out and half the garment unfurled behind to a low, thick wing of pink elastic.

"He managed to shut his eyes to a good deal, I can tell you that," she said. The wing grew broader. "Everything to do with running this hotel, for one thing. He might as well have married a woman who kept a farm or a hat-shop or any other establishment. It wouldn't have mattered what." As the last hook came out the whole tension of the room relaxed and with a remarkably flexible movement the woman turned her back and plunged under the pillow for her nightdress.

"But I didn't mind that," she said, drawing it down, her voice muffled for a moment in the tent of pink rayon. "—Because he was looking at things outside—and very, very far out they were, too."

"What *did* he look at?" said her niece, propping herself up on one elbow.

"Stars," said her aunt. "He looked at stars." She came round and sat down on the other side of the bed facing the window, and they both stared out. But now the mist had reached the window-sill. The house no longer looked out either to sea or plain. It had become airborne, floating in a space where grey clouds, shredding out now and then, revealed only the endless other drifts moving up behind.

"Every clear night," said the aunt. "And if it wasn't, he had his maps and his books."

"You mean he had a hobby," said her niece, speaking in a curiously stilted voice, as though by keeping the situation flat she was saving herself some great disappointment should the revelation on stars come to nothing.

"Hobby!" The woman put a fearful scorn into the word. "It was a passion! He knew every star in the sky and the name of every one of them!"

"Oh no," said her niece still in her cool voice, amused and cool. "After all, there are billions. Only a few have names." But she was sitting up now.

"And every constellation," said her aunt, ignoring this. "And as for planets! The moon, of course, was as familiar to him as his own dinner-plate. Did I tell you, by the way, that he made his own telescopes?"

"You never told me anything," said the girl.

"Of course, the sea's no good for that sort of thing," the woman went on, "and sometimes he had to walk miles inland. Sometimes he even had to climb right up to the top of that hill you see from the back of the house. I used to wonder why he chose a place by the sea at all."

"I suppose because you were there," said her niece.

"No, I doubt that," her aunt replied after a moment's thought, speaking to the girl in an objective and formal voice as though to another grown-up. "But there was lots of room here of course, and he could spread himself around—especially in wintertime. And there was money going too. The kind of stuff he needed cost something, I can tell you. And stars are extravagant. Like diamonds—you've got to pay even to look at them, and the closer you want to look the more expensive it gets. But I didn't mind that." She bent forward suddenly, craning her neck to see herself in the mirror of the dressing-table at one side of the window.

"What else did he look at?" said her niece, watching her steadily. "Did he ever look at you?"

The aunt was plucking at her hair now, pulling great clumps of curl forward across her temples. She looked affronted by what she saw.

"What a thing to ask!" Her eyes glaring at herself in the mirror.

"But if he was always looking at stars . . ." the girl persisted. There was silence in the room except for the woman's hand rustling about her hair and the invisible sea moving like a faint wind amongst the clouds where they were floating.

22

"He saw me *against* stars—that's the point," said her aunt. "Not against pot-plants and cruets and all those plushy sofas squashed back to back down there in the lounge. I had a background then, you see. An unusual one. It didn't last long and it may look as though I were back just where I started, but you don't get over an experience like that so quickly, I can assure you. It places you, in a way, for life."

"And there's that woman on the staircase!" exclaimed the girl. "She has a background too. You must have noticed."

"Oh, her!" The woman on the bed shifted her heavy legs about with scorn.

"It's a coincidence, though. The two of you with your stars. You envy her a bit."

"That great fat thing with the ashet!"

"Because people can actually see she's got stars behind her."

"A horror! He always said it was the worst painting in the place." Her restless scorn had now shifted her right up to the top of the bed where she started to ease back the bedclothes, but before climbing in she said over her shoulder: "Lie down now and go to sleep."

The child moved a little lower on her elbow, but she watched as her aunt climbed into bed and pulled the clothes up to her chin.

"What happened to all the books and telescopes and things?"

"In the basement, of course. In cupboards, on shelves. The maps and diagrams are all rolled up just as he left them."

"What will you do with them?"

"I shall sell them, of course. Sometime when I can find the time. Didn't they cost enough in the first place?"

"I know what I'd do if I were you."

The woman's legs jerked irritably beneath the bedclothes.

"I'd bring them all up and use them myself."

"Use them? What exactly would I use them for?"

"You could learn about stars."

The woman groaned, lifted her arms from the bed and let them fall heavily against her sides.

"Do I *look* like an astronomer?"

"An amateur astronomer can look like anything."

"And where, can you tell me, would I find the time?"

"It's quiet enough in the winter, you've said yourself."

"I can just see myself!" The quilted mound quivered painfully

23

for a moment. From the other side of the room, through the half-dark, the young girl studied her critically. She said: "It's not enough these days—with stars—just to have backgrounds. You have to be right up amongst them. Maybe you're old-fashioned."

"Oh yes, of course. I'm old, amn't I? You'd think that."

"Not old. I said old-fashioned."

"Are you going to sit up like that all night?"

"People will soon be walking about the moon. It's silly to be still thinking about backgrounds."

"So it's silly now. As well as old. You're fairly coming on."

"If you took it up properly you'd be different from that woman on the stairs, and all the other ones that come here. You'd have something nobody else ever thought about."

"And you've just told me everybody's acquainted with the stars these days."

"No, not those ones on the sofas. Not them."

The woman lay for a long time absolutely silent and without moving. It was silent in the room and throughout the whole house as though everyone had been already sleeping for hours, slumped deep in the mist which was now curling through the tops of the open windows. But the woman was not asleep. From time to time the girl lifted her head to look at her, and after a while she stealthily propped herself up on her elbow again and remained in this position, staring across. Her aunt moved suddenly and said sharply: "Are you *still* sitting up?"

"I can't go to sleep until you do."

"What on earth do you mean by that?"

"Haven't you got to have somebody here who sees when you come in and out, somebody who knows if you're asleep or not? I might as well wait now until you're properly asleep."

"Oh, what nonsense! Oh, my God, what's this now! Look what you've done. Now I have to get up and start looking after you!"

She flung back the clothes with a groan and stumped across to the girl's bed, touched her shoulders gingerly at first to press her back into the pillows, then gently, and finally, when she lay flat, bending down to say in a low voice close to her ear: "Don't ever do that. Don't stay awake again. I don't need you. You understand. I don't need *either* of you!"

She pressed the clothes around the child, patting her clumsily. But the head peered out once more to say: "So you've made up

24

your mind. You'll bring up that stuff from the basement?"

The woman pressed the head back with a sigh and moved over to the other side of the room. But before getting into bed again she stood for a long time, her arms folded, glaring at the floor and reaching starkly down through the stained patches and the flabby carpet roses, down through spinning stars and inky vacancy down, down into empty, hissing gulfs of space. Nothing impeded her fall—neither the familiar clutter of stuff in the basement, nor the child in the bed.

Sometime during the night the girl woke up to see that the mist had thinned out and a few black strips of sky were visible. There were no stars, though she strained her eyes staring for them. Then she remembered with a pang of excitement the stacked basements below. She thought of them bursting with the light of great suns, red, yellow and white, thinning out to the dimmer light of those more distant, and out, far out into the black spaces which were not vacant but full of invisible stars still waiting to be discovered. Satisfied, she slept again.

FAMILY HOUSE

ANYONE visiting this house for the first time found himself unexpectedly and uncomfortably exposed before going a step from the iron gates. Tough soles and a thick skin were needed from the moment when, turning in from a soft, country road, he would find the thickly-sown, cutting little stones of the drive working their way over the tops of his shoes and through his shoelaces. And if, while removing them, he were to raise his eyes, he would meet the unbroken, aggressive glare of rows of unscreened windows. For there was no hiding from this place. The gravel was not only harsh but also noisy underfoot. There were no soft bushes to screen the visitor while he made his way to the front door, and nothing about the place made a concession to nerves, withdrawals or second thoughts of any kind. It was a large house—not distinguished by age or design, but formidably plain and square, built in a smooth, grey stone which had begun to take on the polish of marble simply through the care spent on it since it was first built. No one, after meeting the people who lived in it, could think of it again as a house which was owned. It was not owned, but painfully served. It existed not for shelter or comfort, but to announce its own immense gravity and the fact that it was packed from top to bottom with a massive deposit of possessions. The foundations of any ordinary house would have sunk askew, the walls and roof, long before this, have bulged and cracked under the strain.

A family of five lived there—two sisters and three brothers who had been together since they were children. Although the men went back and forth to offices in the city and the women went down to the village with shopping-bags like other housewives, they had no real communication with anyone else, but remained in their tight group—all five of them—thin, anxious people who, like their parents, uncles and aunts before them, had hurried up and down in service to the house. The brothers—Joseph, James and Edgar Findlay, seemed to have effaced themselves so completely in the world that they had become almost indistinguishable to outsiders. They were tall, gaunt men—dark without being interesting, and with a melancholy so grey and unromantic that people did not in the least wish to enquire what might be behind it. There were a few years between them in age, Joseph, who was fifty-nine, being the eldest, but they might have been triplets for all the interest that was taken in them as separate individuals. They were seldom described by name or profession, and any epithet, good or bad, which came their way, did for the three of them and sometimes for all five. The women were never apart and were not expected to need the luxury of their Christian names, Edith and Clara, to distinguish them. They were conveniently known as the Findlay sisters and could be told apart, when necessary, by the fact that Edith, who was oldest of the family, had grey hair, streaked with black, and Clara, who was the youngest, had fairish hair, going grey.

But the house was never spoken of except by name. It had a definite position on the map and in guidebooks; it stood high up and could be seen from a long distance, and the paths, the lines of trees and hedges, the position of the long, wedge-shaped flowerbeds surrounding it had all been designed, from the beginning, to point out the house dramatically and give it an importance which it might well have lost as time went on. For the family who made their pilgrimage daily up and down over the thick layer of sharp-edged stones had never asked why this house and everything in it must be cherished long after it had ceased to provide any comfort for themselves. Habits laid down long before they were born had become laws for them, and because a time was coming when there would be no one left to whom this special care could be handed on, the house exacted from them—the last of the family—a greater effort than had ever been made before. As it grew older it was merciless in its demands. Year after year it was buttressed and strengthened. Ladders were never away from the walls while it was painted, pointed and chiselled. There was a

27

continual scraping, hammering and screwing going on inside and out. Yet underneath it all remained the gnawing anxiety that some day something would begin to crumble or rot, that something absolutely essential to the safety of the house would start to rattle or swing suddenly loose. Ivy, too eager to hide the sharpness of its staring eyes, was torn from around the windows. Hedges were continually being cut back so that its view should be unimpeded, and the branches of old trees, dripping too near the roof, were lopped back to raw stumps at the first patch of damp which appeared on the ceilings.

The family who lived in the house made no demands for themselves. In their own eyes they had very little importance at all, and compared to the house and the heavy accumulation of stuff which it contained, they felt themselves to be lightweights. Their modesty was unnatural; they had never been noticed and did not wish to be, and most of their leisure time was spent inside the house, as though, if they were seen too often, their peculiar lack of distinction might take something from the importance of the place, and let down those people who stared confidently at them from their frames on mantelpieces and the tops of writing-desks. Yet inside the house there was little room for the five of them. It was not so large, after all, and every room was crammed with the possessions of those ancestors and relations who had been a great deal wealthier, more popular, generous, artistic, more widely travelled and more extraordinary in every way than themselves. People had obviously strewn gifts on them wherever they went, had photographed them leaning against giant tree-trunks in California, holding their hats on the decks of Atlantic liners, sitting at the centre of intimate picnic parties on the banks of unknown rivers, or smiling and waving from the windows of train carriages. If they had also sacrificed themselves to a house, then the service had taken the form of a perpetual treasure-hunt and they showed no signs of the strain, except for a wanness under tropical skies, or a certain puffiness about the eyes owing to the difficulties and uncertainties of getting the kind of food they were accustomed to. Most of the time, however, they had been flamboyant creatures, always on the move; and as though to carry on this tradition in the only way possible, the two sisters kept the treasures which had belonged to them always in motion so that, with constant shifting and rearranging, the objects might still seem

28

to have a restless life of their own.

So they polished and dusted, and carried the fragile tables, jingling with curios, from one corner to the other; or placed some ornament nearer the window at a certain time of day so that the sunlight might, for an hour or two, strike the rare metal or glass; or turned some piece of china round into the shadow so that a chip or crack might be hidden. They knelt, side by side, both straining at the handles of huge bottom drawers which held leaden wads of white linen, yards of lace and silk, and the caps and aprons, tunics, collars, petticoats and stockings of national costumes from all over the world. These they were constantly folding and shaking and wrapping up with fresh supplies of mothball, and when the time came to shut the drawer again, they would push with their heads down, gasping, and straining the muscles of their stomachs in order to confine the bulging piles of stuff to their former space. The pressure behind the door of every cupboard and beneath the lids of chests was terrifying even to those who were used to it. At times the five of them could feel the pressure inside their own heads, and a suffocating weight would lie on their chests when they woke in the night and thought of the straining house ready, perhaps, to split, ready to crack if it were not carefully handled. When, on stormy nights, they thought of the fragile things poised on tables, and the heavy objects hanging from the walls on old cords, every nerve in their bodies would tighten with the effort which, even flat on their backs, they made to resist the fraying and the splintering which might be going on there in the darkness. Above all, it was the long attic at the top of the house which crushed them. In the daytime they were conscious of it, like a great layer of heavy atmosphere. But at night, alone in their own rooms, staring at the ceiling, they felt their own identity lost under the mass of stuff up there which weighed on their lids even when they had shut their eyes, and bulged through grotesquely into their dreams when they were asleep.

The family seldom took a holiday away from the house, and to one another they showed the special loyalty of a group of people living under a tyrant whom they respected and even reverenced. The rigid timetable which they kept to, and the discomforts which they endured for the sake of the house, had kept down all superfluous flesh and feeling and prevented any extravagance showing in their expressions or behaviour. They were all silent people,

29

chillingly resigned—the men, relieved to be away from one another in the daytime, were also relieved to be back again in the evening to a relationship which seemed to go on forever, safely, monotonously, unlike the precarious relationships which they caught glimpses of on their way back and forth to the house. There had been certain incidents in the past—times when someone had tried to advise or interfere, or shown some sneering disregard for the house and its property by trying to remove one of them away from the others into marriage or to some prosperous post abroad, or into debts just deep enough to give a taste of risk and pleasure. But all that was a long time ago. No interference from without had come for many years.

It was from inside the house, however, that the greatest disturbance was to come—beginning with an unimportant incident which occurred in its pressure-centre—the attic. It was a mild Autumn afternoon, and the elder sister, Edith, had gone up to look for a small table-lamp which she knew had been lying for many years under a heap of unidentified stuff. Indeed, nothing had been moved in the attic for a long time except the soft, outer layer of cloths, pillows and bedspreads which covered the broken, upturned furniture and the tangle of springs and wire like flesh covering the sensitive bones and nerves of an old invalid. In the course of years, however, one or two lanes had been hollowed out through the pile and one deep cave made out of two sides of tightly-wedged furniture, covered over at the top with various lighter objects which included folded tents and fishing rods, umbrellas, golf clubs, curtain-rails and a pair of broken crutches. Over everything else were two heavy lids of linoleum which had, at one time, been sliced into curious shapes to fit the awkward cupboards under the stair. At the far end of this hollow Edith had found the lamp she was looking for, but in pulling the flex she had also dislodged a heavy, mantelpiece clock. The square block of black marble and metal, built with side pillars to resemble a Greek temple, fell across her foot, all its machinery jangling and whirring for a second as she screamed.

It was nearly suppertime. The whole family had been sitting together downstairs waiting for her to come down, and now they came up to the attic—not quickly, for that was not their habit, but close on one another's heels, and apprehensively. They noticed, before anything else, that their sister was angry, and because they

30

had never before seen an expression like this on her face, it appeared to them more like some momentary madness, caused by the pain. Two brothers bent over to examine her foot—the others bent with equal solicitude over the clock which chimed softly, once, as it was gently lifted and put into a safe corner.

"Not even the glass smashed," murmured the younger sister as she peered into its face and ran her fingers round the rim. Edith now began to sob wildly, and three of them helped her down the attic stairs to her bedroom, as one ran to phone the doctor. They were now amazed and alarmed at this breakdown of her reserve. It was, after all, nothing so serious, as the doctor assured them later that evening. She must lie up for a day or two and have her foot bound—three days at the most, if she wished to be on the safe side.

It was very soon clear that Edith not only wanted to be on the safe side, but that she had made up her mind to stay there indefinitely. She rested for three days and, when her foot was healed, discovered that she was far too tired to move the rest of her body. With the voice of authority which belonged to her as the oldest of the family, but which she had never used before, she informed her brothers and sister that she had decided to stay in bed and regain some of the strength which she had lost in the house over a great number of years. They accepted the announcement silently and did not discuss it any more than they had thought of discussing other unaccountable things which had happened to them. By keeping silent, and simply not paying too much attention, they had vanquished all sorts of mysteries—from the appearance of apparitions to the turning up of unexpected visitors. Nevertheless, coming from within the family, Edith's words struck them as ominous.

On the day after this—a Sunday—the four of them went up and down many times during the afternoon and evening to visit her. Propped bolt upright against her pillows, and framed by the gilt, knobbed bedhead, their sister allowed herself to be identified for the first time. So this was Edith—this stern woman in the fancy bedjacket who stared back at them without a hint of guilt or misgiving in her blue eyes. On the days following they came in with their trays and books and newspapers, on tiptoe or shuffling awkwardly according to their moods, but as time went on they became more wary under her gaze.

For Edith, who had seldom sat down in her life except to get nearer some bit of work, now seemed to want only to lie and watch them coming and going, following all their movements with a close attention embarrassing to people who were unused to walking sympathetically in and out of sickrooms. She would discuss the affairs of the day with them, or listen to the account of some mishap in house or office, but not as though she could ever be involved herself again. Though looking attentively, while they spoke, at their faces, she gave the impression that she was studying the movements of their lips and eyes with amusement, rather as a foreigner might listen to a language he does not quite understand, while unwilling to be done altogether out of his entertainment.

After ten days, when Edith's foot had long been completely healed, her sister sat down on the edge of the bed one afternoon when she had removed the tea-tray, and carefully took Edith's hand in her own. It was not easy to take this hand for it was a large one, and felt hard and strong under Clara's timid fingers. But, flushing slightly, she kept an awkward grip on it.

"Now, Edith," she said, smiling gravely at the space of wall directly above her sister's head, "you will tell me what is wrong, will you not? There is something wrong, of course, or else you would not stay in bed long after the doctor has said you may get up—you would not cause us such serious worry for nothing. No, Edith, you would not, and you must tell me at once what is the matter!"

Her voice, slow and persuasive at the beginning, ended quickly on a note of nervous disapproval. Edith, meantime, had withdrawn her hand to flick up the lace of her collar, and answered calmly enough.

"Why, of course I will tell you, Clara. But surely I have told you all often enough what is the matter. I will tell you again, if it is any help. I am seriously tired—that is all. I have been like that for years, so I did not expect any of you to notice. But lately the pressure has grown worse, much worse, so there is nothing for it but to give up for a while until something can be done about it."

"Well, I am glad you have told me at last," replied her sister, smiling her strained and patient smile. Not finding Edith's hand again on the coverlet, she soothed her own mechanically as she talked. "Of course we can take life more easily after this—I shall see to it. You will rest in the afternoons, and Martha can stay later.

But, at any rate, I can relieve your mind on one thing. The blood-pressure you mentioned just now; do you think Dr. Fisher has taken no account of these things, or that we should ever let him overlook anything as important as that?" Clara leaned forward, widening her tired eyes in an effort to make them look triumphant. She spoke slowly and emphatically: "No, Edith—the last time the doctor was here he said that there was absolutely nothing wrong with your lungs, your heart or your blood-pressure. Everything is normal. It is nerves, Edith. There—I've told you now. It is only right you should know what he said—just a little worry about yourself after the shock of your accident. You have given yourself too much time to brood, that is all. And you must not talk about this blood-pressure again!"

"Oh, but I didn't say *blood*-pressure!" exclaimed Edith with a frown. "It is not a pressure from inside at all. It is from outside—from the house. Don't say you haven't felt the weight of all that junk, Clara! Don't tell me you are going to put up with it in-definitely—that ton weight on top of us till we die!"

Clara shuddered at 'junk' as though her sister had spoken an obscene word. Never, not in the worst moments of the spring-cleaning, had such a word been even whispered between them, and, seriously alarmed, she got up swiftly and began to arrange the little objects on the mantelpiece, with her back to Edith as though she had not heard.

"Moving them about will not help in the least, Clara, as you know," Edith remarked quietly, as she watched her. "We have been doing it for years to try and relieve the pressure. There is not a thing in this house which has ever been in the same place for more than an hour at a time. But it does no good. The only way is to get rid of it all. Indeed, it must be done, and I will not be able to get out of bed until it is!"

When the doctor came on a special visit the next afternoon he was in no hurry to be away. He went softly about the large bedroom, looking about him easily and picking up various objects from desk and mantelpiece which he said were of rare value—collectors' pieces, he called them as he turned them about in his hands admiringly. He studied the photographs for a long time and asked about the relations, and as he crossed over to the bed, he tapped the chairs with his fingers and slid his hand down the length of the wardrobe with an envious sigh. It might have been the house which he had come to examine and to praise for its excellent health and appearance, and he seemed almost reluctant to have to turn his attention to Edith.

It was not an uncommon thing, he told her, when he had settled down at last, to feel, in certain cases of mild nervous disorder, the kind of symptoms which she had described to her sister. On the contrary, it was quite a common experience to have the feeling of heaviness in the limbs—a sensation of pressure in the chest or head—yes, and even a feeling of suffocation—of being unable to breathe freely for the weight on the chest—a sensation, perhaps, of cramp about the heart. He smiled, and stretched his fingers tightly across his chest, then bound them around his head to express the familiar meaning. In most cases, he assured her, after a little rest, these common nervous symptoms disappeared very quickly—once the patient showed herself willing to get up and get on with her normal work. And this—he impressed it upon her as he got to his feet briskly—was the most important part of what he had to say. For there was absolutely nothing organically wrong with her. He repeated this as he went out of the door, and again to the family who were waiting downstairs to hear his verdict. But he was in a hurry now, and no longer took any notice of the precious things which jingled along the shelves of the hall as he strode past with his heavy tread.

A few days later Clara was having supper upstairs alone with her sister. A heavy responsibility had fallen on her—not only for the whole house and its upkeep, but also for the care of a woman whose thoughts, day and night, were now directed on this house with a ruthlessness never before known to the family. Edith's eyes could no longer be said to rest on objects; she now raked through them with a glance so reckless and scathing that the more fragile stuff could not be expected to last long under it. This evening, however, after the meal, she lay for some time with her eyes shut, and Clara, praying that the obsession was passing, drew in deep breaths at the open window. It was a beautiful October evening. Below her the weekly gardener was brushing up the leaves, and soon the smoke from his bonfire drifted through the room. To Clara the smell was a narcotic, reminiscent of autumn days stretching back through monotonous years, and of the blue haze which hung in the wintry, upper rooms of the house—scarcely opened except for the spring and autumn cleaning. But Edith opened her eyes and sniffed the air with triumph.

"You must begin with this room, Clara," she cried, suddenly sitting up straight and staring about her sharply. "That bureau over there has worried me for a long time. You see how it is packed with letters and papers which must be burned at once. No, of course they are not valuable. Why should they be? I don't intend to look over them. They must simply be taken out, bundle by bundle, and put on that bonfire. It is better than choking the chimney. Yes, Clara, of course I mean what I am saying! I am not ill and I am not joking."

Just before darkness fell that evening, Clara came slowly from the bedroom and down the stairs with her arms full of papers. Her brothers followed her out into the garden, keeping some little distance from her, like sober attendants on a bride, and automatically catching at the white strips and ribbons of paper which blew about her in the wind. At first the flames did not seem strong enough to consume the dense wads of superior notepaper, but after a while the sheets blew open, revealing for a glaring second time-honoured secrets of home and business, scraps of ancient family scandal and a smattering of long-forgotten endearments. Exclamation marks and question marks quivered together on the paper, and formidable lists of figures curled up swiftly into scrolls of fire. When the flames died down there was nothing left but some flimsy black scales floating in the air, and a grey ash on the ground.

The fire had not brought any colour to Clara's face. She was paler than ever as she walked upstairs again to Edith's room. It was her sister who was flushed, as though the flames had burned her cheeks.

"The men can help you tomorrow," was all she said. "It is a beginning, anyway." She turned to the wall without another word and Clara left the room.

"The doctor said it was particularly important not to give in to her," she said to her brothers as she wished them goodnight. They could not tell from her voice whether this was an apology or a challenge, and she looked preoccupied—uncertainly opening and shutting drawers and continually glancing about the room as she spoke as though sizing the place up after a long absence.

"What is this?" she asked, picking up an object from the sideboard as she was turning to leave.

"What is that?" replied James, looking uneasily at it. "Why, Clara—what are you talking about? You can see it is a brush with a curved handle. It has been there for years—and with a tray to match. There are two others like it in the drawer."

"Yes, that is true—and what are they all *for*?" said Clara with unaccustomed sharpness.

"What are they for? Why, surely they are crumb-brushes, Clara. You must have known they were for brushing crumbs off a tea-table!"

"Then must there be three of them?" exclaimed Clara. "Do we make more crumbs than anybody else, in this house? Is it likely that this one will get worn out with brushing in our lifetime—that there must always be two in reserve? It is very unlikely that I, at any rate shall use another brush while I live—far less the two of them. Do you even know how old I am?"

"But of course, Clara," her brother replied hurriedly, "and there are certainly not an excessive quantity of crumbs about the place. Why must we discuss the brushes, if it upsets you? They were not ours, in the first place. You have forgotten that they came to us with the napkin rings and hot water bottles when Aunt Helen gave up her house. If they are not used, they can be handed down. What has your age to do with it, Clara? You are too sensitive about that. We remember you are the youngest. And we do not expect you to use three crumb-brushes."

Clara tossed her head and left the room. But her brothers remained standing together long afterwards, apprehensively staring about them, and puzzling over the meaning of various objects which they had caught sight of for the first time.

Two days later, in the absence of the gardener, Clara made her own bonfire—a magnificent affair, far bigger than the last, and lighting the whole garden up to the tops of the highest trees. When the three brothers came out of the house to see it they exclaimed in admiration. This time they could show little interest in what was being burned, for great flames destroyed the boxes and packets before they could be identified, but they drew nearer, step by step, to warm themselves, and their eyes shone outrageously in the light. Every now and then, as the garden grew darker, the fire threw a shimmer of light upon the front of the house. When this happened the woman and the three men stood motionless to stare at the quivering windows and wagging chimneys and at the grey

36

stone which swelled and trembled as though it were no more solid than parchment. Now Joseph, the oldest man, went striding off quickly towards the house and returned in a few minutes with a heap of papers which the flames tore from his hands and devoured with a roar as soon as he had thrown them down.

"Papers are not enough to keep it going," said Clara as the fire subsided again. She went back to the house, running this time, and returned, out of breath, with a couple of heavy wooden trays.

"There was no time to pick and choose," she explained. "I took the largest of the half-dozen behind the sideboard. At any rate they will keep it going while we find more stuff."

They waited for a moment to see the flames lick round the tray-handles which were carved in the shape of crouching monkeys, gripping melons between their fingers.

"What a sin to waste them—and all the people who must be wanting trays!" cried Clara, shuddering with disgust and pleasure. All four of them now started to run towards the house, looking back over their shoulders to judge how long the fire might last. Clara sped upstairs—but not to her sister's room. For the moment she had almost forgotten about Edith. Instead she ran to a spare bedroom, and opening the drawers of a large chest, she began to shake out rolls of cloth and undo the great bags of woollen underwear. Mothballs bounced about the floor as she dug down into the piles with her fingers, but at last she had pulled out as big an armful as she could carry. The men were in the garden before her, however, making for the corner where a thin smoke still rose, and carrying between them as many inflammable objects as they had been able to lay hands on. With their awkward loads and anxious faces, they had the look of people working to save their possessions from a burning house, having caught up the first things which came to hand. James, in the lead, was carrying a basket-chair, piled up with raffia table-mats which he tossed on, one after the other, when he was still some distance away from the fire. Bursts of flame and a crackling like a forest going up forced them to stand aside when the chair went on; and the work-baskets, tea-cosies, clothes-brushes and picture-frames which followed the chair were lost at once in a blaze which sent sparks flying far above the chimneys of the house. This was no ordinary fire. It was more exhilarating than an explosion of sky-rockets. Beyond the vibrating circle where they stood, they caught glimpses of a house which appeared to rock gently on the quaking ground. Clouds, flowers and iron railings trembled together, and the agitation of their own faces made them appear to one another like persons undergoing, moment by moment, the most violent changes of emotion from quivering despair to the wildest glee. When the time came for Clara to unwrap her bundles of underwear their spirits were dampened.

"Perhaps they will smother the fire," said Clara as she threw on the pants, vests and combinations bequeathed from uncles and great uncles who had died young, long before they could wear a hole in the wool. But when she saw the flames slowly eating through the outer layer she added: "There must be thousands of people who could do with them—people without a stitch to their backs. What a waste and a sin!"

But the sin and the shame of it stirred them to even greater efforts, and they prodded at the fire until it leapt up again to devour a clothes-horse and a couple of small wooden cake-stands in a matter of minutes.

It was dark before the fire at last fell apart into a smouldering heap of ashes. Clara and her brothers were so exhausted with their orgy of destruction that they could scarcely stand upright, but as they approached the house they lifted their heads and stared up at it boldly. A little of the stuffing had already been taken out of it —even through the darkness they could feel that. The stone did not seem as smooth to them now. They could imagine it dented, here and there, where the surface caved in over certain hollow patches, odd corners which were not packed so tightly as before, and in spite of their exhaustion they felt a quiet satisfaction in the evening's work.

After supper Clara went up to see her sister. She was sitting up in bed, reading, looking fresh-cheeked and rested, and she glanced up with a smile when her sister came in. There was no mention of bonfires, but Clara asked casually, as she drew the curtains: "I suppose you will be getting up tomorrow?"

"Hardly so soon," replied Edith. "No, not yet—it is not quite time for me to get up and come downstairs, if that is what you mean. But I will certainly dress and get up for tea in my bedroom. That will be a beginning and help to cheer you all up."

They were not cheerful as they brought up the heavy trays to

38

her room next afternoon, but they sat with an expectant air, talking absentmindedly and listening for the sound of the lorry which arrived at this hour every week to remove the rubbish. They heard it at last a long distance away, coming up the steep road below their garden wall, and while it laboriously turned the corner of their drive, they excused themselves one by one and went out to meet it, accompanying it for the last few yards of the way as though guiding a triumphal car to the chosen place. When the three dustbin men saw this place—not the mean pair of ashcans, nor the paltry pile of tins, papers and grass-cuttings, but a great hillock of soft stuff, studded with glinting ornaments—they stopped some distance off and approached it reverently on foot. In five minutes, having prodded through the top layer, they returned to the family who were waiting nearby.

"Say—what's going on here?" asked one, pointing to what he held up in his other hand—a green china mermaid, who also pointed with a puzzled air to the wave on which she sat. "Are you moving off or what? Sure, that's a funny way to be doing it—clearing out all the fancy stuff and hanging on to the plain. Maybe you've made a mistake, folks. We're not buying and we're not selling and we're not mending and we're not shifting the stuff to any other place. There, it's on the lorry—Cleansing Department—and that's us. In other words—your things are for the dump!"

But as they only backed away, nodding and smiling, he went after them.

"Tell us what's up," he shouted. "For all I know you've got heirlooms and all tucked away under that little pile! And what about *her*?" He brandished the mermaid in front of them, but James waved him back nervously and angrily, exclaiming: "Take it away! Take them all away! There is nothing to discuss. There is illness here—a nervous breakdown in the house. The things are to be removed in the normal way, and there is nothing more to be said!" Still shouting he disappeared with the rest of them inside the house.

The men now got to work on the pile with gusto and without wasting further words. The inmates of the house might be cracked, but the stuff they unearthed was unbelievably whole—basins and ewers, teapots and metal trays which had not taken a dint or a crack in fifty years, china baskets of unchipped violets and draped dancing figures without a pointed toe or finger missing. They lay together, smugly shining there amongst beaded shoes and piled soup-plates, as though on their usual spring-clean outing.

The family did not come out again, but the men worked on in frenzied enthusiasm in case they might suddenly appear with a changed mind about their possessions. They now went at the pile without plan or method, scarcely looking at the stuff, but grimly lifting up the clinking armfuls towards the lorry. Small ornaments fell and were ground underfoot as they staggered about, and they began to shout and threaten one another over each coveted piece. Like some deep archaeological site, the heap revealed layers of life in the history of the house—layers which, although only laid down that morning, contained objects which had not, before that, seen the light of day for a generation. The flimsier stuff, skimmed from the tops of drawers and shelves, had been deposited first, and this the rising wind took up and whirled along with the dust and leaves. Clawing at the ground, the men ran, shouting, after ghostly, lacey evening gloves which spread themselves against tree-trunks, and oriental fruit-baskets and initialled collar-boxes which bowled, lightly as hoops, in front of them.

At last, the furious slamming of the lorry doors brought the whole family to the windows in time to see the men drive off at a breakneck pace down the drive and around the corner. Behind them, where the dazzling hillock had stood, there was now only a churned-up patch of ground where fragments of glass and china lay, and on the long grass nearby stray ribbons and tassels hung mournfully. When the dust from the lorry had settled, the others looked at Edith who had stood beside them in her dressing-gown and was now turning to go back to her room.

"You are surely not going back to bed, Edith," said Edgar reprovingly. "Not now. Not after you have seen all the changes that are going on these days. Will we expect you down for supper tonight ? Surely you will dress and come down for a little while and tomorrow you will feel yourself again. Don't pretend you haven't noticed the gaps in the cupboards and the open space on the top landing. We have heard you opening and shutting the drawers all morning."

"I feel a different person—I admit it," Edith replied as she walked away, "—different, but not absolutely better yet. You certainly cannot hurry an illness like mine, Edgar. In a day or so.

One more day, perhaps, will make all the difference. It depends on so many things." Her eyes rested for a moment on the things as she looked back from her bedroom. Calmly she stared through the other doors and at the heavy brass lamp on which a nymph, still smiling, writhed in an effort to hold up the fringed parchment shade, and beyond that to a massive wardrobe with its magnificent false top, and at the brusting trunks wedged so tightly under the beds that the mattresses above had grown hideously deformed over the years. Finally she lifted her head and gazed, without hatred, up the steep stairs towards the attic. They noticed then what they had never seen before—the extraordinary determination of her chin, so like the chins in all the framed photos of the house, but now to be seen jutting out with a witch-like ruthlessness which outdid all the rest.

"Sell or burn." She murmured these words, as she gently closed the door behind her. Less than a week ago it would have seemed as though the devil himself had spoken, but now they stood around savouring them, listening for more. But there was silence in the house, except for the sly creaking of the bed as Edith climbed into it again.

The auctioneer's men started to work early the next afternoon. The gaps in corridors and cupboards widened behind them as they tramped about, and great spaces opened out in the rooms whose surfaces had already been smoothed of ornament. They worked slowly and cautiously, half expecting that the inmates of the house, who stood about crossing items off lists, would change their minds, or stampede to the front steps to say a last goodbye. But there was no interruption, and when they came to the attic they had the place to themselves.

Downstairs, the family—all five of them—were sitting round the table in the dining-room. There was nothing on the table, and they sat silently in the fading light, looking before them and listening as intently as people at a séance, waiting for the vibrations to start. The first indication of movement in the attic was the faint smell of dust which sifted down to them from three floors above— a familiar enough smell, but one which this evening gave to their nostrils a sensation lively as the tingle of snuff. Then they knew that the soft quilt of stuff on top was being gradually moved. It was not much yet, but they could feel it slowly lifting from them, as though a heavy swathe of hair was being lifted up and cut from their aching heads. Next they heard the grinding of things being forced painfully from the positions they had held for years, and the formidable thud and rattle as they were dragged down from stair to stair on to the landing below. It seemed as though the whole house was splitting from the top, and automatically the family below raised their hands to their heads. When they removed them again the noise overhead had stopped. Up there was silence and emptiness. Still the grinding and thudding went on in the corridor beside them, but a pressure had been removed from the top of their skulls and from the nerves at the back of their necks. It was even easier to hold up their heads, they discovered, and they lifted them quickly now to watch Edith who had got up from the table and was whipping off the photos from the mantelpiece and windowsill, from desks and bookcases and the tops of china-cupboards. In a few seconds the eyes which had not wavered for years—eyes grave, wistful, stern and piercing, but all terrible in their watchfulness—had disappeared. The photos, in a neat pile with faces down, had been placed in a corner of the sideboard. It was as easy as that to be rid of onlookers. The people round the table allowed themselves to smile at the audacity of this idea, but nevertheless a conspirator's brightness shone from their own eyes as they glanced about.

Though relieved of the pressure in their chests and heads, they slept badly that night. Like people unused to a rarified atmosphere, they were restless and their nerves were on edge; and after twelve o'clock the wind began. At first it was only a breeze from the open windows—a welcome fluttering of curtains and loose papers breaking the stillness. In half an hour the wind had risen to a hysterical note, and gusts of rain, sharp as nails, struck tiles and windows and swept through the chips of gravel on the path, grinding them together with a sound like pebbles grinding on the shore. In the early hours of the morning, when the gale was at its height, the house, without its ballast, shook like a hollow ship at sea, and from all parts came a drumming, a rattling and a banging as though doors and windows had been suddenly prised open to let the furies in. But nobody got up to investigate. As though by a mutual agreement from they day before, the lay rigid the whole night through—letting the house rip.

In the morning Edith was up first. The others, waking slowly from their first, deep sleep, heard her voice calling to them from overhead, and giving themselves time for only a glance at the flooded garden, they dressed and went up to find her. She stood in a corner of the empty attic, surrounded by all the buckets and basins she had collected together and listening with interest to the variation of notes struck from them by the rapid drops of water falling from the roof. Craters and grey rings of damp covered the ceiling and the floor was thick with drifts of plaster which had blown far and wide, so that even the webs in distant corners were hung with a fine white dust.

"But there is more to see down below," said Edith, after they had listened to a full range of musical notes for some time. Following her down through the house, they were soon aware that, in the attic, they had only seen where the softening-up had taken place—a crumbling at the top which had convulsed the body of the building with more spectacular results.

The house had plainly given up. It had allowed the screws to loosen and the hinges to crack, and let the watery blisters rise under the face of paint. Tiles, sticking grimly to the roof through the storms of years, had been lifted in a matter of minutes, like slices of bread off a board. The glass lay everywhere. Long splinters were piled under the broken windows, and shining crumbs of it, fine as sugar, crunched under their feet in odd corners as they moved about. Throughout the morning they came on the fragments inside old shoes or in the folds of newspapers. They cut their fingers on it in the fringes of rugs and down the sides of armchairs. In every fireplace a heap of soot had fallen and lay, thickly quilting hearths and rugs and thinning out to sift with the leaves and plaster around passages where the cold wind still blew. It was difficult, they discovered, to get out of their own front door. Pushing against a bank of sodden leaves and twigs, they came face to face with a great, jagged branch which had fallen against the steps, and was still quivering and clawing at the door with a persistency which made them draw back at once into the hall with a feeling of panic. For as long as the scraping went on they remained inside, whispering and peering occasionally out into the garden through the slot of the letter-box.

Only when the wind had died down did they begin to hear the complaint of the house itself. There was a creaking and a wheezing about them, and a far-off rattling of unidentified broken things from places which they had not yet investigated. They could hear the heavy shifting of the house through all its loosened boards and joints, like a patient cautiously turning over to feel which of his limbs pain him most, and from overhead a faint whine and whistle in the chimneys and a half-hearted hiss as another puff of soot came down. But above all it was the huge sighing of the building which they heard, as a last gust of wind blew through it from end to end. They recognized it at once as a sigh which came from the bottom of its heart—a heart from which, in the last week, they had extracted as much life-blood as it was possible to take away without a complete collapse ensuing. The foreboding which, since morning, had increased in all of them except Edith, they now diagnosed in one another as the growing pangs of guilt.

Edith had now to work harder than she had ever done before to disperse the atmosphere of this guilt which hung about the place and threatened to thicken and congeal in the empty spaces where they had felt such light-heartedness only a few days before. She set about the task bravely, but at times it was too much even for her.

"It is a case of complete breakdown, I am sorry to say," she would remark, as she came across further signs of damage in the next few days. "We have done everything we could for it all these years. No people could have done more. But now is the time to make a change. Luckily for us, we have done most of the moving already—we have only ourselves to take away now. If other people can move themselves, so can we."

But they were not convinced. Indeed if they had taken pick-axes and sledge-hammers to the house, they could not have felt more responsible for the damage. Nevertheless, it could perhaps be patched and propped again. The harm was extensive but not, after all, so serious. If necessary they could even pack the place up with furniture again—they could replace and rebuild and re-organise, and in a few years they might manage to make up to the house something of what it had lost and suffered at their hands. They would take it upon themselves.

"We will take it upon ourselves." This was the phrase they repeated over and over again in answer to all the consolation and suggestion which Edith offered them. Already they were sagging under the weight. Again they had begun to assume the resigned, identical expressions of a united family—still shaken, but ready for their folly to be forgiven and forgotten. Very soon they would try to go back, not to where they had started, but far further back to a state of absolute and unquestioning innocence. Decidedly, they were to give up the rest of their lives to regain favour with God and house.

Their elder sister now began to search the place methodically from top to bottom, as though her own life depended on it. She would disappear early in the day, to be found hours later, moving about on her knees in some dark corner, or lying flat on her back, prodding and knocking on a low slant of roof above her head; or they would hear her in some distant part of the house, stamping slowly about in a circle, as though engaged in some ritual dance of her own. There were times when they wondered whether she might be searching for hidden treasure, known only to herself, or thumping the walls to find some secret cupboard where the family fortune lay. Most of the time, however, they took little notice and seldom mentioned it amongst themselves. The possibilities in human nature had only lately been opened up to them, and it was a discovery which, given time and their usual routine, they hoped would one day be completely forgotten as though it had never been made.

Meantime Edith appeared to have lost interest in the damage in the house. She passed by the wastes of damp, the cracking plaster and broken windows many times every day with scarcely a glance, and made no comment when, after six days, slater and plasterer had failed to turn up. Nor did she comment on the limitations of her three brothers who stood about much of the time with their loose, clean hands at their sides or deep in the pockets of jackets which they had never removed. She had nothing to say about all this because she had better things to hope for. She was hoping i n fact for bigger and deeper damage—damage long-standing, spectacular and terrible to cure. Dry rot was her aim.

She found what she was looking for one evening in a small unused bedroom downstairs, which until lately had contained a chest-of-drawers, a bed, and a marble washstand with ewers. There was nothing here now except one cane chair against the wall and a picture over the fireplace. Where the furniture had been, pale shapes, complete with knobs and spirals, were traced on the wallpaper, and above them, one long rectangular strip where a school photo had hung, keeping in living memory for over sixty years two hundred boys in striped blazers and tabbed socks.

The remaining picture was a sombre reproduction in brown and white, but its subject was a garden in midsummer, where a family of young men and women were giving a tea party to their friends. There was nothing sombre about these people; they were obviously a frolicking crowd with generous and careless habits. Fruit of all kinds had been allowed to spill from baskets into the grass where tame birds pecked at it. A puppy was lapping up the milk running from a jug which had been knocked over in the midst of some game, or perhaps by the foot of the girl in a white dress who was swinging in a hammock above. Behind her in the distance could be seen an imposing house, not unlike their own, and at the gate stood an eager young man, identical with the other men in the picture, but showing by his anxious face and his untidy necktie that he had seen the world and found it wanting, and was now only too thankful to be back. As she stared at this picture— "A Homecoming"—Edith stamped mechanically but strenuously at the floorboards beneath it.

She did not need to stamp long. After a minute her foot went softly through the crumbling wood and a long piece of boarding fell in, covered on its inner side with a thick web of greyish-white strands, blotched here and there with blue and yellow patches. Edith fell on her knees and peered down into the area which had suddenly split open under her eyes. It was a place of primeval dampness and darkness, smelling of must and decay, but seeming, at first sight, to be nothing more than a disagreeable hollow under the floor. As she became accustomed to the darkness, however, she saw that what she stared into was not an empty hole but a world, well-established and powerful, where a secret growth had been going on, over months or years, spreading insidiously about the roots of the house. Here and there, springing out of the darkness, white blotches could be seen, stuck like tufts of cotton wool to the rotting wood, and between the black cracks spongey, yellowing mushrooms grew out. Further down, spread widely over the level places, was a layer of poisonous-looking red powder. Only one corner had been opened up, but Edith knew she knelt over a place where life had spawned and spread in the darkness over a vast area, wider and deeper than anything she had imagined during her rapping and stamping of the past week.

"This, at any rate, had nothing to do with us," said Edith, when she had summoned the family together. "The place will die of it sooner or later, if nothing is done. No doubt something will be done. But not by us. We brought it safely through its choked drains and its damp spots. We patched it up where it was thin. Pruned it down where it bulged. We can't forget the money spent to give it space to expand at the back, the cost of the paint it soaked up, year after year, to prevent the rust from getting it! But the cure of this is beyond us. We have our own health to think of. We are not surgeons or nurses to stand by at operations of this scale! Let it go to somebody else. As for us, there is nothing else for it—we must get out and stay out!"

As they stepped forward, one after the other, to look down into the opening, they breathed an air which smelt not only of decay, but also of certain freedom. This time they saw there was nothing more for them to do. Under these boards conscience could be finally buried. They would pack up and leave the place forever.

On a dark morning in the middle of November, they stood together for the last time outside the front door of the house.

"We have everything to look forward to!" exclaimed Edith after a long silence, while they braced themselves for the final departure. It was true, at any rate, that they were looking straight in front of them now—down the stony drive, and beyond it to the bleak stretches of empty fields, already beginning to darken under the rain. It was not, after all, the whole world which was before them, but a small hotel nearby, from where they would carry on the long-drawn out negotiations over the head of the house. California and the decks of the ocean liners were as far off as they had ever been, and it was too late to group themselves, as their relations had done many times before them, for an exuberant send-off photo on the front steps of the house. The men required every scrap of jauntiness still left in them simply to carry the luggage down to the gates, and the women, worn out with their own displays of excitement and enthusiasm, had let their faces fall again, and now longed only to settle as soon as possible under some other roof.

They did not look back when they came to the gates, and when they were beyond them they did not immediately shake the dust of the place from their feet, for nothing as soft as dust had been under them. But the three men put down their cases and sat down outside to remove, for the last time, the cruel pieces of gravel which had lodged in the heels of their shoes. This done, and walking with greater confidence and dignity, they passed out of sight of the house forever.

THE SPARK

"I FIND it strange, Mr. Abson, that your face doesn't change much at the things I've been telling you. But you do listen, don't you?"

"I listen, Mrs. Imrie. I find what you say very interesting."

" 'Interesting'! But you do *feel* what I'm saying to you? About the little puffs of smoke between the tiles . . . the dog howling at the back?"

Abson was thoughtful for a few minutes, his round, black eyebrows raised, melancholy eyes fixed on the floor.

"Later, Mrs. Imrie. Things come over me later. When I've had time."

"When you've had time? But you have lots of time, Mr. Abson. Who's disturbing us? You're a person of feeling, aren't you? A person would need to be inhuman not to respond to what I've just told you."

"That's how I'm made, Mrs. Imrie."

"How? Not inhuman, I hope?"

"I mean I go over things later."

"Later? How late?"

"Indeed I am not!" exclaimed a girl who had just opened the door. "It's all your crazy clocks running on again!"

"I'm not referring to you, Brenda," said her mother. "I'm talking to Mr. Abson here who feels everything later than other people."

The girl shrugged herself through the room and over to a corner where she hung up her coat and stared close and long at a small mirror. As she watched her daughter combing out her hair the

48

woman at the table seemed at ease, as though her own nerves were being combed out strand by strand from the knotted frizzle they had got into while sitting too long with the passive Mr. Abson. But after a while she turned to him again, speaking, however, in a more patient and relaxed tone.

"How late do you mean, Mr. Abson?"

The man gave his peculiar half-sigh. That is to say, he drew in his breath, held it for a while, and expelled it almost without a sound. But, halved like this, it was also irritating, as though he had no wish to give generously of his feelings—even feelings of desperation—like other people.

"How late, then?" Mrs. Imrie repeated.

"At night. When I go to my own room. In bed probably. I go over things when I'm in bed. I suppose that's what I usually do."

It was quieter in the room. The girl had stopped combing her hair, or she was combing it very lightly. The woman took up some sewing again. "You mean things don't strike you right off? Even funny things you see or hear?" Mr. Abson turned his eyes towards the window, but said nothing.

"I suppose that means you don't sleep well."

"Not always."

"I'm glad I'm not troubled like that. With me it's when my head touches the pillow. Or when would I ever get my work done next day? I've no time to think day or night, it seems!" She sewed steadily for a bit, and once she whispered: "The whole roof caving in . . .!"

After a while Mr. Abson gathered up some papers from the table into a brief-case and prepared to go into the other room which was officially his for the evenings if the family were not entertaining visitors in there. They had only a very hazy idea of his job for he had not talked much about this. But they knew his firm made tiles and pots and mugs, and they associated him with a peculiar foreign jar they had once seen there—long, black and white, narrowing at the top to show that nothing was to be got out of it and nothing put in except perhaps a bare twig or two. And yet with a mournful, drooping lip to it.

"Don't go unless you must," said Mrs. Imrie. "It'll probably take a bit to heat up in there. Jim and May will be back soon and we'll have a cup then."

"I'll come back later then, if I may," said Abson. He went out and they heard the door of the other room close behind him.

"Always later!" exclaimed Mrs. Imrie. "I'm afraid later's not much use to me. I've got to have the laughs on the dot, and the crying too. And I like a gasp when it's tragedy—even a blink would be enough. *Some*thing. When I told the butcher about them throwing the twin babies out of the window and the fireman nearly gone himself with the smoke, he doubled over as though he'd a pain here—doubled over his knife. Mrs. Liddel did more. She wailed out loud."

"There *was* a safety-net, wasn't there?"

"Has the world gone quite heartless? Yes, there *was* a safety-net. And lots of people down below, including that mother—watching her two babies being thrown, one after the other, out of a fourth-storey window!"

"Anyway, they're safe. No damage done."

"Talk about sleeping! Imagine that poor woman's dreams when she does close her eyes. Will she ever get it out of her head? No she will not. Some people have reason to lie awake at night."

"We don't know what's in Mr. Abson's head."

"No, we don't. Whatever it is, it doesn't show on the face. The strangest thing about buildings when they collapse is the slowness. It's like a slow-motion picture. A sag here and a bulging there, and a slow, slow puff of dust."

"I've seen something like it on TV."

"The sparks are dangerous. I believe they can travel miles."

"And still keep alive?"

"Seemingly. In a wind."

"Surely not miles?"

"A long distance. You think they're dead, and the next thing you know there's a fire blazing away miles from the first place."

"A single spark," said the girl.

"But if it's alive, after all—and travelling fast."

"A dark spark," said the girl again, brooding on it.

"And more dangerous for not shining," said her mother.

They sat in silence for a few minutes till the girl took up her comb again and began on her hair. This time there was a faint crackling and she laughed. "More sparks," she said, drawing out a strand and letting it float free from her head.

"Look, leave your hair alone," said her mother, "and get that comb away from the table."

Later on, twenty minutes or so before her brother was due back, the girl knocked on the door opposite and opened it. Mr. Abson was sitting there with his papers at a small table. The room had not heated up and as she spoke she could see the little white puffs of breath before her in the air.

"You haven't put on the light yet. Shall I come in?"

"Yes, come in," said Abson. "Have your brother and his fiancée arrived?"

"Not yet. 'Fiancée' is idiotic. Why do you keep using that word?"

"I took it for granted."

"Well don't. You haven't been here long or you'd know the number of girls he's brought home already. We keep off the word."

"What is the play they're rehearsing?"

"I'm not very interested to talk about them. I don't know what it is. All I know is he's a sailor and she's a school-mistress. Have you noticed how nearly all the women in these plays turn out to be teachers? Last year he was a painter and she taught Algebra. In the end they show they can take off their glasses and everything else the same as other women. But of course only for sailors, painters or murderers. Is that fair? Never for anyone else—never a male teacher, for instance."

"Is your brother a good actor, then?"

"I'm not interested in that. But there's one thing. I've been behind the scenes when they're taking the paint off."

"Yes?"

"It's strange, frightening maybe. They take a blob of grease and wipe off a pair of round, black eyebrows, or a frown or a luscious pair of lips. They can clear patches of white fright from their cheeks in one stroke—grease off a blush as quickly as you'd wipe round a dinner-plate, and underneath, when they've wiped off every mark, their faces are dull . . . dull!"

"It's not that. But undramatic perhaps. Unexaggerated."

"No. Dull. When you take off eyebrows, for instance, the surprise goes out of the face. Yours is the opposite."

"Mine. My what?"

"Your face, Mr. Abson. When you wipe it off, yours must be exciting."

There was silence in the room. The man turned his eyes slowly,

51

still keeping his head stiff.

"When I say 'wipe off' I'm not referring to paint, with you, of course."

"No? What, then, could I wipe off?"

"I've no idea what it could be."

"I take it you find the surface dull—no dramatic eyes or lips?"

"But underneath—exciting."

"Where exactly does it break through?"

"It doesn't. But I can infer it, from what you say. At night, for instance, in your own room."

"Miss Imrie, if you're trying to make up for anything your mother said—don't bother. She's been good to me. She likes me well enough even if I do get on her nerves. And I'm not to be here long. Why bother yourself?"

"Miss Imrie! Part of your trouble's politeness. Like fiancée. Politeness dulls the face. It's nothing to do with my mother, though naturally she likes excitement. She imagined that being abroad so long you'd have lots to talk about. But it hasn't worked like that and she doesn't hold it against you. It's a dull street, that's all. A dull street, a dull town, a dull country. We're pretty dull here compared with lots of them, aren't we?"

"And she has a feeling for drama like your brother?"

"She likes the applause and the gasps when she has something good to tell."

"Something good?"

"Ah, you know what I mean. Don't fold up. Don't start moralising. I mean good and bad at the same time. Everyone likes sparks and fire-bells. Why else would they come running?"

"And the screams?"

"There were no screams. And no one was hurt."

"There would be bigger crowds for screams, I can tell you that."

The girl sat still and watched him. After a while she sighed, took the comb from the pocket of her jacket and drew it smoothly down one side of her head from the middle parting, bending her head right over so that the hair swung out away from her neck and ear. Her upturned eyes showed a rim of white round the lower lid and gave her a look of fixed surprise.

"It's not quite dark enough yet," she said, "and maybe not the right sort of day—but often, when I do this, I can get not just crackling, but actual sparks as well. Frost and darkness are the

52

best. I know," she smiled, "that it can't happen often with men. There's got to be plenty of hair for it—something you haven't got. But more spectacular still . . ." she paused and smiled again into the dim room, "is the last thing I take off at night. It's not just sparks but flashes. The quicker it's done, the brighter. If I rip off the vest and toss it away I can get great, blue flashes that sting my arms and back. And if the room is absolutely black it's like lightning—crackling, stinging lightning. But the stuff's got to be silky, nylon and that sort of thing. Nothing dull or thick. Not everyone believes this. People can get very stuffy about electricity too, you know, as though it ought to be confined solely to lamp-bulbs."

"There's your brother now," said the man, unstiffening to the sound of the key in the front door.

"Is it ? There's another thing. Some people think you're getting sexy if you say 'sparks in the hair'. 'Electricity' is as good as an invitation, and if it's electricity and underwear they're waiting to be eaten up."

"Yes, it *is* them," said the man. "I can hear the girl too."

". . . Waiting to be eaten alive or ready to pounce themselves. It comes to the same thing," said the girl. "No, that's my mother's cousin. She's got a key and comes in on Tuesday nights if there's anything she wants to watch. No, it's early for them yet. The sad thing about those ones—whether they're waiting or pouncing—is they're still dull, terribly dull and sad."

"You've little idea at your age how tired people can become," said the man.

"At my age! Some of my friends are as tired right now as they'll ever be. Tireder, for instance, than my mother ever was or ever will be. Tired wasn't what I was talking about. It was dullness. A mean, suspicious, greedy, beady-eyed dullness, if you can imagine that!"

The man gave a laugh. He put his hands to his face and rubbed it hard for a moment, first his forehead, then his cheeks. He was breathing quickly.

"What's that for ? Are you cold ?"

"Maybe. I'm trying to wake up, warm up. Anything to scrub off those words."

"Those words were meant to go over your head. They're nothing to do with you. Not one of them landed on you—so you

53

can stop scrubbing."

Abson's hands were suddenly still, his fists clenched at the sides of his head. He turned on her angrily exclaiming: "And you! Look—you can stop nagging! Stop lecturing me!"

"That's better," said the girl, leaning her elbow on the table so that now the other wing of hair hung down to touch his papers. "I don't mean to nag. I think a lot *of* you, and a lot about you. And do you know *how* I think of you? I think of you as a sort of dark spark."

There was a tremendous crash from the outer door on the word 'spark' and a sound of voices filled the hall. The wall behind them rattled with the buttons of overcoats being flung at the pegs on the other side, and there was a thumping on the wainscoting where heavy shoes were kicked off.

"That can't be just the two of them," said the girl, straightening up and folding her hair back behind her ears. "Maybe they've brought the whole group back. There's five there at least. Do you hear five?"

"But have they *got* to have the wind through the whole scene?" a voice was calling out plaintively in the hall. "And has it got to be a *gale*? Two pages! Tenderly! Have you ever tried speaking *tenderly* with a howling gale at your ear?"

"A dark what?" said Abson.

"It's the last scene," said the girl. "They're talking about the bit where the two of them—I told you about the sailor and this woman—they're waiting for news of his son in the storm. There's a bridge been blown down or something."

"A dark *what* did you say I was?" said the man.

"Just a minute," said the girl. "Listen! How many actually are there? I'm not going out there till I know. If it's five then it means Ben's around. I'm not going out there if that Ben has attached himself again. Well, it can't be helped. I'll never know if I don't look, will I? Are you coming out?"

"Not yet," said Abson.

"Later then," said the girl. When she opened the door a brilliant shaft of light and noise cut through the dark room. The man inside had a glimpse of a boy sitting on the bottom stair taking his boots off and a young woman leaning against the wall unknotting a headscarf. The girl's sudden appearance in the hall caused a moment's silence then a burst of acclaim from at least

54

five voices. She passed through them, leading the way into the other room and they went after, dropping the boots and water-proofs, shaking the rain from their hair. They followed her and the door closed beyond. Suddenly the hall was silent. It was quite silent and empty.

A long time later the group in the sitting-room heard steps going upstairs—or rather the boy who had sat taking his boots off on the stairs heard them. He was now leaning with his elbow on the hearthrug eating toast and he held up his knife with the butter on it for silence.

"Who is it?" he asked.

"I'll get him," said Mrs. Imrie, and she went out to find him already round the corner of the stairs. "Why, you can't go up yet. It's early. Aren't you taking a cup with us before you disappear?"

"For a few minutes—with pleasure," said Abson, coming down slowly.

Like her daughter, Mrs. Imrie felt that politeness at this moment was a mistake. Why 'pleasure' with his face? With his reluctant steps? She had once had someone who, called down like this, had stuck his head in the door, made hideous faces at a group of old ladies and withdrawn. And been loved for it.

"Creaks on the stairs," remarked the boy at the fireplace, watching Mr. Abson who was now sitting with a cup of tea in his hand. "That reminds me."

"Go on!" voices encouraged him. "Give us the story!"

"No, it's not a story. There's nothing to it."

"Go on!" they shouted.

"Not a story—not an experience even. A sensation. A stirring of the hairs of the head. It was this perfectly ordinary suburban villa belonging to a schoolfriend's family—an ordinary red and yellow brick affair."

"All right. Don't worry," said someone. "It was ordinary. We got that."

"I was staying the weekend. I had my dog with me. Well, each evening at the same time—eight o'clock—footsteps going up-stairs. The first time I said 'Who is it?'—nobody'd heard them. And the second night: 'Who is it?' Nobody heard them. The third night—same thing. No one had ever heard them except me."

"The dog?" murmured someone who'd heard the story.

"I'm coming to that. Each time it happened the dog would get

55

up and whine at the door of this room until I let him out. We'd both stand at the foot of the stairs waiting for the last creaks going up at the top. Then the dog would give one yelp, turn his back to the stairs and sit huddled up to me without moving a muscle. It happened three times. In the end the family, including the schoolfriend, had taken an intense dislike to both of us. Can you blame them? Each time they came out of their cosy, plush drawing-room they saw me gaping up the stairs and the dog hunched round the other way. They could hardly wait to get rid of us. In the end I had to carry my own suitcase to the station in the pouring rain. I can still see myself trudging past their long, cream car at the front gate. The schoolfriend hardly spoke to me again—avoided me as though I had the plague. Well—there you are. A gloomy silence in the audience. Didn't I tell you you'd be disappointed?"

"No, not a bit," said a girl from the other side of the room. "The fact that it lacks all drama makes it more real. Now I know it happened."

"Thanks."

"Even in spite of, or because of the dog. Because prowling, howling dogs are common in ghost stories. But yours just sits there on the mat. He's a pet. He's sweet. I know him."

"Thanks again. His name is Brown. I suspected it was a boring little tale."

"Surely not just Brown?"

"Simply and literally Brown. Nothing more nor less."

"Well anyway, I liked the way you made nothing of your sensations. I think that's drama, or is it anti-drama? Nothing more about your hair rising. Or your sweaty palms."

"I don't know what it is, but whatever it is, it hasn't got over the footlights."

"I adore ghost stories!" exclaimed Mrs. Imrie.

"Mr. Abson," the boy said, "did you ever do any acting when you were young?" He was leaning against the fireside wall with his knees drawn up and he now gave his full attention to the older man. This attention was compelling as though silently, deliberately, almost while they were unaware, he had smoothly pivoted the focus of the whole room round in one direction. By the steadiness of his eyes, the absolute stillness of his thin hands—clasped together and just touching his lips as though he were preparing for an absorbing story—he silenced the rest of the group. They might have been under iron command not to move. Nobody moved or spoke.

"No, I never did," replied Abson. Mrs. Imrie gave a faint, a very faint, exasperated sigh.

"Well no, I suppose that's not absolutely correct," said Abson, nervously smiling. "I was, as a boy, I remember, once given the part of a tree in some play or other."

"Yes?" came the boy's voice, quick and serious. There was unusual power in this young man. By split-second timing, by the sheer force of his expression and tone of voice, he had prevented a burst of laughter from the rest of the room.

"Well, I suppose you wouldn't really call it a play—it was probably a kind of ballet," said Mr. Abson, still smiling, though there were no answering smiles from the others. "It didn't, you'll agree, need great dramatic gifts."

"On the contrary," said the young man at once.

"I beg your pardon?" Abson looked surprised.

"On the contrary it would need rather special dramatic gifts to express this."

"Well, hardly human ones."

"Superhuman, then. Did you enjoy it?"

"I think I did, now that you remind me. I'd really absolutely forgotten the experience."

"Perhaps there were others."

"Others?"

"Perhaps there were other parts?"

"I don't think so—unless you count noises off. Anything I was asked to do was strictly non-human or background."

"To do a tree you've got to be more human, not less. You've got to be so human you can reach people and even go beyond them. That way you might just hope to arrive at your trees and rocks. Isn't that so?"

"Yes, that's an interesting point," said Mr. Abson.

"What kind of tree was it?" asked the young man.

"An apple tree," said Abson. There were still no smiles.

"In blossom or with apples?" asked the young man.

"Just leaves," said Mr. Abson, remembering so much now that his face was warm for once. His eyes stared from a nucleus of shadowy, scalloped green. "And an interesting thing I remember

57

—it was not to be a tree in the wind. That was definitely ruled out. Yet you'd have thought they'd have insisted on wind to make absolutely sure people knew what they were looking at."

"No, too obvious. All that thrashing and swooshing about, as though all trees must be in perpetual gales to show they really are trees. What rot!"

"Well, maybe you're right. Anyway, I had to make only the smallest movements—a kind of microscopic growing."

"Oh God—that's difficult enough!"

"Not much more than a vibration—I'm not sure about this."

"Your producer was a master then?"

"He was quite a talented young man, I think," said Abson mildly. "A vibration, or was it perhaps the dry bark cracking a bit in the sun?"

"God knows!" exclaimed the young man, at last permitting himself to smile. At once the rest of the group released themselves from his control. The red-haired girl put her head back on to the knee of the man behind who after simply lifting up strands of the long hair and letting them drop, began plunging his fingers up from the roots, tugging so roughly through the knots that the girl had her eyes screwed up each time his hand came down. It looked like torture but when her eyes were open the expression was blissful. Mrs. Imrie put the cup she had been holding all this time down on to its saucer. Neither the ghost nor the tree had exactly electrified the atmsophere for her. She decided that at a suitable moment she would give them the roof crashing in the night with the sparks flying off, and the butcher bent double over his bloody trembling knife.

"Well, I suppose I should be getting up now," said Mr. Abson. "I've very much enjoyed . . . but I think I'd better . . ."

"With your early start in the morning . . ." Mrs. Imrie agreed, rising briskly to accompany him to the hall. But the boy who sat at the fire was before her. It was now almost an acrobatic feat to cross the room over the outstretched legs but he was up and out at the same moment as Mr. Abson started to go slowly up, one hand on the banister. Through the open door they saw the young man go round to the side of the staircase and walk down the passage, sliding his own hand up the banister as far as it would go. For the last few inches he had to stand on his toes reaching out, his long fingers stretched hard against the wood, his body, straight and tense from head to foot, leaning forward at an angle along the banister. This sight gave the one or two who were watching a strange frisson of dread or elation. They watched a contact missed by inches, an effort to reach still further, doomed. Mr. Abson's hand moved smoothly on up the banister. He disappeared round the bend of the stairs without looking back. For a few moments longer the boy remained stretched out. Then his arm dropped like a weight. Mrs. Imrie's daughter joined him in the hall.

"Poor ghost," said the young man, turning slowly from the stairs. "One of you should take a look at him now and then. Just once in a while—look at him, will you?"

"I do. Honestly I do. Before you all arrived we were having a long talk."

"Or he'll fade out. He'll absolutely fade out."

"Don't you think we look after him well?"

"Look after—yes. Look *at* him!"

"Why should he fade out? I see him as a sort of dark spark. He can be brought to life all right. But it takes constant fanning. Bellows even."

"Use them then!" He went quickly past her into the room where Mrs. Imrie had already started the conflagration. Chimneys were crashing in the street, red, green and orange flames unravelled from window to window, and from one a white bundle dropped, then another, to the gasping crowd below. Great swirls of living sparks were being blown for miles along the rooftops. No gush of water could quench these. No hosepipe, however long, catch up with them.

Mr. Abson stayed with the Imries for two months more and then his work, whatever it was, took him to a neighbouring town where he remained another three months. And there he died. Three months ago. They had almost forgotten him. Or at any rate his face was not absolutely clear any more. But the manner of his death which they found in a newspaper, hearing further details from an acquaintance who lived in that town, jolted their memory in a peculiar way. He had failed to get out of the way of a lorry, the paper said. He had stepped out, said a witness, and stood still.

"No, it was not deliberate, if that's what you mean," said Mrs. Imrie to a friend who had come in. "If it says 'failed to get out of the way' then that's exactly what it means. I wouldn't say, now I come to think of it, that I ever saw him do *anything* exactly deliberately, would you, Brenda ?"

"Never. It would be that he didn't know whether to put his feet backwards or forwards. I've seen him do just that on the thresholds of doors."

"You will never really know, will you ?" said the friend.

"Never know what ?"

"Nothing. It's all right."

"It's terrible," said Mrs. Imrie. "Poor man, he should have shown more in his face. That would have helped him. It would have helped people to take notice of him too."

"He would be clear enough to the lorry-driver," said her son. "It's going to add another ghastly hazard to life if you're only visible to motorists if you've got an interesting expression."

"He only thought of things later when he was in his own room. That wasn't good for him, was it ? Like secret drinking or something. I should have interrupted him oftener."

"Why are we talking like this ? Could we help that bloody great lorry bearing down on him ?"

"Oh, how I sometimes wanted to give him a push!" exclaimed Mrs. Imrie. "If I could have given him a push when he was standing there—one hard push—it would have saved him!"

"Rooted. Rooted to the spot," said the girl. "What does that remind you of ? Are you thinking of a tree ?"

"Am I *what* ?" said her mother.

"If he'd even learnt to dance oddly enough," said the girl. "There are people who learn to dance simply to help them move their feet properly—to balance themselves. Did you know that ? Hospitals send them."

"Hospitals now!" cried Mrs. Imrie, holding her hand to her head. "So now you make out he was a sort of patient. Some kind of case, I suppose."

"It never even crossed my mind. I simply remember he sometimes asked about dances I'd been to."

"Near enough a case," said the friend, "if he just stood there."

"What are we talking about now ?" said Mrs. Imrie. "Has it come round to this again ? 'Failed to get out of the way'—I interpret that simply as I see it set down on the page."

"If you can see it simply," the friend said.

During the next few days they could have been no more acutely aware of Abson had he been following them around from room to room over the whole house. His death lit him up for them. He flickered with a red, unnatural light which flared or sank as their feelings about him flared or died. He was not silent. His identity demanded constant discussion and examination. Yet what did they know about him? They had scraped their memories. At the end of the week the girl, for the second time, rang the young man who had sat by the fire.

"You'll come round and help us out, won't you?"

"If I can. Are you still brooding?"

"Oh, we're stuck. It's hateful. We'd almost forgotten him. And now this. We've got to start again, and there's nothing to go on. He didn't talk about himself and neither did we."

"Why not forget him again?"

"How can I? I've got to get him clear first, if he's to be properly washed out. What was he like?"

"Look—I met him once only—at your house."

"But you had a feeling for him. Say something about him."

"It's you who must say it. Or you'll be haunted."

"Haunted by nothing! All I can think of is a spark and a tree. And don't ask why. I don't remember how they came in or when."

"Well think of them, then. Think hard!"

Later that evening, still having nothing to go on, she did think of them; for she was standing outside the open door of his room looking in at the place where, according to him, he had gone over and over things. What things? It was bare-looking now—a small room but with a high ceiling speckled in minute and scabby stars. A tree might grow in here. With an effort she could see it—this dry, grey tree with branches twisted at right angles round the corners of the ceiling and roots that had to bend back to fit the wainscoting. A rustling, creaking, cracking thing, dry to its sapless marrow. At first the dark spark settled lightly there like a crumb of dry ash, dead in the dead, bedroom air. Nothing kindled it here. It needed nothing, but took its life from some stupendous unknown fire blazing away miles from here. And gradually a microscopic speck of red began to burn at its centre. No movement fanned it, but still it expanded, fraying at its edges into palpitating spangles of rose-colour. Suddenly it ruptured, falling away into other sparks which went rolling and spinning along the branches, dropping down and falling apart again, multiplying, sprouting buds and shoots, roots, leaves, blossoms and fruits of green and yellow fire. The tree burned in silence. No part of it was reflected on the walls or the star-scabbed ceiling, and not a spark or speck of ash fell to the ground. At last a single white flame burst from the root and ripped up the length of the tree, reducing it in one flash, like the slashing upstroke of a knife, to ash and blackness. Then to nothing. Spark and tree went out.

"I feel better about him now," the girl told her mother and brother that night after supper. "I can put him out of my mind."

"How's that?" her mother asked.

"When you put everything together, looking back, you can see he was really alive."

"Was he?" said her brother. "But now he's dead."

"He wasn't dead all the time though. Not grey as we thought. If he'd been dead alive as well as dead dead—that would finish me! But I can forget him!"

"But he's dead *now*," said her brother. "He stepped off a pavement."

"I prefer to think of it as going up in flame," said the girl. "It suits him—the way I'm thinking about him now. The way he was really alive all the time."

"Prefer all you like," said her brother, "but that's the way it was. He stepped off a pavement."

"Don't remind me of that fire," said her mother with a shudder. "Don't ever bring that up again."

REMOVAL

REMOVALS had always had this extraordinary attraction for him. Yet attraction is too weak a word. For the removal van—any removal van—worked on the boy like a gigantic magnet of solid steel which could pull him, as it would a slim filing, round the corners of streets, out of shops or houses, dragging him backwards as though by the hairs of his head out of any occupation or conversation he happened to be engaged in. He did not discuss the fascination with anyone, seeing no one else had it as strongly as he had. It was simply taken for granted that he would be around, in the town or its outskirts, wherever other peoples' possessions were piling up beside their front doors.

The town was a fair-sized one, built high, with steep, busy streets running down to the dark sea on one side. On the other side was the residential part of the town, spreading out into villas, bungalows and summer houses, with a gravelled patch where the caravans stood, far from the sea. Beyond all this the roads narrowed and wound down into a shallow countryside cut into fertile strips of field and dotted with farms. There was a wood which in high winds made a sound almost indistinguishable from the sea, and one field completely covered in tall, white marguerites during the summer. Scattered about the world there are still people who imagine that the only time they were ever really happy was on some stormy evening in this wood, or during a hot after-noon spent in the field with the cold daisies crushed under their ears. But not the boy. Or he could have spent his whole time on the other side amongst the crash of boats unloading or up beside the sheds where they were being built and where all day long the hammering and sawing was going on. But no. His only curiosity was with these giant vans which stood for hours, blocking both sea and country, outside some house, waiting for it to disgorge its contents.

The boy had to be there when the stuff spilled out. He liked to look through uncurtained windows at the rooms emptying and whitening. He got in the way of huge men in black aprons, sweating down flights of stairs with grand pianos or who came out balancing chairs on tables and pots and pans stacked on chairs, like conjurers in the final act of a spectacular turn. They were good-natured enough, but if he got under their feet they cursed him lustily, and the curses, blown out on great, rasping breaths, sent him sprinting round to the other side of the van where from a distance he could watch them, necks crimson, their eyes bulging, give the last tremendous heave to a sideboard or a great double wardrobe. Occasionally, when everyone else was down there in the street, he would even dart into the house and have a quick look round the empty rooms before they were finally shut up. The silence and emptiness fascinated him, and for a few minutes the place was his own. He could slide his hand over the square, grimy marks where pictures had hung or pick at the little shreds still clinging to the nails where a carpet had been roughly torn up. And from scraps here and there, from skeins of cobweb filling odd shapes on the wall, he could visualise colour schemes and build up his own elaborate furniture. Then he would dash out again as quickly as he had entered and that would be the end of it. He would never set foot there again, but for the next days or weeks until another house came up, he kept that particular roof over his head. He retired into it when he wanted to. He made his plans there and preserved an extraordinary privacy whenever he felt himself too much jostled. But the moment he got wind of a new owner moving in he disgustedly forgot the place. Any thought of sharing it was out of the question.

He was not always lucky. Sometimes many removals would go by before he managed to look round a house, and for weeks on end he would allow himself to be jostled like everyone else—by parents, relations, teachers, neighbours. He got himself hooked up on barbed questions and nudged into making paltry confessions. He did not mind this. The parents and the teachers were being chivvied themselves. There was a perpetual jostling movement

64

going on the whole time from above and below and from every side, and on the whole he enjoyed fighting his way through the crowd as long as he could finally strike a patch of absolute privacy for himself. A patch in a daisy field had not been enough, nor a circle of rocks on the beach. Very early he had been bitten with a passionate desire for private ownership.

Three years had changed him from the child who made a dash up the steps of strange houses, into a young man of sixteen who sauntered in, hands in pockets, with scarcely a glance behind him. These years coincided with a great spate of removals in that town. The new housing scheme was spreading out as well as the dozens of large villas which were going up on the outskirts, and so his passion took him one afternoon in early summer to a less familiar part of the town from where he had word of a removal. The place was on the verge of the country—not near the farmland, but at the other end where flat fields with garages and roadhouses linked it to the next town. Here large, white-painted houses stood, widely separated from one another by lines of frail, new-planted trees and elaborate walled gardens, freshly dug from the fields. But there was already a prosperous air. The gleaming garden walls were already well padded with little cushions of rare rock plants, and the new-laid gravel leading up to each door was as bright and sharp to walk on as a thick crust of diamonds.

It was very quiet when he arrived on the scene. A few bits and pieces of furniture were still lying about ready to be lifted, but the removal men had almost finished the job and were sitting wedged in the entrance of the van with thick wads of sandwiches spread out on the top of packing-cases. From the kerb of the pavement below them, a draped, marble figure was diffidently holding up a bunch of grapes. The house itself looked empty and it seemed the owners were already gone, for there was no car in the garage. The boy went round to the back of the van and walked unhurriedly, unnoticed, along the path to the front door. It was half-open and he stepped inside. There was no question of creeping in. The place was now his, and what was more—his best yet. It had certain features that he'd never had before, giving, for instance, an immediate impression of light and space. And things were on a large scale. The picture marks on the walls of the main room were enormous, the dark patches where mats had been lifted showed that they had been outsize mats, if startlingly dirty. It was the sort of house he could retire comfortably to for days afterwards, even if he managed to set foot in it for only three minutes and never set eyes on it again. He went quickly upstairs and opened one door after another—just wide enough to stick his head in and take a long, cool stare round each one. He was quick about it but not furtive, for he was no amateur now. He even had an instinctive feeling about which doors led merely to cupboards or musty little boxrooms. He had no time at all for these, and in this particular house it was even a question whether he had any time, other than a glance, for the third bedroom whose door he had just opened and was about to shut again.

It was the smallest bedroom—a rather dull box of a place like many he had seen before in other houses, but his practised eye caught the thing that was different about it and made him pause. The clearing of this room had obviously been a careless job and various scraps and pieces had been left behind. There was an old rug rolled up at the fireplace, a wastepaper basket stuffed with envelopes. A long newspaper cutting was laid along the mantelpiece, weighted by a large, white pebble. But what he particularly noticed was a small, framed photograph on one wall, and two, cut-glass beads on the floor under the window. Against his better judgment the boy stepped inside the room and shut the door behind him. First he picked up the beads, then went over to study the picture. It was of a young girl. Perhaps she was about fifteen, but the profile was already a very conscious one as though she had long ago discovered that this was the side of her which must always be presented to the public eye. It was an intriguing face and could lead an observer to wonder whether the full face would reveal something quite different from the profile which was pensive, reserved and rather severe, under a pile of dark hair. Her neck was the most remarkable feature—long and unusually slender, but it was held stiffly and the stiffness was almost certainly due to her having put her hair up for the first time shortly before the picture was taken. He ran his eye down the newspaper cutting without picking it up, for it was a long and tedious account of a choir concert with the singers names listed at the bottom. He had no doubt that hers would be amongst them and after some thought he picked a name for her—Marian Martin. It was the best he could do amongst a lot of names he disliked more. Time was running out, and down below the men would be getting through the last of the sandwiches. But he was rather more involved than he had ever been. The beads, the choir, the photo had slowed him down. He now unhooked the little picture and took it over to the window to have a closer look. When he raised his eyes again he saw that, for the first time in all his life of removals, he was caught.

He was looking down on to a long back garden enclosed by walls. But the constriction in his chest came not from these walls—for he could see over them to further gardens and beyond that to fields—but from a long, wavering plume of smoke rising from a bonfire lit in one corner. An old woman who had been poking it was staring up at him intently, yet without surprise. She even gave him a nod, to which, after a second or two, he responded with a cool wave of the hand which held the photo. But the back of his neck felt rigid. She was obviously expecting him to go down and he went quickly enough, only to find her waiting on the path at the side of the house. He corrected his speed at once, and was soon sauntering behind her round to the back garden where they stopped and faced one another. She was tall—a gaunt, brown-skinned old woman with dark eyes shining from the hollows behind high cheekbones. Black hair, only lightly streaked with grey, was drawn straight back across her ears and hung in a heavy loop at the nape of her neck. She was leaning, both large hands clasped over the stick with which she had been prodding the fire.

"Well," she said after a pause in which she never took her eyes from his, "so you're the cousin." Behind the hoarse, old woman's voice there was the hint of a foreign accent. He allowed her question to hang vaguely in the air and finally float off and escape with the plumes of smoke which he followed enviously with his eyes. In no time the curious questions and the demands would start piling up around him. In no time he would be in the thick of it, jostled and prodded. Meanwhile he smiled, and the smile seemed to annoy her.

"Well, I never imagined they'd send a child round to close up," she said. "I'd expected a man." This fairly stung him. Nervousness instantly vanished in anger, and his smile became insolent.

"What's more—you're late," she went on, staring at his mouth, "very late. I've my own place to attend to, and men to feed. All right—so you're here. Then I can go. I see you've done all the clearing up you intend to do." Her eyes fell to the photo which he

67

still held in one hand while with the other he fingered the beads in his pocket. They now felt like diamonds and he didn't care for the sensation. The old woman didn't go, but turned to a nearby shed and wrenched the door open. There was a dark jumble of stuff in one corner, pierced here and there by pitchforks, rakes and a variety of garden shears. Around the walls hung knapsacks and boots dangling by their laces, and a new tent, still snowy-white, was crushed down amongst sacks and old mackintoshes. There was a smell of musty rubber, onions and oil-paint.

"Look at this!" said the woman. "You've had an easier job inside than I've had out. Here, you can help! Some of this stuff is for the men to lift, the rest goes to the dustbins." She bent down and with her back to him began to toss things out without looking round. A thick, folded groundsheet whacked him on the chest, and he swerved from a climbing-boot which came at him with its nails gleaming. It was rough treatment for a house-owner —rough even for a cousin of the house. While her back was still turned he thrust the photo for safety in amongst the prickly twigs of a flowering bush. When he came back to the shed he remarked with dignity: "I've never seen you before, have I?"

"Why should you? My job's the garden—and I've been exactly three times. Before they decide to move off." She turned abruptly round and stared at the climbing boots. "You might imagine by the mess in here that it was all camping and climbing with them— when all the time it was nothing but moving about from place to place. I've scarcely seen them on the outside of a car myself. Now, that's all right, young man—cousin or whatever you are! Don't glare at me. They're yours, not mine, and I'll say what I'll say. Why should I hold my tongue for any of you? Can't you see. Money's the trouble here. Every object's brand-new. Used once and flung into a corner!"

The boy flushed and drew his brows together. The woman's taunts were beginning to get under his skin, as though it were the thinnest of family skins. At the same time, a vague idea of these people, whoever they were, began to form in his mind. He felt a pride and shame, not for themselves, but for how they might reflect upon the girl whose face at this moment was shining, clear as a half-moon, out of the bush.

"And as you know, that girl—" the old woman spoke as though following his secret thought, "—that girl wa sactually given a harp! Well yes, if you don't mind—a harp!"

"Go on!" exclaimed the boy defiantly, bracing his shoulders. He was as tall as the old woman. Now he seemed to tower over her, and he glared.

"Go on?" she jeered. "How do you mean—go on? What else is there to tell. She draws her fingers once or twice over this harp and that's the end of it. Brand new as it came out of the box!"

"Out of the box!" exclaimed the boy sarcastically, then failing to find anything more cutting to say he flung his head back and laughed. Still the smoke was fleeing over the wall into the sky and still he longed to be away. But now they were fairly crying out for him to defend them. Besides, the old woman's goading had made him strong. She turned back, muttering, to pull something else from a corner of the shed.

"Camping!" she made a contemptuous sound and shook out the folded tent before him. There was no denying its snowy whiteness.

"All the same . . ." began the boy.

"All the same—what?" said the woman. "Maybe they camped in the back garden!"

The boy drew a deep breath. He shouted: "You know nothing about it! I've been with them! Stop talking about them! I've been all over the place with them!"

There was an abrupt silence in the back garden. The woman's fingers stopped scruffing about in the canvas of the tent. Neither of them moved. But round at the front the men were moving about in the cramped van. There was a scraping and bumping as they shifted bits of furniture, stretched their legs in a new position, and settled down into silence again.

"I've been with them!" shouted the boy, waving his head wildly and throwing his arms about. "They've been all over the place!"

"Over the world, eh?" The old woman was grinning.

"I didn't say that. The continent."

"Ah, the continent! They were in the mountains, were they?"

"Yes, the mountains. Switzerland."

"You were all climbing these mountains? Camping and climbing? Well—funny thing. They never walk a step around here. Keep calm. You're too hot. Why don't you sit down?"

It was true his cheeks were burning, his eyes smarting. He actually looked as though he were just preventing himself from bursting into tears. He sat down on the edge of an old box, his

69

head turned away. The woman, the fight gone out of her, stood for a while looking out over the garden with her arms folded. The tent which she had dropped was spread out like a great crushed flower at their feet. The brash boots lay hopeless on their sides.

"And the girl was there too?" She asked the question carefully, without scoffing. He nodded. After some time the woman sat down too, crossed her legs and rested her chin on her hand which was brown and bony, rimmed with black earth round the nails. She stared long and intently out over the garden.

"The view from the tops of those mountains!" she exclaimed at last in her hoarse voice.

"Yes," said the boy. He did not commit himself.

"No, I mean the distances, the distances!" she rasped, clawing out into the air with her huge hand. The boy turned his head now to stare cautiously at her, and after a moment looked away again, reassured. "It's not as clear as all that," he said rather glumly. "When the mist comes down you couldn't even see your own hand."

The woman kept her hand out and brushed it impatiently to and fro in front of her eyes.

"No, no," said the boy wearily. "You've got to wait—maybe hours, maybe days—for a rift or a hole."

"Yes—a hole," said the old woman, bending forward intently, "a hole you can put your eye to. But it's better than nothing. And what then?"

"Then you see whatever there is to see. Maybe another mountain, maybe a bit of the valley with a house. Maybe just a scrap of blue or green."

"A scrap of waterfall, eh?"

"Or it might be a cow or a person."

"And you've just come out of this tent?"

"What?"

"You've been inside this tent. And now you're outside looking through a rift?"

"Yes."

"This tent—it's been propped up on some flat bit of the mountain?"

"Sometimes. It could be just a ledge—a narrow ledge with a drop of hundreds of feet below." The old woman hissed between her teeth and chafed her elbows as though an icy blast had caught

70

her.

"And before you come out you make a little hole, a little crack in the tent and look through?" she demanded.

"I suppose so."

The old woman groaned deeply. "You put your eye to this little rift in the tent. Then you come out, and we'll suppose the mist's all around—and you wait, maybe for hours, for another little hole, a little crack to stare through?" This time the boy was silent.

"God . . . help . . . us!" exclaimed the old woman, drawing out each word slowly, vehemently. She stared a long time, her mouth set grimly, her eyes narrowing on the scene in front of her. Yet everything here was clear and peaceful. The gardens diminished into the distance until the walls were strips of white, the green and black fences fine as tooth-combs. Nearby a large white cat padded along a rockery, stopped to sniff a purple flower, padded along and stopped again, its tail quivering. It was extraordinarily silent, and the air so still that the thin plume of smoke was now going softly up into the sky with scarcely a waiver to one side or the other. Blue shadows of leaves were stuck like transfers to pink and white painted back doors.

Suddenly the old woman shouted: "Don't talk to me about the wind!" The boy jerked his head round, startled. He had even raised his elbow as though to defend himself.

"When it wasn't mist it was the wind!" cried the old woman. "The wind was worst. If you listened, there was nothing you couldn't hear in that wind. Such a moaning and gasping, such a retching and groaning and crying! And how am I going to get it out of my ears? Twenty years away. Do you think that makes any difference? It's still here—here in my ears!" She pounded the sides of her head with her fists. The boy had now turned his whole body away from her except for his head and his eyes. They both remained frozen, motionless, for some minutes—the boy with his eyes fixed on the woman's face; the woman, her hands to her head, staring forward with sickening intensity as though penetrating clean through the peaceful scene, deep, deep down into unspeakable abomination.

The boy had screwed himself not to yell out, when suddenly her face changed. She focused again on the wall, the cat, the flowery stones. Her hands fell to her lap and she turned her head slightly towards him.

71

"But you—you hear nothing," she said sardonically. "Or perhaps only music—harp music!" He smiled faintly. Cautiously now he turned his body towards her, and eased his neck which had grown stiff as though with momentary paralysis. He began to revive in the mocking air between them. He began to feel equal to her again. And now she had slapped the palms of her hands down on her knees and got to her feet abruptly. She began to haul out the last of the stuff in the shed.

"Come on," she said, when it was all out: "this lot round to the men—the rest stays for the rubbish. Well, come on. Aren't you going to tell them, or do you want to carry it round yourself, piece by piece?"

"You can tell them," he said. He had recovered some of his wits.

The old woman straightened up slowly and stood over him, very tall. "Look here, I've nothing to do with this stuff. Whether it goes or stays is your business now. So you'd better get on with it. Are you going to let them drive off?"

Reluctantly he walked round the side of the house and slowly up the front path towards the van. The men were finished eating but they were still inside the van. They were arguing. One of them had spread out a newspaper and was prodding a headline with his finger, but he stopped at sight of the boy. Behind him the others craned out, astounded at the intrusion. The boy himself looked apologetic. There was no sauntering now. Once, all had been plain-sailing, but then he had reckoned without the tents and the harps, without the monstrous memories of old women or the secrets of sly, smiling girls.

"More stuff back there!" he called, pointing behind him. But he no longer felt himself to be an owner of houses. His voice scarcely penetrated the van and the men pretended not to hear, but fell silent as though on guard of a huge cavern stuffed with loot. In front the empty street opened out to him and again he longed to be off. But this time there was going to be no quick get-away. What was behind weighed heavily on him. Back there he had his ties—he had relations of a sort, a friend certainly, he had a heap of stuff to shift. But there was more than the stuff to shift. He knew it was up to him to make some final reckoning with this place unless it was to haunt him for the rest of his days.

"Back here," he called again, retreating down the path and round to the side where he stood waiting. He watched while the men slowly eased themselves out from the upturned tables and chairs and jumped down, one by one, their boots crashing on the empty pavement. Low flowering bushes bent on either side of them as they came up the path and round the house. They were laughing good-humouredly enough as they brushed past him, and one of them gave a little tweak to the lapel of his jacket, as though, in spite of the calling and the pointing, they knew him to be an absolute outsider to the whole affair. He was still in the same spot when they came back a minute or two later with the stuff. There was not enough for the four of them. One was trundling a lawn-mower with the spades, forks and hoes over his shoulder, another carried the folded tent—boots and knapsacks swinging from his elbow. Two men between them were carrying a heap of water-proofs and a sack stuffed with rope. The last man had nothing. He bent and from the path in front of him picked up the head of a small, crushed yellow rose which had got torn from a bush in the first upheaval.

"Here you are, laddie," he said, offering it with a friendly and sardonic grin. "Thanks for all your help!"

The old woman was treading out the last wisps of bonfire when he went round to the back again, and when every spark was extinguished she strode to the shed, locked it, and heaved her side against the door to make sure it was fast. And as he watched, he marvelled at her. He could remember no other old woman whose movements had seemed so strong and so determined. Exodus was in her bones. All ordinary removals must seem trivial to her now, yet she went about things as though unaware that not until the final scene could she come into her own. She could make all tramping down of fires, all turning of keys, testing of closed doors —absolutely final and irrevocable. At last she faced him, slowly brushing her large hands down over her hair, over her chest and down the long folds of her stiff skirt, letting them finally hang loose and open at her sides. It gave him a strange pang to see this movement—this long and final brush-off. Their contact, such as it was, had ended.

"Well," she said, "your job's done. And thanks." For the second time in the space of a few minutes he was being thanked. He gave her a quick look, but her eyes were grave. Now the long, blue shadows of chimneys stroked slowly down over the rockery, where the white cat was kneading herself into a cleft between the cooling stones. The removal van had driven off some time ago, and in the distance they could hear a factory hooter blowing from the town. It seemed hours since he had entered the place, but one thing was certain. Though this would never be his house, however long it stood empty, yet it was only with a tremendous effort he could bring himself to quit it. But it had to be done. And there was still one last object to pick up. He went to the bush and drew the photo out from under the prickly leaves. Crouching, with his back to the woman, he rubbed his sleeve over the glass and slipped it into the pocket of his jacket, then, straightening up, he stood for some time looking up at the stripped windows of the empty house. Still with his back turned, still staring up, he twisted the yellow rose into his lapel—casually, almost absent-mindedly, yet skilfully, like a mature and confident man smilingly displaying himself, with his buttonhole, to the gaze of flattering eyes at windows. He held the attitude for a full minute and, still holding it, walked out of the garden where the old woman was now busy picking up the odd scraps of rag and paper strewn around the shed. She had not looked his way again.

The road where the van had been was still absolutely empty and silent. Facing the front, the gates and garages were all wide open ready for the cars to come back. Paths, hedges and doorsteps —all gave it the clipped, smoothed-down appearance of a place awaiting a succession of punctual and prosperous returns. But on the side where the van had been the road had a churned-up look, and the house, after its ugly exposure, appeared to be nailed and settled down all round, absolutely tight and silent. The boy began to move off cautiously with his hand over the rose to hide it from anyone who might happen to be around, but also to keep it secure in his buttonhole. After a few steps he had begun to loosen up, and when the first home-coming car passed him, both hands were in his pockets and he was taking long strides back towards the town.

A CONVERSATION ON FEET

Two women were walking in single file along a high ridge overlooking the sea. Behind them the path narrowed steeply and at its highest point disappeared into a mere sandy track running along the cliff's edge, but in front it gradually broadened and flattened out until eventually, far down below, it became part of the smooth, white promenade which stretched round the whole of the bay. At the far end of this bay was their hotel. Just at that point on the path where usually they began hurrying forward to be in time for supper the younger woman fell behind a little. She seemed to be smiling to herself. These two things had a vaguely disconcerting effect on her friend, but she attributed this feeling to the pressure of time and began to glance from her watch to the hotel which was still a long distance away. But in a moment the other had made up on her and they were walking side by side again.

"It was a curious sensation," said the younger woman who was called Sarah, "though it must be a very common one. I felt it for the first time the other night when I was taking the short cut from the post office along that path by the ploughed field. I was wearing my sandals. You know the ones I mean?"

"Your old sandals—yes. I suppose it was worth bringing them, if only to save the other ones for evening. Well, what happened to you, Sarah?"

"You remember Tuesday—it was the first really warm day, and the ground was bone dry. The soles of my sandals are so thin you can feel the earth pressing against the arches of your feet. It's as though you were walking barefoot."

75

"I don't wonder, Sarah. They're nearly done—those sandals. They'll hardly survive another holiday. One of the soles is actually worn right through at one part. And there's nothing you can do about that—not with crêpe. When we get back to town you could try that shop again, but I doubt if they'll have them now—not exactly those ones anyway."

". . . barefoot. It was not so much the feeling of simply walking on top of the ground or using the ground to get along to some other place. There was no division between earth and feet. I discovered for the first time what the ground was actually made of and how the different parts of my feet were shaped. Of course, there's no such thing as a flat piece of ground. You can feel al sorts of unevenness—those tufts of cold, slippery grass and perhaps at the next step a mound of fine, very warm earth that fills up your shoes like dust, and even on the dryest day cold hollows, rather damp where a stone has been dislodged. And the stones themselves are all shapes—round ones rolling under your feet and those sharp little flinty ones that get wedged inside the soles of your shoes."

"What happened, Sarah? Did you hurt your foot?"

"Suddenly in a flash, no, not a flash—it's more like a beat, or is it the feeling of actually missing a beat . . . ?"

"You didn't fall, Sarah? Why didn't you tell me? Was it on your back?"

"Suddenly in this instant I knew what it would be like to fall in love. Do you understand what I mean?"

There was a very short silence. Then Nora, the other woman, spoke again: "I know the path you mean, of course—you could hardly call it a path; it's almost part of the field, and full of stones as you say. Was it your foot or did you actually fall down?"

"Suddenly I had an idea what they were all getting at—the songs and the poems and especially those scraps from dance-bands that blare out from radio stores as you go past. For the first time I actually felt the love in them."

"Through your feet?"

"I'm trying to tell you—that's how it was."

The path was clearly broadening now and it would have been possible to walk side by side and still have plenty of room to swing about or gesticulate freely with the arms. All the same, the two women walked within some carefully prescribed limit of their own.

They seemed to take enormous care about this as though it were necessary to control not only their own movements but also, by looking straight ahead, to curb the tremendous energy of the sea below them on one side, and on their other side to ensure the continued balance of the huge black boulders which appeared to have been savagely ripped from the hills above and tossed right to the cliff's edge where they had stood for a millenium—as though still rocking with their fall—in mocking positions of appalling insecurity. Occasionally one woman would fall behind for a moment to let another person go past—someone coming up from the town, climbing slowly—someone perhaps who was staying at one of the boarding-houses where supper could be as much as an hour earlier than the hotel meal.

"Those songs you mentioned," said Nora, making an effort to place her feet absolutely steadily on the path which, though it had broadened out, had not begun to be smooth; "—were you referring to popular songs—pop singers? I mean the ones that rhyme 'blue' and 'you' and 'true'?"

"That kind of thing—yes."

"I believe they are not very difficult to make up."

"No, I don't think they could be."

"I should think almost anybody could do it."

"I'm not sure about that, but at any rate some people must find it easy."

"And make a great deal of money. It is not difficult to find words to rhyme with 'love', either."

"Oh no. I can think of two or three straight off."

"I expect they are exactly the same ones I am thinking of—'glove', 'dove', 'above'."

"Yes, you're right; those are the ones."

"Can you think of any more?"

"Not just for the moment."

Nora had fallen a step or two behind her friend through some momentary depression. It seemed as though something which was important to her had not been proved.

"No, it's got to be clearer than that, Sarah," she said, making up the short distance between them again. "I'm sorry, but all this about shoes and feet—it's not like you. I wish you hadn't brought feet into it, Sarah."

"Why not?"

"We've known one another long enough, haven't we? I'd have thought that by this time you might sometimes find it possible to be a little more direct with me—that's all."

"Well, I'm direct as I can be, Nora. I can't make it much plainer—what I felt—can I?"

"Do you think so? Well, it's just your way, isn't it, Sarah, and I daresay you'll tell me some other time when it suits you."

"Tell you what?"

"Oh, that you've met some man or other that you like."

"Some man I like!"

"All right. Do you want me to use the word 'love'? I don't intend to go into it. I'm just asking you to be a little more open with me. We'd get on better, and it would be more human, to say the least."

"But I haven't met any man."

"That's all right, Sarah. You need say nothing more about it—not another word. What do you take me for? Have I ever asked you one single thing about your personal life?"

"Never, Nora."

"Have I, in all the time we've known one another, ever tried to find out anything about your private affairs?"

"You never have, Nora."

"Or even about your family or any of your friends?"

"Never at any time."

"All right then, Sarah. Let's leave it at that. Only please don't treat me like a creature who knows nothing and feels nothing. After all, it's not the first occasion that a woman on holiday remembers—or even actually meets—some man she's attracted to. She has more time, of course."

". . . Or who's attracted to *her*."

"Of course—that goes without saying."

"It's better to say it, all the same. Though in this case neither seems to fit."

"Meaning . . . ?"

"There's no particular man in it."

"Ah, so we're back to that, are we?"

"We seem to be. Only it was you who brought in the subject of men."

"I must say it seems rather odd," said her friend, laughing lightly. "If it's no particular man—what is it? Just men in general,

78

I suppose."

"Yes, as a matter of fact that seems to get nearer it. You could say the feeling was for every man."

Now there was a long silence and the older woman looked about her with a grim, hurt smile. In front of them the whole sky seemed to have darkened slightly, but the sun was still hot on their backs. As though materialising suddenly from the empty spaces behind, a large family went tramping past—bringing a murmured exchange of greetings as they went by. Even in the short time they took to pass it was possible to see that between them they were sporting an extraordinary variety of footwear—Nora saw Wellington boots, high-heeled shoes, galoshes, sandals and plimsolls; the smallest child wore a pair of scarlet sand-shoes with white gulls on them. The six of them had managed to churn up the soft path for some distance ahead, and although walking with her eyes on the ground, she found it difficult to decipher the various footprints they made. Yet it seemed important to her that she should make out at least one clear set of marks before the hard white concrete fifty yards or so in front hid all human trace.

Sarah said, as though having thought the whole matter through clearly and completely: ". . . And not necessarily all men either—all women, if you like—or stones, chairs, railings, milk-bottles—or just bits of glass . . ."

"Kettles?" asked the other woman. Her smile was wild and despairing.

"Yes, if you like," said Sarah politely.

The path took a last steep turn and they were on to the concrete which brought them down quickly and smoothly into the narrow end of the long High Street. On one side was the dark green sea rolling in over a beach of black stones—on the other a row of small, expensive shops—a jeweller's, a tea-shop, a chemist, and a shoe-shop displaying in its window every type of summer sandal. Even though the going was now so smooth one of the women seemed to be limping slightly. She looked very tired.

"It's a relief to get off the subject of feet, anyway," she remarked, glancing once at the shops and then quickly away to the dark sea on the other side. "Or was it shoes? It may be harmless enough—the way you talk; and feet are all right. But you can go too far like that."

"On my feet, you mean?"

"Don't smile at me. I'm often unhappy about you, Sarah. And I feel we are neither of us open enough with one another. I am at fault too—I admit it. And in your case all this love you have for stones and men and women and chairs and kettles hasn't made you very expansive, has it? Has it even made you very loving, Sarah—that's what I'd really like to ask? I mean to any thing or person in particular?"

"I think you're probably right, Nora. I wouldn't say it has."

"I mean if the feeling's spread so wide over everything, it's bound to get fairly thin."

"Yes, if you think of it like jam—I suppose it is."

"I don't think of it like jam," said Nora. But she seemed less tense now, and her walk was easier. Even Sarah wore a more good-natured expression. And the hotel was now so near you could see the children at the upper windows leaning out over their damp, striped towels and tipping the small stones out of the heels of their shoes on to the window-sills.

"If ever you want to tell a love-story about yourself or anyone else I wouldn't begin with your feet, if I were you,' 'said Nora with a faint smile. "Feeling everything through your feet is one thing, and explaining it is another. You see, people don't really want to hear that sort of thing. Don't bother with your feet, Sarah."

The other woman said nothing. By this time they were near enough to hear the clatter from the dining-room as the waitresses finished laying the meal and began to light the little lamps at each table. Yet the sun was still blazing down, red and purple, on the chimneys of the house. Nora felt a slight chill at the strange waste of these lamps—the little lamps burning away in the full blaze of the evening sun.

"I suppose what you really meant all the time was that you felt something in your heart," she said in an even and encouraging voice.

"No, Nora. It was my feet. I'm sorry. My feet."

"That's all right," said Nora.

Ahead of them the sea was now slashed with sharp little white lines, yet further out near the horizon there was no movement to be seen—only a smooth, grey surface, lightly scratched, as though with a sharp knife. But near at hand waves broke on the black pebbles with a comfortless sound. The women walked on towards the front door of the hotel, moving steadily and slightly apart—any contact between them visible only when the ends of their identical silk scarves went fluttering back behind them, linked momentarily in a sudden chill gust of wind blowing from the open sea.

SUNDAY CLASS

THIS semicircle crouched around the teacher are dead on time with their answers. A well-drilled lot, they flick them back, one after the other, while the question is scarcely out of her mouth.

"Flowers."

"Birds."

"Good food."

"Homes."

"Friends."

"And loved ones," snaps the oldest girl jealously.

Now they all turn their heads to the boy at the end. They know there is nothing left for him except 'good books', 'good music' or perhaps 'sunshine' at a pinch. They wait for it. He stares stubbornly down towards the end of the room.

"Come on," urges the woman, Miss MacRae, her eyes wavering from her lapel brooch to her wrist-watch. "Some of the things God wants us to be grateful for?"

"Dinosaurs," says the boy.

There is a pause while the woman shifts the fur about her neck. She looks warm. "To be *grateful* for," she warns.

"I know that. I said 'dinosaurs'."

"I suppose you know what they are?"

"I know all about them. Always have."

"And you know how to spell them?"

"It doesn't matter."

"What did you say?"

"It doesn't matter."

"Can you not think of anything else?"

"No. I'm thinking of them all the time."

"*All* the time?" Her eyes narrow in suspicion.

"Well, someone had better think about them. They were around for millions of years. I'm grateful for them!"

There is reason to be grateful for the swinge and whack of the monstrous, scaly tails in this stifling hall. A quiver of relief runs through the others in the circle as they momentarily throw aside good books, homes and loved ones. They stare up towards the high sealed windows expectantly. In this East of Scotland town it is common enough to see things swirling in the air even at that height. On the stormiest days tufts of foam have sailed past and whole sodden newspapers flattened themselves out against the glass. Besides being a meeting-place for various classes during the week this hall is sometimes used for a dance, and on Sunday morning the sweaty dust of Saturday night still hangs in the air. On the platform stands a grand piano, swathed in green cloth. Along the wall behind it are various Bible pictures, maps and travel posters. There is also a chart showing a fair-haired young man balancing on the apex of a large isosceles triangle, and at graded levels beneath him a variety of animals stare wonderingly up, except for one or two leathery creatures near the bottom who continue to stare glumly at their own tails. The chap standing at the top looks glad to be where he is, but not surprised. He is not naked, as in some charts, but wears a casual sports shirt and flannel trousers. His pink, open palms are turned outwards to show that he has nothing to hide. His bare feet are also turned outwards.

Down both sides of the room, separated from one another by thin, wooden screens, are a dozen or so small circles seated around a man or a woman. From behind each screen comes a strange murmuring, discreet and low. It is like the murmuring of visitors in a hospital ward—sometimes placating, sometimes insistent or impatient, but always mesmerically soft. The boy who has dinosaurs on the brain keeps turning his head first to the stage and then to the door. Sometimes he tips his chair forward and cranes his neck as though to see around the neighbouring screens and to catch another murmur, perhaps to compare one murmur with another. Then he returns his attention to the woman in front of him, watching her mouth closely like a lip-reader or like somebody following a conversation in a foreign language. This irritates

83

her more than anything else.

"I'm afraid that's not quite good enough," she insists. "I want something more."

The rest of the class fix him with their eyes. They are afraid that now for the sake of peace he will hand her a good book or even a single perfect flower. But the boy broods. Now he is dredging through the deepest pits of the sea. Things not quite good enough for Miss MacRae spurt from fissures or prod the blackness with phosphorescent eye-stalks. Further up are creatures frilled, beaked and scalloped, some whip-thin, others round and smooth as bells. And far above in steaming tropical forests the ground crackles and glitters with ferocious insects. He has made his choice. He scratches his knee thoughtfully, then raises his hands and demonstrates something in the air.

"There's a sort of insect—" he ruminates. "A giant fish-killing bug with claws that fold up under its head like a clasp-knife . . ."

"I am taking no notice of you," Miss MacRae interrupts instantly, her eyes riveted on him. "Everybody else can understand what I'm asking. Are you different from everyone else?"

He is silent. They are all silent, studying Miss MacRae. In striking contrast to her lack of love for wildlife she is made up of scraps from various birds and beasts. She is sporting a tuft of bright-coloured feathers, a couple of paws, a tail and a head and a carved bone or two. Her gloves are suede and she has a small purse-bag made of real pigskin lined with coarse hair. There is nothing artificial about her except the butterfly brooch in her lapel and the deep-set button eyes in the furry head that peers over her shoulder.

At the top of the room a handbell is struck loudly—signal that it is time to reassemble in the larger adjoining hall. Although most of the group snatch up magazines and Bibles and stampede off as usual, a few—mostly the older girls—linger as though protectively about Miss MacRae. Today there are mixed feelings about her. Her dismissal of dinosaurs and her withdrawal from fish-killing bugs has shown her to be wildly outside and utterly alone. It seems there is no place to put her now. All the same some of them feel for her in their hearts, and the oldest girl strokes the face of the little fox consolingly.

But the boy remains uncompromisingly stern. He gives them all time to clear off to the next room and in the meantime he takes

84

a closer look at the chart on the wall behind the platform. This look confirms something he has suspected for a long time. Now there is no doubt about it. Miss MacRae is the true, self-appointed mate of the chap standing on the sharp, topmost point of the isosceles triangle. Her place is up there beside him. But could the man bring himself to step aside one fraction of an inch to make room for her?

THE SIEGE

WHY should anyone imagine that because she was now alone she would immediately begin to do things on a much smaller scale? Did it mean that she was expected to cut everything by exactly half because her husband had died—outings, phone calls, friends, food, rubbish? There would be time enough for that. At the moment it could only underline the drastic change in her life. For instance she never even started to get the small portions which were offered to her—tiny packets of this and that, diminutive tubes and bottles and jars and those dainty cakes of soap that melted away after half-a-dozen washings. This was the expensive way of doing things as everyone knew, and apart from that she didn't intend to be diminished, because that meant instant death. Before long people would begin to offer her dainty portions of love and economical little squares of friendship, exactly enough to last over a certain period with nothing wasted. So she kept to the medium size in everything. It was a normal, decent size and gave her enough weight when she went shopping to keep her properly balanced amongst the crowds on Saturday morning who were staggering home obviously loaded up with stuff for endless family parties. The great thing was to keep a sense of proportion.

All the same shopping took up a longer and longer part of each day. It began to eat up the friends and the interests in a mysterious way. Sometimes, walking home with a bag of sensible sized packets, it seemed to her that the sense of proportion was beginning to have a curiously chilling effect on her whole existence. Her day was now divided up in accordance with a strict schedule. No top secretary ticking off a list of pressing social and business engagements could have kept a closer watch on the clock. There was a time for everything, from the stroke of ten in the morning when she snatched her shopping-bag off its hook till half past ten at night when she placed her slippers side by side under the bed. But it was the shopping which tired her most. She was as tired as though she were continually buying stuff not only for a husband but for a large family and a hoard of hungry relatives—and critical and demanding relatives at that. She felt she must be far, far more tired than anyone else she saw on her expeditions.

After a time she made a change in her life, or at any rate in her shopping which seemed now to take up so much of her attention that it could almost be called her life. She gave up the medium sizes. They had been a failure from the start and had tended to contract her in some way. Instead she bought the giant-size packets, the outsize tins and jars and bottles which were advertised as being in the end more economical of both money and energy.

"This is going to save me an enormous amount of time," she would say to the shop assistants who were surprised to find themselves handing over monster tubes of toothpaste and mustard every week along with the rest of the stuff. But the truth was that when she had finished her shopping, made up her lists for the next day and got everything sorted out into its proper place she had very little time left and almost no energy for anything else. The lack of energy worried her. She was quite well of course. There was absolutely nothing wrong with her. But sometimes she felt so weak that she could hardly be bothered taking off her outdoor things when she got home from one of her shopping expeditions. Often she was still in her hat or in her heavy shoes till quite late in the day, which gave her the appearance of somebody who had simply looked in for a few minutes between outings, or who was sitting with one eye on the clock, just waiting to be called for. Nowadays she did not meet many people she knew outside, but when she did she made it clear that she would be very glad indeed to give and accept invitations whenever she had managed to get things properly sorted out. She used this phrase often and most people tactfully agreed that it took a long time to do this. They were not to know that sorting out meant stocking up. She went on steadily, silently building up her impenetrable inner wall of bottles, packets, tins, boxes, and pots and pots of jam of top-quality standard.

87

Her kitchen, facing north, had never been exactly sunny, but it had been a pleasant enough place to sit in. Certainly it had not been gloomy. Now the extra shadows gradually filling it would have been scarcely perceptible to anyone on an occasional visit. But a regular visitor, had there been such a person, would have noticed that the change in light had come about because the upper part of her window was slowly becoming blocked. The wide ledge which formed the top of the lower window was now being used as an extra shelf. Immense, rectangular packets were wedged side by side along the whole length of the ledge. They made a low barricade—cheerful enough at night in electric light, because most of them displayed red, yellow and blue pictures of exuberant children hanging over plates or laughing housewives with wind-blown aprons and eager husbands. But in the daytime they definitely made the place much darker and also stuffier, for the window could no longer be raised from the bottom. But there was nowhere else to put them. All the shelves in the flat were filled and the cupboards crammed.

She would have been quite ready to admit that her life was becoming difficult—in fact she was far past the stage for a mild admission. She could more easily have screamed or shouted it. Not that her life was empty—that word sounded absurd in the crammed flat. Nor could she say that the time hung heavily when she considered the amount of arranging that had to be done—the hours spent in shifting stuff here and there, finding room for new jars and packets and stuffing empty corners with boxes of biscuits and multi-coloured outsize dusters. She had a problem now with the tins of polish that had accumulated. There were a few small things she could still polish but these used up only the merest smear on the surface of the tin of wax. For nowadays if she were to find even one decent-sized surface to use the stuff on it meant that first she had to go through the slow, backbreaking job of clearing a patch of the floor or the piled-up tables. Finally she broke her lifetime's rule of never polishing under the rugs and, as a consequence, had one or two rather dangerous skids alone in her own front hall. She did not go out nearly so often now since she had got used to the idea of having one large order delivered to the flat regularly every week, and at first she rather enjoyed the visits of these two men tramping through her hall into the kitchen, goodnaturedly quizzing her about the amount of stuff they were carrying. After a bit, however, a sourness entered into the business. It became difficult for them to go forward without knocking things over. Instead of talking to her they began to breathe heavily and complain to one another, and at last she asked them simply to leave the things outside the door which they did with a jarring crash which made the whole hall vibrate. Then she would laboriously carry the things in one by one to the back of the flat, going to and fro with the absorbed and anxious expression of someone stranded on an island hurrying to bring in provisions from a shipwreck before another devastating storm carries them away.

It was at about this time that certain food manufacturers got wind of her, and one firm in particular began to take an interest in the fact that she had regularly ordered the largest size packet of a new breakfast biscuit which had recently come on the market. It did not take too long for the young man who arrived to break down her reserve. She had indeed at one time been anything but forthcoming with strangers, but a virtual imprisonment amongst tall bottles and packets and an extraordinary increase in her grocer's bills had changed all that. While the young man unpacked the gadgets for his camera she spoke with almost terrifying enthusiasm about her breakfasts and she was snapped with her arm round a giant packet, her chin resting on top of it. She was not smiling. It was only a pity that this picture could not be in colour, for below her face there was a vast prairie cut by a narrow road which went on and on until it was lost in the blue and purple haze of more and more distant prairies, fading at last into the sky or the sea or whatever it was that lay miles away from that first blade of wheat in the foreground. Over this golden expanse her pale face peered like the moon coming up where the sun should have been.

The photograph appeared over a short period in the advertisement columns of several magazines and newspapers, and then it dropped out altogether. All the reports suggested that it had not gone down very well with the public and there was a feeling amongst some of those who actually made the stuff in the packet that it was a pity the picture had not been studied more carefully before letting it go out. Not only was the woman not smiling, but her face was so tight, her expression so hopelessly withdrawn from the outside world that she seemed to have no connection whatever with the vanishing road and the wide blue horizons of the packet she was embracing. In the time it took for this picture to appear and disappear, several persons who had known her showed that they were very anxious indeed neither to see or to speak to her again, some got in touch for a short time to satisfy their curiosity, and a few friends became very worried about her and made it their business to call at her flat or persisted in ringing her up on the phone until they got an answer. Those who called were for a while luckier than the rest. She kept them on the landing outside the door but she was pleased to see them and looked as though she were about to cry when they left. Usually, for lack of news on her side and the uncomfortable on-the-doormat position of the visitor, the conversation was jerky, full of silences and new beginnings, consisting mainly of questions and answers and ending in a way which was disconcerting in its terrible politeness.

"But I'm keeping you, amn't I, standing chattering away like this ?"

"No, no, no!"

"Would it be bothering you, then, if I came in for a couple of minutes. I mean, it must be weeks, no—actually months since I've seen . . ."

"The flat isn't . . ."

"*Really* months . . .!"

"I am getting things sorted out here."

"Of course you'll be busy."

"And there is such a tremendous amount of stuff to sort."

"But you aren't moving, are you ?"

For a moment the other's anxious face relaxed. The idea of moving even seemed to amuse her. It was as though someone had asked her if she was going to loosen all the screws in the place and throw out every precious weight which kept the flat from flying apart, or unpack some huge box after weeks and months of her life had been spent in getting the stuff wedged more and more tightly inside.

Nobody, then, got over the doormat. She might wave and smile as they went downstairs, with an expression of anguish in her eyes, but there was simply no room for another person in the place and that was all there was about it. For a long time she was not disturbed. The regular order still arrived and was set down with a crash and a curse, but apart from that it became very silent in the flat and in the summertime she had taken to sitting for long periods by the kitchen window, staring out. Though she was in a top flat she did not often look at anything going on down below. She was sensitive about peering down or putting her head out. On the whole she felt nearer to the sky than to the ground, and was content to sit with her arms in her lap watching the windings of smoke from chimneys on windy days or the movements of birds. From being only vaguely interested in clouds she became knowledgeable about their various formations, and about what sort of weather might be predicted from a sky which was scrolled or feathered or spanned from end to end with long ridges of fishbone cloud.

At last the phone rang. She lifted it, shocked and eager, and heard the voice of a woman she had not seen for months saying: "Well! Lovely to hear you again! How *are* you?"

"I'm fine—very well indeed!"

"It's this. We're just up for a couple of days. We were wondering if you were free?"

A long silence.

"Hullo?"

"Yes."

"Oh, there you are. Well, it's this. Are you free today?"

"Am I what?"

"*Free!*"

There was silence again, and then the apprehensive voice, apprehensive but emphatic: "I don't know that."

"It's a bad line. Can we call for you in the car this afternoon— say between two and half-past? We've got everything ready here for a picnic. We'd love you to come if you're . . . I mean, you're not doing anything else, are you?"

"Well, there's always a lot to do. But that's splendid. A picnic! Are you going to the sea?"

"Probably. It depends on you, really. Where would you like to go?"

"Me? But I can't go. I can't possibly go."

"You're doing something else. There's nothing wrong, is there?"

"I'm still laying in my stores."

"Your what?"

"My stores."

91

"What a line! It sounds like 'stores'."

"Yes."

"Stores of what?"

"The usual stuff. Tins, bottles, cleaning-things. You can run out fast enough if you're not careful. I want to get them properly sorted out. I can hardly just walk out and leave everything. Not just yet, anyway."

After a moment the other voice said, as though relieved: "Then you're taking lodgers?"

"Lodgers!"

"Well, paying guests?"

"Goodness, no. There's hardly room for myself here, let alone *lodgers*. And what it will be like when I finish laying in my stores—if I ever do finish. It's endless, isn't it? Please go on about the picnic."

There was silence at the other end. Then a quiet voice, now rather remote, asked: "What are you storing *for*?"

"I don't know. I wish I *could* come."

"Did you say 'I don't know'?"

"I said 'I wish I *could* come'."

"Yes. Well, another time perhaps."

The silence was so long that it seemed there was nobody at the other end. And then a voice said: "I hope you'll get a good day for your picnic. The clouds were perfect last night. You can usually tell by the sky if it's going to be good or not. And this morning there's a lot of cirro-cumulus about. I hope you'll be lucky."

"Thank you. I hope so too. Cirro-cumulus. I'll remember that."

A voice, full of tears, said: "Like long, long fishbones across the sky. You can't mistake it."

"I'll remember. Well, lots to do. Goodbye just now."

"Goodbye."

"And don't overdo things."

"Oh no."

The phone went down at the other end. Real silence, over-whelming and uninterrupted, returned. Even at that height, four flights above the ground, it was the silence of some crushing weight overhead. It gave the place the atmosphere of some huge, water-logged boat stuffed with rotting junk and slowly sinking through nets of dense black weed. The woman still sitting near the phone had her hands over her mouth. Darkness and silence were now pouring in. She was sinking, drowning. But in order to fool herself she took the greatest care that the sound which came from her lips to break this silence should not be a choking or a gasping or a shriek for help. Panic-stricken, she removed her hands from her mouth and gave a long, loud yawn.

OVEN GLOVES

LONG intervals might go by between one new outfit and the next. But when she decided the time was up she didn't stint herself. It was an all-over change from head to foot, and from the skin out. This time, after much thought and saving, Mrs. Finlay bought a new coat, new hat, gloves, shoes, dress and underwear. She bought a new handbag to replace the last which was getting shabby and a new brooch for her lapel. But although not one scrap of her former material hung about her, this change was not at once visible to a careless glance. For if the body still keeps its recognizable character while every single cell of blood, bone and tissue repeatedly renews itself, so she renewed herself every few years or so without any spectacular change in appearance. Her hat was still brown felt, though a shade darker and crisper. Her tweed coat, speckled pointilliste-fashion green, yellow, brown—came over as the usual fawn. Her shoes were better, dearer, but still light tan and with the same sprinkling of minute, expensive holes across the toecaps and the curl of darker leather round the back. On her lapel the yellow bird with ruby-glass eye, whose wing had got slightly bent, was replaced by a yellow bird with green eye and swifter-looking flight. New, powerful corsets, the same brand as the last, braced up her over-fifty figure. She was the same, yet miraculously different in every part. But that was not to say only scientist or mystic could have spotted the subtle change. Given favourable circumstances, any human, interested person might have seen it—that something clearer, sharper, smoother. Above all, the expectant aura of the woman.

Mrs. Finlay did not even unfold the outfit for a few days, and it was over a week before she put it on for the first time to air it. Her husband met her when she was returning from this outing and he was coming back from the engineering firm where he worked. They saw one another at a distance, converged at a junction of streets and walked the hundred yards or so home together. He did not notice her new hat, coat, gloves, shoes or handbag. But he saw the parcel she was carrying—a parcel beginning to ooze the blood of red meat. It was well after five o'clock.

"That's surely not the supper you're carrying there, is it?"

She turned her head and stared at him, steady-eyed under the darker, crisper hat, but said nothing. She held the parcel well away from her coat.

"All right, all right. It's just if you think your supper's still dangling, dripping, at the end of a string your stomach gets a kind of fright. It turns over, you could say."

Still she said nothing. The parcel twirled slowly from her gloved fingers.

" 'All right', I said. It's just a joke."

"Is it?"

"Look. I remember now you've got fish. I saw it myself this morning. It went out of my head when I saw the meat."

"And now?"

"And now—what?"

"That fish. Is it back in your head again?"

The man said nothing. He brooded over it—the fish in the head. He took a sidelong look at her. And he saw the change in her, for he wasn't as slow as all that. He saw the darker, clearer, smoother look that irritation gave her. You could almost say it suited her. The fresh, sharp, uncrumpled look of anger. It suited *her*, but what about him? There was the whole evening ahead.

"Here, I'll carry that. It's birling round and oozing a bit at that corner. It'll mess up your coat."

"What about it?" She was slowing up as they came nearer the house.

"I'm saying—do you want your coat messed up?"

"Well. Should I mind?" She was almost at a standstill though they had not reached home. She presented herself to him—every bit of herself. The coat, the gloves, hat, handbag, shoes—all gave him his last chance. The most enormous compliment coming

95

one split second after that would be too late. But his eyes were fixed on the parcel.

"Here—give it to me!" There was a grotesque struggle. The string had twisted itself so tightly round her finger that he had to use both hands on the job. Even then he could scarcely move it. She didn't help him. At the first sign that it might be loosening she clenched her hand. The worst of it was they were nearly at the house now. Any neighbour watching would think he was putting on a show of ferocious, delayed gallantry almost on his own doorstep, and she resisting as though her life depended on it. Suddenly she snatched the hand and parcel away and marched before him into the house. The door slammed behind them both.

Now here was a strange thing. Once inside, she began to be very busy and quite calm again. Calm and almost triumphant. For a while he was so taken up with this that he didn't notice the stranger thing. Ten minutes, quarter of an hour, twenty minutes went by and still she busied herself taking out cups and saucers, rattling the knives and spoons cheerfully as she always did. But there was a difference. She hadn't taken off any of her outdoor clothes. This fact made the gentle, cheerful bustle going on almost menacing. It made him, standing there in his soft, hand-knitted sweater and shabby slippers, look hopelessly unguarded. He was all frayed and soft and the holes in his slippers, instead of comforting his feet, exposed him. Her outdoor clothes in the small room looked stiffer, even more confident and splendid than before. Like armour.

After twenty-five minutes of it he said: "Aren't you going to take your things off?"

"My things?"

"Yes, aren't you going to take your things off?"

"What things?"

He shrugged, sat down and opened the evening paper. But he didn't look relaxed. He read cautiously, intently, as though deciphering the double meanings of headlines, and as for the curt, short statements of fact—they were hard to unknot as coded messages.

He raised his eyes once to say simply: "Your hat and coat."

"Yes?"

"Aren't you going to take them off?"

"No."

"Why not ?"

"I'm cold."

Outside a warm, slow Autumn wind was blowing, and once or twice a big leaf, twirling lazily, went past the window. It was a steamy evening. There was a smell of bonfires, and in the corners of cramped town gardens lay the damp piles of late grass-mowings and rotting flowers. Inside the kitchen was like a furnace—the sort of heat which brought a dampness to the forehead when the door was first opened. They liked it like this. Since its repainting the window was stuck at the top, and it was seldom warm enough even in summer to have it up at the bottom. Nevertheless the woman's husband immediately bent down and opened up the stove. A great flare of heat leapt at him and he banged it shut again. The pans, kettle, shovel, pokers—everything near the stove gave off a shining, blistering heat.

"If you're cold then there must be something wrong."

"Maybe there is."

"Maybe you've got a cold or something."

She continued her cheerful, gentle, bustling activity round about him—activity with its hard, inner core of triumph. The tablecloth flew up, billowed like a sail above the table and flipped down again, stirring his hair and scattering a few toast-crumbs which had been hidden in its folds since breakfast.

"No, I've not got a chill. I'm just cold."

Places were laid for three, their daughter being due in from her office before six o'clock. Several times the woman looked into the oven where the fish-pie with its crust of cheese was browning. For the final look she put on oven-gloves—big, soggy-looking pale blue mittens with tabs at the wrists for hanging up. When she stood up straight again, fully-clothed, oven-flushed, and with clowns hands dangling at her sides, he let out a crack of laughter. He couldn't help it—it was more like a nervous spasm than a laugh and his face immediately afterwards was serious, even extremely anxious. The laugh had come directly from his empty, nervous stomach and issued out without making any difference to his face, without even stretching his lips. They looked at one another gravely.

"Well, those oven gloves don't exactly go with the rest of you, do they ?"

"Did you want me to look at the fish in suede gloves ?"

"Don't be silly!" He looked uneasily across the room, following her glance to where her new gloves lay meekly folded together over the back of a chair.

"Suede, are they? Those look good. Where did you get them? I knew there was something different about them when I saw them."

"Something different about them?"

"Well—new."

"Different from the oven-gloves you usually see me in?"

"For mercy's sake! What's this about now?"

She sat down on the low arm of a chair. She looked interested, quite pleasant again and very collected, as though willing to use his help in some investigation she was undertaking. She frowned —not angrily—simply trying to remember.

"Oven-gloves! That's funny, now. Do you know something about oven-gloves? I'll tell you. Christmas after Christmas, two days before on the dot—I got oven-gloves. In an envelope with or without a Christmas stamp—and sometimes birthdays too. Year after year after year and as far back as I can remember. The very first present I ever had after we were married. Oven-gloves. From my mother-in-law."

"My mother," he sat up now. "Look here, my mother's dead!"

"I can see every single pair yet. Dozens of them. Felt and wool, felt and wool, and as the years went on—nylon, terylene and the rest. You could make quite a study of material through the ages just from those oven-gloves."

"Some of them hand-made," said her husband, sitting well forward so that their heads were close together.

"That's so," she agreed pleasantly. "On the whole, though, the bought ones were better for the purpose. Hand-made ones could suddenly fall apart when you had your finger on a roasting-pan. If the stitching was loose at all, you could get a blister the size of a saucer in seconds."

"Most of them embroidered!"

"No—sorry. That's where you're wrong. Stitched with coloured wool—yes. Embroidered—no. Who would know best about that? You or me?"

"Those ones with purple daisies?"

"Oh yes. Those were embroidered. But not by your mother. She got them at a sale. She told me so herself. A bring-and-buy."

98

She stripped off the gloves gently, patted them together and hung them on the hook beside the stove. She began to cut bread, too many slices for three people, and as she cut she gesticulated with the knife.

"There's one thing I kept asking myself—still do, in fact. Do people ever actually wear out oven-gloves like other gloves? If they baked and roasted day and night? Or perhaps if they kept peering at the stuff, taking it out, putting it back, shifting the oven shelves up and down, up and down."

"Look here, my mother's dead!" he exclaimed for the second time, but now up on his feet.

"Are you trying to quarrel with me, at this late date, over your own mother? I never quarrelled with her—never in my life. We got on better than most, in fact. Are you working yourself up about gloves! Or maybe you're trying to say I've never baked enough or cooked. I simply asked if you could wear out oven-gloves like other kinds. Well, I don't know. Maybe they're more like boxing-gloves. Do boxing-gloves wear out? Of course they must. But how long does it take? After how many rounds? And oven-gloves—after how many meals? I've never spoiled a pair yet. So I've never cooked enough. Is that it?"

The fish smelt strong and good. Everything was ready for supper. In fact the woman had been so busy since coming in that she'd gone over the mark. There was this great pile of cut bread, and she'd put everything out on the table—two jams, two kinds of cake, galore of scones and some old biscuits she'd found at the foot of a tin. And going continually back and forth from sideboard and cupboard she'd managed to bring out all sorts of oddments they didn't usually bother about—little flowery butter-dishes, odd bottles of sauce and a second salt-cellar. There were a couple of old table-napkins. She even plonked down a flower-vase in the middle of the table. If it was a feast she was preparing it was a wild one, wild and empty.

"If you take my advice you should get to your bed after supper," said her husband. "You look hot. It's maybe a temperature you've got. Don't sit around all night with a chill on you."

"After supper?" said his wife with a laugh.

"Well, before, if you want. As soon as Rita comes in."

"But I'm going out now!"

"You're going out?"

"I'm going in next door to the Philips."

"You'll not be here for supper?"

"I've told you. I'm going in next door."

"With a fever?"

"Who said 'fever'. 'Fever's' your idea."

"What are you going in there for?"

"I've something to show her."

"To give her?"

"No, to show her."

"You'll give her something all right. You'll give her 'flu. Don't you care whether you give that whole family the flu?"

"Look, I've left everything ready, so there's no need to panic. When you're taking out the fish use the oven-gloves there. Or if you don't like those ones, there are a dozen more in the drawer. Plain or fancy. You can take your pick." She took up her own new, suede gloves from the back of the chair, stroked them on to her fingers and went out.

When the daughter came in her father was still standing in front of the fire. He looked dazed and was staring glassily at the empty flower-vase without uttering a word of greeting.

"Hullo," said the girl, following his gaze. "Fish, it it? What's up? Oh no! Not visitors tonight. Don't tell me!"

"Your mother's gone out—gone in next door. Gone into the neighbours with a temperature."

"With a what?"

"She's got 'flu."

"Did she say that?"

"She didn't need to. Her face was like fire. She said she was cold. Do you know since we came in she never even took her coat and hat off."

"That would make her hot enough. Did she say she felt ill?"

"She said nothing. But you'd have worried if you'd seen her."

"I'll go in and fetch her."

"No! Don't do it. Don't touch her. Leave her!"

"Well . . .! Are you all right yourself?"

"I'm damned hungry—that's what I am! Here, let's fetch out that fish before it's black to the bottom!" He unlooped the oven-gloves, put them on slowly, held them up and stared at his two hands. He moved his pale-blue, padded fingers.

"What's up now? Fancy yourself as a boxer?"

"I'll tell you another thing. Your mother's got gloves on the brain tonight. She mentioned all kinds. Boxing ones too. Oven-gloves! You should have heard her on oven-gloves!"

He slid the dish out gingerly and put it on the table amongst the knick-knacks—the extra dishes, cream-jugs, the useless jam-spoons and butter-knives.

"Napkin-rings!" said the girl as she sat down. "Well, when did you last see those?"

"Believe me, it's no joke. There's something going on in her head."

He broke the crust of cheese, and steam rose from the boiling fish. Because of the heat they both ate it with frustrated, genteel nibbles from the ends of their forks—an eating-method slow to cure hunger and anger. The man's face was red. After her first helping the girl asked: "Have you any idea why she was going in there?"

"Yes, giving them something. No, showing. That's it. She had something to show them. She didn't say what."

"Of course! Her new outfit. How do you mean 'she didn't say what'? It was obvious, wasn't it?"

"What was? What outfit?"

"Well, what else would she be showing them? She told me she'd be wearing it the first time this afternoon, and obviously she never took it off."

He went back to the small bites even though the fish was cooler. Then he laid down his knife and fork.

"Outfit? She had new gloves. Didn't I congratulate her on those gloves? That's what led to all the glove-talk. I mentioned new gloves, and she flares up about oven-gloves!" He did not pick up his knife and fork again. He waited, his eyes moving rapidly around the useless objects on the table. His daughter was silent too but she continued to eat, raising her eyes to look at him each time she brought the fork to her mouth. Nothing had spoilt her supper. Indeed in the last few minutes she seemed to be relishing the stuff more. At last she spoke.

"Yes, she would have new gloves, father. She'd have new gloves, new shoes, new hat, new coat, new handbag."

The man brought his eyes round to his daughter where she sat, still eating and taking little looks at him. The looks added nothing to him—tended rather to diminish him, like little bites. And her

101

sudden resemblance to her mother was peculiar. She even had her look of grieving triumph. He muttered as though to himself: "She had this parcel in her hand when I met her."

"Something else to go with the outfit. A scarf, maybe, or stockings."

"No. Steak."

"Ah . . . Well, don't let it take your appetite away. You haven't finished your supper."

Her father shoved back his chair, glared about him as though for something to contain an explosive exasperation, then grabbed up the empty flower-vase from the table and brought it down again on the edge of the sideboard. The daughter went on eating. As though his one act had drained him of all energy, the man turned and limped slowly to the armchair at the fireside.

"I'll bring over your cup," said the girl after a bit. She poured out new tea, carefully carried it across and set it down beside him on a low stool. She was now treating him like an invalid. Consoling him. Perhaps he was an invalid. He had now withdrawn from combat and all responsibility. In this situation, at any rate, he was all invalid. There was nothing left of him.

"Nothing more. I couldn't touch it."

"That's unusual for you, isn't it?"

"Yes, I don't know what's up. I couldn't face another bite."

"Well . . .!" She stood back, marvelling. "So it's the pair of you!"

"How do you mean?" He put his limply-slippered feet on to the rung of a nearby chair. He rubbed his leg slowly down from thigh to knee.

"So you've got what she has?"

"What's that?"

"You told me. 'Flu."

"I said nothing as sure as that. I said 'might be'. Might be 'flu or chill."

"All right, then. Might be. And it might be you've caught the bug."

He pondered it. Stared at it. And saw some hope in it. "It's not very likely, is it? When it's not even sure she's got anything herself."

"It's how you feel that counts. How *do* you feel?"

"Awful!" His mournful eyes, swivelling round the room and

steady only when they penetrated the wall of the house next door, gave this long-drawn-out-word a ring of truth like a gong.

"Bed's the place for you, then."

"Yes."

"The sooner the better!"

"Yes, yes!"

"Better get up then. There's not much time."

He seemed, with his stubborn staring, about to take her up on the meaning of this, thought better of it, and instead turned to stare at the clock. He rose slowly, groped his bumbling, invalid way across the room. At the door he stopped, alert, and pointed.

"Here, get those oven-gloves out of sight—get them on to that hook there!"

"All right. Do you want the place tidied, then?"

"Nothing of the kind. It's not that. We don't want any more glove-talk." His eyes circled the room again, and then stared for a moment at the empty flower-vase. "A pity you couldn't have got some flowers," he said grimly.

"What! Me? Well, why me? Why not you?"

"Look here! What would I look like bringing flowers home?"

"Well, I never heard a mention of flowers before."

"It's just that empty flower-vase puts me in mind. And the way she set it down. It fairly got my nerves on edge."

"Banged it down?"

"No, no. Careful, very careful. And dead in the centre."

"Look, why not get to bed?"

"Yes." He let his hand fall limply on the door handle, shuffled through. And was gone.

Ten minutes later the woman came in from next door. The girl smiled to see her head-to-foot, skin-out newness. She helped her off with the coat. "How did she like it, then?"

"She loved it. She saw the fleck in the coat—saw something I'd never seen myself—how it went with this piece of pale felt at the front of the hat. Oh, but she's bright. She's really all there."

She removed the hat carefully, then paused with it lifted above her head, her eyes turned up, to listen.

"He's gone to bed," said her daughter.

"Why?"

"Felt something coming on, most likely. Thought he'd better go to bed."

103

"Oh, so he decided it was he was ill. Not me. I was to go to bed. Did he tell you that?"

"He said something earlier on."

"And after you'd talked a bit, he felt something coming. He felt *me* coming, you mean!"

"You can't just expect him to notice a change of fleck at the first go-off. Give him time."

"Is that what you call all this? Look at me—new to my toe-caps. Gloves, handbag. A change of fleck indeed!"

"I know that—but all the same . . ."

"Talking about gloves," said her mother, "your poor father's got a thing about oven-gloves. And all because his mother made them. But why he should bring them up today of all days—havering on and on! Don't ever let him get started on that tack, or I'm warning you, you'll never hear the end."

"I've been well warned," said the girl.

"Did he say he felt cold?"

"He didn't say. Perhaps he did."

"We needn't worry. He's got my old coat up there—hanging over the bed. That'll keep him warm. That'll make his ears glow!"

The woman sat with her hat on her knee, and the girl with the new coat on her lap. They sat on, their eyes matching up the flecks with the pale felt of the hat, the handbag with the scarf, the shoes with the dark felt, the gloves with the shoes, the shoes with the flecks.

PROMISE

AT FIRST Carter—who had been referred to more than once as an amateur of promise—painted only at weekends and occasionally on holidays, until one day while seated precariously on a tiny stool on the edge of a cliff, and bending lovingly to press out blobs of blue and white paint to match the blue and white waves below, the word 'promise' struck him sharply unawares. He was fifty-one, a heavy man with a cheerful red face, a head neatly halved by its exuberant crop of dark hair behind a bare brow and eyes of a confident, unbrooding blue. Nevertheless when the word struck him a second time his glance faltered. The waves took on a cruel edge in an icy colour which was not to be found amongst any of the tubes in his box. For a few minutes more his brush half-heartedly stroked the canvas, then he laid it down and considered the word. Why should it come to mind now and with such unwelcome force as though spoken aloud not with the usual mild respect but accompanied by a whole battery of hoots, whist-lings, gibes ? He turned up his coat-collar and began to screw on the tops of the tubes with chilled fingers. He had started painting late in life, and if the word had struck before it had glanced off again, producing only a qualm or two which were quickly forgotten. But not this time. The idea that he might have little time to replace 'promise' with any better word came over him with stunning force. How chill and inappropriate to his age the word now felt! How scandalously skimpy the covering it afforded his fifty-one years! He was not to forget that afternoon. The gulls which up till now had appeared on his canvas, stroked tenderly in with pure white, now swooped far above him, screaming bitterly. His peace of mind was gone.

He began to go out more often, especially on the odd holidays from his school teaching. Where before he had been glad to relax for at least half of this precious time, he now set himself resolutely to his task. He sat for hours on high, windblown banks staring grimly at picturesque groups of cottages and measuring with his paintbrush the distance between horizon and foreground. He sat in wet woods, peering between the branches of trees at cloud effects. He sat on deserted shores, bravely sweeping the Atlantic Ocean on to the minute and fabulously expensive canvases which he had brought with him in batches from the city. At certain out-of-the-way hotels, if he could find enough old nails already in the walls, he would put on the occasional small exhibition at the end of a three-week visit. A typed price-list of pictures would appear on the tables beside the menu-card to be studied on rainy days with an almost ghoulish intensity by those holiday-makers who had run out of reading matter. Or, on the encouragement of the proprietress, the work might be displayed modestly but persistently round the dining room itself, propped on empty tables against pepper-pots and milk jugs—small, delicate paintings, cold in colour, through which patches of bare canvas showed like gooseflesh. People, if they looked twice, thought it odd that such a large, healthy-looking man should paint them. He had his occasional sale. Old ladies and engaged couples who wished to be reminded of the place sometimes bought them. But the sunbathers went past with averted head for the sight of them was diminishing and chilling, and they had a thinning effect on the blood.

Carter painted on. But there was this change. Now when he was not painting he was walking, and as he walked he staggered a bit. For he had discovered with a shock that the earth was not smooth at all, but rough. He was a heavy man and he sweated as he waded through prickly grasses or took short cuts through the squelchy sun-warmed bogland between hills. And sometimes the ground stung him as he went by—roots and low branches lashed and stroked him, tripped him up, and sheltered hollows, smooth to the eye, were bristling and jagged to the feet. The earth had curious lumps and grooves, patches of warm and cold. Its surface—tufted, feathered, stubbled—could change in seconds from rippling to thrashing movement. The going was tough and while he reminded himself that it was partly for his health he did it, one thing became clear. He was no longer walking through landscapes. He forgot the horizon and the middle distance as he plunged along like a half-blind man through the thorny, tangled chaos which swirled around him or shifted underfoot, while overhead, through jerking nets of small flies, the whole sky changed its pattern from one glance to the next. But it was the actual air which struck him most in those moments when he sat down to recover his breath. He was too tired to look for views. Instead, for the first time, he stared ahead and saw with a shock that the air was full of spinning stuff which rose or slowly sank according to its weight. Sharp points of dust and sand, seeds, minute feathers and wings floated by, met, disengaged, and sailed on.

Not only had the landscape burst from its frame. He could be brought up sharp by something incongruous in his path, something repellent and fascinating like the white flower he had seen growing out of the oozing neck of a dead bird, or the rock, calm and smooth as sculpture, which he had shifted to reveal a huge circle of ants, furiously whirling like some obscene spinning-top. These sights affected him in a strange way. Sometimes after such a walk he found it difficult to balance on his small painting-stool. The fact was he felt ridiculous perched with his bottom on a narrow sling of canvas a few inches above the ground—as though trying to keep himself upright and steady while all around him the thrashing, floating, crawling movements of the earth and sky went on. His dazzling 12 x 8s, too pure to touch, affronted him. He would sit for ages holding one on his knee, bent over as though defending it with his arms from the surrounding chaos, yet he was always thankful to see it spotted even if it was only a leaf scraping across or a spider slipping with its ugly shadow down the icy surface. For a while, tired of nursing them, he gave up painting altogether. He went on plodding about the countryside. But he would notice, on his return to his job after a week or two away, that even the city had lost some of its geometry, the hard, polished balance he had taken for granted. He found himself staring down into the deep wounds in streets where workmen operated all day on the gigantic entrails of the city—sometimes working on into the darkness with crimson lamps and spectacular silver flares. In spite of himself he was moved by this appalling struggle which went on day and night

107

to keep the place on its feet. There was a continual leaking and spurting-up to be sealed, a never-ending splitting and crumbling to be patched. The city, where it had worn through, belched gas and its lifeblood oozed out from ancient arteries. How then had he had the audacity, the naivety to think of the place, far less paint it as though it stood mile-deep on solid concrete with air crystal clear and stone smooth enough to lick? There was no such thing as crystal air. He looked at tall tenements through siftings of soot and dust. He saw them moving like flimsy backcloths behind racing seas of mist or stained a heavy purple facing the fog-blackened sunset.

When eventually he went back to the country and to his white blocks again he found himself painting in strange places—in lanes hollowed into tunnels where thorn scraped against thorn over his head, or on parts of the shore where, his back to the sea, he watched quivering tufts of yellow foam melting and mysterious bubbles forming and bursting on the sand. Seeds fell on his canvas. He would scrape them off, imagining what strange things might not flourish from the oily brown paint. "And hell—why not?" he cried angrily on one windy afternoon when his canvas was peppered with seeds. "Stick on then! I'll make you grow there— I'll make you shoot up quick enough!" And around these seeds he painted thick red and purple flowers with furry emerald stalks. Expanding and feeding upon his prim landscape, they eventually overwhelmed it. That evening he took home a patch of tropical jungle to prop against his wall amongst the grey landscapes and powder blue seascapes. Later leaves fell on him, small twigs and berries which, half-impatient, half-curious, he did not bother to brush off the canvas. Some stuck there, and some he made to stick with big, oily gobs of paint which he laid on with a knife. One afternoon when he had left his half-finished painting and walked some distance away to see what could be seen from a rise in the road, he came back to find a dragonfly, still struggling weakly, stuck to an outsize mound of scarlet paint on his pallette. As he watched, its great wings stopped vibrating and it sank its body in the luscious grave, one leg still quivering in the air. Already outlined in charcoal on the canvas and awaiting its scarlet was the roof of a nearby cottage. Carter scooped up the paint with its embedded insect and spread it carefully on this roof. He went on working all afternoon until he had finished, and always out of the corner of his eye he was aware of the weird thing on the tiles. Back home in the evening he studied his work—a commonplace enough effort if ever there was one, but having, like his seed-grown flowers, its saving touch. The giant insect, wings shrivelled but still glinting, spanned the roof from one gable to the other, its legs trailing against chimneystacks. A beginner's work all right—a beginner half a century old and with a touch of the fantastic, not to say the macabre. This mediocre little landscape was at any rate wide open to heaven knew what strange monsters from mind or space. Carter smiled as he looked. It had been easy to do. Truer to say it had been done for him, dropping as the seeds and twigs had dropped out of the air.

He became less wary, when he went back to the city, of painting in the blustery streets, where before he had taken every precaution to protect picture and palette from the weather. Grit made the surface of his canvas rough. Sometimes scraps of blown news-paper would skiff the paint, sticking momentarily and swirling up again, and once in a bored moment, tired of straining his eyes to find the symmetry of windows and railings, he held on to a scrap that had settled and spread it out on the canvas to read. It was a grim scrap—on the one side a gas-oven suicide, on the other a triple car-crash. He couldn't always be lucky with what came out of the air. The whole place was swirling with disasters overhead and underfoot. All the same he let it stay where it had fallen. He even managed to stick it down by applying thicker paint under its corners and daubing over parts of it so that in the end it was firmly sunk in the picture. It looked incongruous at first, but at least it helped to take the deadly smoothness from his paint. He decided it added not only a flick of lively white to the thing but also a touch of reality.

"Incongruous?" he said aloud to himself as he was packing up to go. "And why incongruous? This is a street, isn't it? Sheltered or not, don't tell me its never seen a car-crash!"

"Pardon me?" said a bowler-hatted man who was going past with a briefcase.

"I said 'don't tell me this street has never seen a car-crash'!"

"Oh, certainly," said the man, slowing up. "We've had a car-crash here all right. Two years ago just about this time we had a car-crash at that corner there. One dead indeed."

"I can imagine it."

109

"You read about it?"

"No, as a matter of fact I didn't."

"Well, it didn't make a headline, oddly enough."

"That's hardly odd these days, is it? Anyway, what's a head-line? If you want unpleasant facts to stick, you've got to stick them down yourself, I find. That's what I've done, anyway."

"I don't think I've quite . . ."

"Yes, they've got to be dug in, embedded. Nothing really makes an impact unless you've actually dragged it out of your own soup, does it?"

"Oh, you're a painter, aren't you?" said the other with a smile. "Of course you must have your own angle on things."

Carter's heavy shoulders shook in a spasm of silent laughter. "Painter! That's good. But thanks all the same. Things drop on me. The finishing touch you could call it, but sometimes the only one that matters. Left to myself . . ." He shrugged and smiled.

"You underestimate yourself, I'm sure," said the man politely, moving on.

"And I'll bet you've had the odd suicide around here!" Carter called after him. The man did not look back, though inclining his head at an uneasy angle which indicated neither assent nor protest.

For Carter, as he stood at the window of his flat that evening, the tall buildings opposite had changed again, or the air between become denser. But he felt this even more intensely when the curtains were drawn and he sat with his back to the windows, his mind blank to the day's events. It was then he sensed the impact of the dark air outside and felt, as though against his skin, the dust and stinging grit—saw through closed eyelids scraps of a tragic whiteness float by to paste themselves against walls and windows, and underneath, skiffing the gutters, the desolate flicker of red and purple tickets from late buses. Every now and then he was roused and his windows shattered by motorbikes bursting past, and after each explosion had died away he felt the air slashed as though by razors and the surface of buildings scorched and seared with sound. All lines were bending. Horizons, railings, walls which he had once thought straight as measuring-rods were endlessly warping and thickening under the invisible weight of air and noise, and day and night there was a melting of edges—roof into rain, iron into sunlit air.

Very gradually Carter's outlook changed to meet his discovery

110

of the new, tilting, bending, melting world he had set out months ago to explore. Slowly his paint fattened up, if only to bear the odd bits and pieces scattered over it, and a fruity roundness grew inside his canvases. With a tremendous effort which added lines to the sides of his mouth and took much of the amiability out of his eyes, he climbed out of the weekend-holiday class of painter. He painted in winter as well as summer—not only in vacations but on half-days, in the evenings and sometimes in the early morning before he set out for school. He did not rely on the sun. Sometimes he exchanged it for a powerful 150-watt electric light bulb. And as his paintings fattened up, Carter himself became rather thinner. A certain easy flamboyance which he had displayed before in his general get-up faded slightly. He had been known as a colourful character as far as dress was concerned. Curious buttons had been his specialty and an unusual line in ties and socks. Now the buttons were seldom in evidence. People who missed them had begun to say that you were just as likely to find them, if you looked hard enough, amongst all the other paraphernalia in his paintings. If shells, bugs, seeds, small stones and paper snippets—then why not buttons?

"Yes, why not indeed?" Sometimes the occasional visitors to his room would turn to find him at their shoulders with this question spoken in a serious, not to say a severe voice. He had been known to be good company before. There had been plenty of genial jokes and long evenings of full-blooded gossip. But this flatfooted "well, why not?" soon became his answer to almost anything that came up, in painting or out of it. It was an absolute deadener to the gossip.

"What tremendous fun you must have, messing about around here!" exclaimed the assistant head of the school on his first, uninvited appearance at Carter's rooms. "If only I had time to go in for this sort of thing myself. How *do* you make time, by the way—from your work, I mean?" They talked over this matter amiably enough but throughout the discussion the second head kept glancing automatically at the palette knife which Carter held in his hand. It amazed him how such a gentle instrument, so pliable it could be bent back in a curve by the flick of a finger, could assume the appearance of a rather dangerous weapon simply because of the awkward way it was held. He left earlier than he had intended, a streak of scarlet paint along the sleeve of his

111

jacket, and overcome with the reek of oil and turpentine in Carter's place. On the way home he glanced a good deal at the streak of scarlet. He thought of blood and the difficulties of his position. He thought of blood again, of middle age and its vagaries, of weird insects which drew blood, and fleshy, tropical flowers that stung.

It was true that Carter's attitude to his schoolwork was changing, but no one could use the word 'slackness'. Rather the opposite. He was obviously intent on keeping that part of his life in its place. If outside he had begun to see swirling lines and shapes which melted into one another, he viewed things very differently inside the school. Even the appearance of his classroom had changed. Boys were no longer looped from desk to desk, or crouched ready to flip missiles into the air. The free and easy relationship was over. Strictly vertical figures now sat at bare, horizontal lines of desks. The design had become formal, even abstract. If he was now aware how full of stuff the air was between him and every other object, he did not allow this to detract his attention from his pupils. Paper scraps or sifting chalk—he continued to see them with a new, unwelcome clearness.

Nowadays Carter went out very little and the long walks were a thing of the past. In the last years he had given up holidays abroad. He brooded continually, however, on the places and objects he had seen, and memory made his paintings lush. Spires, glittering with shell or glass or crusted with plain city grit, shot up alongside flamboyant flowers with staring eyes, and oily, orange suns, heavy as copper balls, stood out from a background no longer pale but purplish-black like skies seen from rocket height. From the memory of the Italian lakes he had introduced square patches of rippled water on to his canvas, or cut thick, tufty doormats from the Irish fields. Great bogholes, sinking through layers of underpaint, sucked down trees which had changed from the limp shapes of former days to great rubbery leaves and branches which flailed the air in their struggle to breathe. But above all it was the paper which caught the eye. Into almost every picture he had stuck his scraps. Some were cheerful, sparking from the canvas like exclamations—bus and train tickets, scraps from travel folders and theatre programmes, strips torn from music pages, and occasionally the disembodied, gleaming teeth of a smile from a toothpaste advertisement. But others, like the first scrap stuck to his paint, were gloomy accounts of accidents and killings, or strips of murderous black headline threatening war. Seen in profile these paintings bulged with their bits and pieces and scraps. Carter grew concave. His appearance suggested that it would be better for him if he could simply settle down every evening and tuck in to those oversize loaves wedged between wine bottles, the chunks of cheese and fleshy piles of fruit which appeared from time to time in his still life paintings. Yet he prospered. His palette, which had once been a small rectangle of enamel, discreetly daubed with pastel colour round the edges, now became a great oval platter of wood, heavy to hold and heaped with an exotic substance to be scooped and kneaded into shape with knives and coarse brushes whose strokes made marks along the surface like the tracks of a heavy insect. He held two or three small exhibitions of work in his own studio. His paintings began to sell.

People were attracted by their design. They made out the spires, suns, bogs and buildings, but saw them through a rich veil of floating debris as though an explosion had brought the heavy stuff streaking to the ground while smaller motes and scraps spiralled slowly, catching the light as they floated down. They saw houses as though through deep water, seeded with fish-eggs and threads of weed, or behind a skin of ripples which made the iron railings and lamp-posts writhe like eels. But the little scraps of paper, stuck on at all angles, were still the main cause of comment. Seen from a distance they gave the whole thing a flickering quality. Nearer to hand there was reading matter for those who wanted it. Indignant people who could make neither head nor tail of the paintings were glad enough to step forward and find a bit of sober print somewhere. They would see amongst the rest of the stuff a slip of cool, white newsprint lying sideways on a swadge of yellow paint, like a petal coming to rest after an earthquake. And screwing their heads over they would read: ". . . money was again acutely short following heavy calling. The authorities gave a very large amount of help both ways. The made money was passed out in loans at $4\frac{3}{8}$ p.c. and $4\frac{11}{16}$ p.c. Money remained tight up to the close and the rate which had been effectively $4\frac{1}{2}$ p.c. throughout the day, with $4\frac{5}{8}$ p.c. for a decent line, eased only to $4\frac{3}{8}$ p.c. by the close." Or: "The overblouse is cut straight above the yoke on the bias below it: the shoulders are rounded: at the back there's a round dipping yoke and the V-slip in front accentuates the dip from front to back. The skirt is gathered on to a wide waistband."

Whatever it was, the moment's reading took the edge off their anger. Their stares calmed a little as though the printed scraps had been cooling patches laid across their eyes. Not every scrap, however, had this calming effect. It was a different matter when an acquaintance at one of the first exhibitions made out part of a plumber's bill in the heavy ridge of paint which held also a few grey gulls' feathers. Backing away, he found himself close to the painter himself. It was the first day of the show and Carter was still straightening frames and arranging price-lists on a side table.

"You don't mind my making a small criticism of this particular painting?"

"Heavens, no—go right ahead!"

"As a friend, I mean."

"As anything you like. Go ahead!"

"It's something you may not have noticed, Carter, but that scrap of paper just there—that one in the right-hand corner . . ."

"Yes, you see I like using these paper shapes."

"Well I'm not exactly blind to the fact. I know you use them. I've nothing against them. But that one happens to be part of a bill!"

"Is it? Well, so it might be. Isn't everything you open a bill these days?"

"My dear fellow, I've nothing against your painting, as such. And I would hardly presume to set up as a critic. What I mean is simply this. Do you want anybody and everybody to be looking into your private affairs?"

"But the whole thing's a private affair. If I minded I wouldn't hang it up there, would I?"

"Ah, but I mean *really* private. I'm not discussing art now. Do you want, for instance, every Tom, Dick and Harry who goes past to know you've had a water-heater installed at £12 9s. 11d. plus the renewal of the bathplug—though I'm thankful to see the cost of that particular item has got torn off."

"There could be worse revelations."

"That's what's worrying me. What will you paste up next? Pages from old bank-books?"

"Look, I believe I know what's really worrying you, and I can set your mind at rest. That's not an unpaid bill, you know."

"Oh rubbish! Paid or unpaid—I couldn't care. But it's part of your private life!"

"All the same, if that *is* what's worrying you, you haven't gone close enough. If you look again you'll see part of a purple 'Paid with Thanks' stamp. I wouldn't be surprised if the whole of it weren't there."

"Well, it's your business. Just a warning. You know how people talk, especially if it's anything to do with money. If it were me, I'd be careful too with my scraps of letters. I've a horror of leaving old letters around, let alone pasting them up on a wall!"

But Carter took little care of anything nowadays except getting on with the job. If people took him seriously as a painter, he accepted that. It was all right too if he got the name of fraud, manipulator, or spoiled schoolmaster. He minded only when it was suggested that he had copied, as near as he could in his bungling way, a painter in South America and another in Finland. He resented that. Whatever others were doing, he had found out for himself that the act of placing a small dried crab, for instance, in a turbulent lacing of green and white paint gave him more pleasure than he had experienced for years. Since the bill incident, however, he had begun to think about his bits of paper. While most of them were simply shapes to him there were others, like his car-crash scrap, which had a meaning apart from the flick of white or grey they gave the picture. He had watched the reactions of people who came up close to read the printed stuff. But there were bits which simply by their associations and even without being read, could produce a reaction. Once he had set up a large circle of pink, green and white bus and train tickets into a smooth expanse of grey and black paint. The pattern was good, but certain people insisted that it was more than that. For them it had the appearance of a revolving wheel of escape—its wedges of coloured cardboard pointing out a complicated choice of routes and destinations, and stamping the drab background with a vivid memory and nostalgia for all past escapades. Were there scraps with stronger associations even than this? He thought about it as he went about the city and watched the reaction of people to the various official and unofficial papers they held in their hands— maps, bills, menus, programmes, tickets, timetables, wrappers, shopping lists, napkins, envelopes. Their reactions to these were various but none were spectacular.

There were certain explosive pieces of paper, however, which he had not reckoned with until one evening in late autumn, when a stuffy meeting after school had prompted him to go home by a more roundabout route than usual. The wind had increased throughout the day and it was blowing hard when he at last emerged at the crowded corner where a few late shops were closing up, and already large queues were forming on either side of the cinema. Here he stood for a moment, illumined in purple by neon lights, remembering that he must buy bread but had no change in his pockets. Before him, serrated by chimneys, was a red sky into which clouds were piling, loaf-shaped. He remembered now as he watched them that he had taken out money the day before and that his notes were not in his wallet but still folded into his bank-book. He drew this out, and still staring at the sky, opened the pages on to the palms of his hands and let loose into a sudden gust of wind eight single pound notes. It was an unhurried gesture, gentle and careful as a man freeing a box of birds. But once they had flown circling above his head his whole body changed. He pounced at them, his hands snatching the air. He shouted at them. He ran first after one and then the other. At the entrance to the cinema he performed a panicky dance—stooping, snatching, running, turning, one moment throwing his head to the sky, at the next doubling down towards his feet. Onlookers joined in, some breaking away from the queue to circle with their hands near the pavement and others running right out into the street where cars screeched to a halt and a woman on a bicycle tipped off sideways to scoop about in the gutter with the rest. For some minutes all was confusion. Carter felt himself wild and calm by turns as he glimpsed people in the half-darkness picking up bits of paper, examining them, and throwing them back to the mud and wind again. At last all the notes were in his hands. But he was not satisfied at once. Standing there in the full glare of the cinema's lights he counted them over several times, his head stubbornly bent, marvelling at himself as he did so. So the scruffy bits of paper had changed him in a few moments from a quiet, absent-minded chap contemplating sunsets and bread, first to a prancing clown, through various attitudes of doubt and fear, till he reached this final role—the middle-aged gentleman, outlined against huge, kissing posters, slowly, suspiciously, thumbing through a wad of muddy banknotes.

He had found what he was looking for. How had he ever missed them—these bits of paper with associations stronger than any he

116

had used before ? This was legendary stuff, unreal almost, but with a lash in its tail like a dragon. Bizarre incidents now came to mind. A man swimming far out into a stormy sea after a ten shilling note until cramp pulled him down. Money boxes flung free from burning houses while their owners forgot to jump. Notes had been fought over, crumpled, spat upon, thrown into corners—but seldom destroyed. There was something indestructively sacred about the stuff. As a schoolboy he had listened a hundred times to his father's account of the man who had torn up a five-pound note. Nothing remained of the story now except a memory of his father's outraged voice talking to his mother, describing again and again the size of the fragments—the tall man at his desk with the pieces flying from his fingers, falling amongst all the other papers into the inkpot, on to the blotting-paper, sliding from the toes of his polished shoes. They were very small, his father had said—like blue and white confetti, and someone else had eventually gathered them up and put them in the wastepaper basket. But they had been torn up so small they came right through the spokes of the basket as soon as they were put in—unlike the old envelopes, the circulars, the scraps of letter.

"They were too small for the basket, you see," his father had said to his mother. "Do you understand what I'm telling you ?"

"But couldn't they have been . . . ?"

"No, you see, you haven't understood—no amount of gumming or sewing could possibly. . . . They had been torn not twice or three times but again and again . . . they were so small, so light they were actually moving about in the draught from the door—flakes, they were."

"But somebody could surely have stepped forward and stopped . . ."

"No, you weren't there or you wouldn't . . . How could they put them together—flakes of paper like confetti!"

Carter finished his next painting within three or four weeks of that autumn evening. It was a large composition with a background of dark green and black bands of colour overlaid with oblongs of pale pinkish-grey paint. Though not the most spectacular it was one of the most carefully designed of his paintings and the effect was a satisfying balance of colour and shape. Set at all angles were the semi-transparent oblongs through which the dark green showed like the sea through patches of fine-meshed stuff. The two crisp, ten-shilling notes which he had pressed into the bottom right hand corner were not at first apparent because of these surrounding pinkish shapes, all lightly scrolled with markings.

The painting was acclaimed on sight by a school colleague as he came along the passage towards the open door of Carter's room. It was leaning against the opposite wall and he opened his arms to it.

"This is it at last!" he exclaimed as he stood viewing it from the doorway.

"You like that one," Carter replied smiling, for the paint was scarcely dry, and praise was welcome.

"Oh yes, I *like* it. I like most of your stuff. But the point is this is obviously the one we're to purchase."

"We ?"

"The school. Of course nobody's ever bothered to look into the fund that was left expressly for decorating the hall. But there's a group of us been following your work pretty carefully lately—and with absolute carte-blanche from the top to buy anything that particularly happens to strike us."

"The head ? I thought he'd practically disowned me."

"Don't underestimate the man. He's proud of you in a twisted sort of way."

"This painting's for the hall, you say ?"

"For the platform wall, to be exact."

"Amongst the former heads ? The Council photos ?"

"It's a place of honour, isn't it ? You're not going to quibble about the placing ?"

"God, no! When do you want it ?"

"As soon as possible. String it up now. They're going to love this!"

"They ?"

"Geography, History, English. And I *think* the woman in Infants is with us."

"Good. Then let's get started. You don't want to look at it longer ?"

"We'll look at it a long time at the other end. If they *like* it— forgive the 'if'—simply a form of speech—you can name your price. The school's prepared to give you anything you ask. Within reason." They smiled at one another. The picture was tied up, wedged inside the car, and Carter waved it off.

He made no attempt to get in touch with his visitor the following morning. His timetable was full and he assumed they would meet at first break. But towards midday he was vaguely surprised he had not looked in to see him, and later unnerved to find that the man was indeed avoiding his eye at the long lunch table. Several other glances came his way, however—curious, amused, and more than one downright hostile. Late in the afternoon he made up on him in a corridor and touched him on the shoulder, murmuring: "Well, about the picture?" at the same instant as the other defensively exclaimed: "Good, I've been looking for you!"

"Have you decided one way or the other? Oh, but I see which way!" Carter remarked as they approached a room and he saw the picture, face to the wall, its back still dressed in tattered brown paper.

"Carter, it's no use. Why did you have to go and paste money on it. Real money! If only I'd seen it right away I could have warned you. Surely you didn't suppose it would do for this kind of school?"

"This kind of school?"

"Well, all right. Any school. Can you imagine the effect it would have on a crowd of kids. The head's dead right this time!"

"I can't tell what effect the picture's going to have on people. That's the fascinating thing. Each reaction's different."

"Ah yes, but not to *money!* We're trying to teach them responsibility, Carter! If we go and hang a thing like that up on the platform—what are you saying to them? What are you saying to the Staff, for that matter? You're virtually telling them they can throw their money around just as they like. They're going to hear speeches from that platform—appeals even. That platform was built so that people could get up on it and tell others the value of things. All right, so the ones down there look up and what do they see? They see a painting absolutely plastered with bank-notes—wadded with them!"

"Two ten-shilling notes," murmured Carter.

"I don't propose to add up the stuff. That's not the point. It's the principle of the thing. But *real* money! Good heavens, you're skilful enough! You could have painted notes if you had to have them."

"I'm not exactly a skilled forger yet."

"And there's something else you may not have considered,

Carter. More serious still. It's a question of temptation. Has it crossed your mind that one of those boys and girls might try to extract the money from your painting? Do you imagine it's going to hang there week after week, month after month—intact?"

"Well, what about it? Paper and objects have disappeared before. Things get taken and once in a while things even get stuck on. No, I'm not fussy. If a thing's public and the object's moveable —what can you do?"

"Ah, *you're* not fussy. But what about the parents? Do they send their children to school so that they can learn to throw money about the place—to paste it into the mud?"

So his paint was mud now. Carter was not surprised at this. Money, once free, scattered insult and panic before it. Hadn't he insulted people himself, dourly totting up the banknotes in full view of strangers who had gone out of their way to snatch them out of the air for him?

When he went home that evening he was aware for the first time how tidy the place was. Jeffreys, the man who now cleared up for him three mornings a week had excelled himself. Not a scrap was discarded, but neatly piled up—from a basic ground-work of whole newspapers, through a variety of page and card, to the sprinkling of minute scraps like snowflakes on the top. Paint tubes were lined up in order of size from the fat and new to the emaciated and twisted, canvases stacked on a floor swept clear of the dust, rinds, sticks, gravel and shells which had accumulated during the previous night's work. Yet he seldom saw Jeffreys except in the holidays or on the Saturday mornings when he was at home. The man worked in the city's parks in the afternoons and took the odd evening job in the suburbs where Carter had some-times seen him, cutting back bushes and hedges and making bonfires in back gardens. It was more or less the same in the studio. He spent his time brushing, pruning, burning so that Carter could breathe again and new stuff grow unimpeded by the mess and tangle of the day before. All this Carter had grown accustomed to. But tonight when he stepped into the clear patch he felt more than usually relieved. He put the unwanted canvas he had brought from school amongst a stack of old paintings and almost at once set up his stuff to begin another. He worked late that night and the nights following. The excitement of the thing kept him going and by the end of the week it was almost finished.

120

A space painting. Blues ranging from ink-black to aquamarine gave it a depth like the sea, but this time vague stars appeared, cloudshapes and a huge white moon. Five blue pound notes floated through this sky, spiralling with the wind and veiled here and there by slanting wires of rain and shreds of cloud. Unlike the ten-shilling notes they were not difficult to spot. These were no abstract blue shapes. This time Carter had made no bones about it. This was a picture of money—money which had just escaped into the air out of purses or pockets, crumpled money which only a few minutes before had been crushed and folded and trapped. There was a feeling that the stuff had broken loose—that there was more floating about just out of reach, whole drifts blowing up where these had come from, and a regular thunderstorm of notes darkening on the deep blue line of horizon. It was a picture deserving plunder rather than contemplation.

He was excited when he had finished it, and slightly ashamed of his excitement. It was as good a composition as the others. Yet this time he was not absolutely in control. These shapes had set up something in his blood—a fever as though some bug had bitten him. Had he himself been bitten by others' response to the stuff? Was it now simply a matter of experimenting with people— testing, tempting, seducing, irritating, disgusting them with these notes which seemed to float so free yet were asking to be grabbed? Well, why not? He discovered in himself a fearful impatience for his painting to be on view. And not only that. He wanted reactions and he wanted them now.

When Jeffreys came in early on Saturday morning Carter had the painting propped on a chair facing the light. But it was Carter the gardener looked at first—Carter who was standing with arms folded leaning against the wall opposite. It looked as though he had been standing there for some time and there was an expression on his face—expectant, uneasy, and at the same time irritable as though he only waited for the first word uttered to send him into a burst of temper.

"So everything was all right when I left last time, was it?" asked Jeffreys, removing his scarf and cap and hanging them on a hook on the back of the door, slow and wary as usual, his face expressionless as an oval of raked earth.

"On Thursday? Well, why not?"

"When you came back—the place was O.K. was it? Nothing

out of place I hope. It's not easy nowadays on account of the stuff lying about. It looked as tidy as usual?"

"Oh just as usual, yes, of course. Why ask?"

Jeffreys gave him a slow look-over. Then without a word he removed, as he had always done, the stuff from the centre of the floor to the sides, heaving a box of loose papers, tickets and colourful junk of all kinds over to a table by the window. He waited there some time, staring out, leaning heavily with one hand on the table while he slowly rubbed the back of his head with the other. He was, however, not bewildered. He was a shrewd man and not inclined to bewilderment.

"When you've finished with the view I'd be glad if you'd come over here and see what you make of this painting," said Carter.

Jeffreys took his time coming across, and then glanced once at the painting between bending to pick up more odds and ends from the floor and turning round to gather up plates from a nearby stool.

"Can't you look at it properly and say what you think of it?" exclaimed Carter again in exasperation. Jeffreys stood still and looked vaguely before him. His eyes did not snatch at the notes. He let them float on serenely, undisturbed in their universe of blue.

"It seems all right to me."

"Yes?" Carter encouraged him.

"I'm not sure what you're after."

"Go on."

Jeffreys cautiously shifted a few empty envelopes with the toe of his boot. "All the bits and scraps you need! I don't mind them round the place of course—no more than dead leaves on a path. It's not that. But when did you start pasting them in?"

"Ah, that's just the point. You see I didn't start. At first they dropped on me. Like your leaves, they simply dropped and stuck."

"Yes, but after that—?"

"Well, after that I began to use them. They interest me."

Jeffrey's smile was crafty. "Some, I'll bet, more than others."

Carter was silent for a moment. He seemed not to hear this last remark. Then he said: "But surely you must see it yourself, week in week out. With all your sweepings and rakings and burnings. Talk about overflowing desks—look at the litter-baskets! The

122

gutters! The world's absolutely smothered with the stuff!"

"It's true people throw their stuff around. I've seen hedges sprouting pink and blue tickets like spring flowers."

"That's what I mean. Even the country ditches are stuffed full of cigarette cartons."

"Ah, you've never had the job of jabbing up chocolate boxes in the parks. Soggy cardboard after rain! There's a job for you!"

"And isn't it my job? I want to catch the scraps too. Frame them."

"Tidying up the place?"

"If you like, yes."

Jeffreys said nothing for a while but stared at the empty wall to one side of the picture. He said softly: "But the money? It's not whirling about the sky, is it? Not exactly bunging up the ditches? In all the sweepings of my whole life I've found exactly three ten-shilling notes and a four and sixpenny postal order. The stuff isn't scattered as thick as that, Mr. Carter, in spite of what you might imagine."

Carter flourished his hands in front of the painting. "But that's just it! This paper's different. You've only to watch the professionals tenderly pinching it between thumb and finger—the richest material isn't given respect like that. Look at the tight wads banded up in bank drawers, locked in secret tins. It needs a drastic shuffling to change that outlook—the opposite treatment to your scraps. Money's got to be scattered around. You've got to imagine it, floating, blowing! Like these. People are solemn about the stuff. I want them to feel it's free. Sailing past in the air!" Carter's cheeks were flushed. His eyes bulged at Jeffreys as he talked.

"Well, are they free then?" said Jeffreys in a pause, pointing to the notes.

"Of course. That's the meaning of it. Doesn't it come across?"

"Oh, I'm not bothering about the meaning of the picture. I'm saying—is that money free?"

"Yes, absolutely free."

"There was a painting of yours once—you said it was done by accident."

"Of course. There've been lots like that. Mostly it's paper. The one you mention got slivers of glass from a broken tumbler stuck in the paint. They fell, I swear, almost in a star shape."

123

" 'If accident's made a picture, accident can unmake', those were your words. 'Anyone who's got a mind to can take it apart again'."

"Exactly! What's a bit added or taken away here and there ? My pictures live. I've no objection to change—none at all. Bits can be taken off and others stuck on, if that's what you mean."

"Ah, but nobody's ever done it, Mr. Carter. Nobody's ever wanted to."

"I know what you're driving at. Does the thing still hold good ? Do I make any difference with this one ? Well, the answer's no. No difference at all!" Carter's voice, which had been steady to begin with, gradually quickened throughout this declaration. The calmness of the other man riled him. Again he demanded loudly: "What do you think of it ?"

Jeffreys stood stolidly silent for a long time, taking in the painting. But at last he brought himself to speak: "I'd like to tear strips off it!" he said.

"Carry on then!" exclaimed Carter instantly. Jeffreys smiled at the provocation in his voice.

"What ? Me be the first to remove stuff from your work! When no one's so much as touched a bone button up till now ? Is it likely ?"

"You want to. Who's stopping you ?" Carter's voice was accusing.

"I'm stopping myself—and that's final. I once saw some papers on a park flowerbed after a night's gale. The usual filthy litter you could say. Another puff one way or the other and I'd have agreed with that. But this time they'd blown themselves into a shape like a sailing-ship—a gigantic affair you could almost see from the gates. White, scarlet and blue—not a spar missing! I didn't want to change *that*. But I've got my job. And it's my job to change the paper arrangements in parks. Not on pictures. You can make your changes yourself. I'll be getting along. Anything else you want done to the place before I go ?"

"Leave it!" Carter cried.

Jeffreys who had bent to a scrap, straightened up, letting it fall from his fingers. "Right you are. If there's nothing else then . . ." He walked over to unhook his scarf from the back of the door.

Carter pointed to the picture: "You've not been much help, have you ? What am I going to do with it ?"

Jeffreys slowly wound his scarf about his neck and began to do up the buttons of his coat, staring thoughtfully at each one. "So it's got on top of you, has it? You can take my word for it—one of these days you'll want to move those notes yourself. You might as well do the job now. Rip 'em clean off! No, not rip—gently does it. Roll 'em off like a bandage!"

"And put what in their place?"

"No, I couldn't say that. I'm not the painter, am I? All I know is you're better off with them in your pocket. Easier in your mind. And your visitors—they'll feel easier too." He opened the door, turning once to say: "You're never going to change the economic outlook that way, Mr. Carter. You'll change the art maybe, but not the other—not if you lagged your drainpipes with five-pound notes!" He closed the door discreetly behind him.

When Jeffreys' footsteps had died away down the stairs Carter approached his new painting. The notes were not difficult to peel off for the paint was thick around their corners and still damp. When they were all off he sponged them carefully with turpentine, washed them with soap and water and placed them on a stool near the fire to dry out. Their peculiar cleanness gave them a fragile and innocent look, as though they had had no traffic with the world since their bank-birth. To preserve this, and long before they were quite dry, Carter transferred them to his pocket. But how bare the picture looked! Apart from the corners the paint underneath the notes had been thin. Where they had been, pallid oblongs floated in the sky—mere ghosts of the rich scraps. The whole thing had lost its kick. Even the moon looked starved. Carter stared about him for something to replace the blanks, but what other piece of paper was fit to fill them? He sat down and looked at the piles of printed stuff which had been cleared to one side. How early in his job had Jeffreys come to terms with paper? After how many hundreds of cartons and sweet wrappings? It was easier for him. He could exercise its power by running after the stuff and impaling it on the end of a prong. Well he—Carter—was halfway there himself. He had come to the end of what paper could say. Meantime he had a problem on his hands. Kicking a stray scrap aside he reached for pots, brushes and palette. These blanks were more than pale oblongs. They were holes which had to be filled up—gaping holes in space, letting through God knows what sights of emptiness and cold. No paper could patch these up. He loaded his heaviest brush with paint.

A MAP OF THE WORLD

AFTER each holiday our cousin Robert pays us a visit. Three times a year he comes, and he doesn't leave it till long after he gets back either. Obviously he isn't the kind that just drops in for nothing. He likes to have something to tell and he comes while his experiences are still fresh in his mind. In the Spring he stays in Britain—a different place each time, though it's more often the hills than the sea. He's never been a man for the same place twice, nor the same people either—so as often as not it'll be some out-of-the-way hotel he's found with a bedroom overhanging this waterfall where you can almost catch the leaping fish in your arms. Or maybe he's come across some marvellous cook who'd once owned a big place in the south of France and for reasons best known to himself is now whipping up exotic dishes in some remote valley in the north of Scotland. His winter holiday simply amounts to a few days in London around Christmastime for the theatres, so it's more a description of plays and we enjoy that too. For he talks a bit about these actors and he'll sometimes act out a line or two of some play he's seen—perhaps comparing two different actors he's seen at some time or other in the same part. "Who, in your opinion, would you say is the best for that particular character?" he'll say to my sister, and she'll mention names and parts better or worse played, lines botched or matchlessly spoken. For she reads reviews and keeps up with everything that's said about the stage as though she were the most regular theatre-goer. Sometimes he listens for a bit, looking rather blank, and then murmurs vaguely: "Oh yes—reviews . . . You've *read* the play ? . . . But, then, the only thing that matters is to be sitting right there up in front with the lights dimming down . . . You've got to really feel this thing between actor and audience before you can know for yourself what the play's all about . . ."

However it's really the autumn visit we enjoy most, for this comes directly after his holiday abroad. And he always brings his map along. It's always a different map, because it's not just that he never goes to the same place twice. Now that he's got more money he never even goes to the same country. We're used to it—it's almost a ritual—the way he spreads out the map on the table after it's cleared, smoothing it out with his hand and sometimes flipping it up impatiently when he feels a crumb underneath or a teaspoon, and at last having it the way he wants it—dead flat—so that he can point out the places to my sister and me. My brother is seldom around at this time. He works all day in an office and in the evening he shuts himself up in his room to study for his exams. But to get back to maps. It should be possible to go out and buy a map of any country in the world, Robert says, but it isn't—such is the narrowness of life here, the parochial island outlook. But he's made up for that. He buys a map of every country he visits and of course he buys it inside that country. This cousin of ours, I should point out, is a widower in his thirties. That's rather unusual, and it's to be hoped he'll marry again before long—at least I hope so. I can imagine him bringing his wife one day and how they'll both smooth the map out with their hands, though she being domesticated by that time would no doubt be more patient about crumbs and teaspoons. Though, again, it might change things for him. She might not like the travelling.

I think the first map we studied was the Scandinavian one which he'd bought along the sea-front in Oslo. It makes a good start—that great, ragged-backed bear pouncing down towards Scotland. It's not so far after all. Nothing is far now, as everyone keeps saying. The world's a small place, and so on and so on. Robert has his little transistor set with him when he comes here, though he's not one that travels everywhere with it. When he's *not* travelling he's afraid of being bored. Sometimes when he's in the middle of a sentence he'll put it on and have to raise his voice a bit over the accompaniment of music, and when this happens Paul comes running downstairs and opens the door a slit.

"What a racket!" he exclaims. "Keep it low, can't you?"

"What is it?" Janet, my sister, says, looking up startled. "Is

127

mother all right?"

"Yes, but I'm not. I've got to work. Remember?" He shuts the door again. It's true that working this time of the night is hard after a day in an office. Only the idea of a different and better job keeps him slogging on. But he doesn't smile about it, believe me. Nothing of the gay student about Paul. And by this time Janet has got worried about something.

"Shall I go up?" she says, raising herself from the map, her fingers pressing into the crackly paper around the Arctic Ocean with a sound as though thin ice flakes were breaking up.

"If you like," I say. "But she'll be all right." Janet jumps up and goes quickly off upstairs.

"And how *is* your mother?" says Robert, reluctantly turning the transistor knob round a fraction.

"She's all right, if she doesn't exert herself. Mornings or afternoons in bed. No lifting. No stooping. No excitement."

"But she"s always done that, hasn't she?" he asks. "Since I've known her. Hasn't she always had these mornings in bed? Or evenings?"

"It used to be just the odd day. But since her last attack . . ."

"And *how* is your father?" he interrupts. The different emphasis makes it sound ironical, and it's meant to be. At once I see this man as he appears in my cousin's mind for that split second in which he allows him to be there. But for that time the older man flounders, blunders, and throws himself about, scandalously selfish, in his own world with his own friends. Defenceless too. How do you defend a spinning, swinging object? If he would walk through this door I could defend him from the ironical smile of my cousin. As it is, I say nothing. Or simply: "He'll be back late tonight. This is the night he goes round to Foster's place." And Robert nods gently and goes on nodding for a long time like one of those toy mandarins who, once touched, continue to nod and smile interminably over nothing.

Everything is all right upstairs but my sister comes down looking pale. Is that what anxiety is—looking pale over nothing, or rather over what hasn't happened but might happen tomorrow or the next day, or next month or in ten years' time? This kind of pallor has been spread through our house for as long as I can remember. Even my father at his most turbulent is touched with it, and my brother wears it constantly—a white, constricted patch on

128

either side of his sharp nose. Anxiety can mix with the colours of a house so that no matter what red and yellow cushion covers, striped rugs or checked cloths are brought in to cheer, they begin to look faded in a very short time. In such a setting it's no wonder our cousin's cheeks look ruddy by contrast, as though perpetually sunburnt. And perhaps they are, judging by the short interval between one holiday and the next. The second map he brought a few months later was a full-scale one of Italy. I remember there was a lot of purplish-red about it and when he bent over it you could see all that sunshine and fruit and wine he'd been describing suffusing his whole face. It fairly glowed—almost purple. He was not talking to absolute ignoramuses though. My sister especially has read a lot about this part of the world and this city in particular, and once or twice she interrupted him to ask enthusiastically about some object—maybe a fountain or a tiled patch of floor, or some figure high up on the corner of a building. She looked up from the map and stared hard at these things in mid-air as she spoke, reflecting, it seemed, on her eyeballs the pale, polished marbles and the sparks of light flung from fountains. But he answered none of her questions—certainly not one about the shade of certain walls and pavements. Honey? Or was it more an apricot? And at what time—morning or evening? A shadow of annoyance crossed her face at his silence. But she was stubborn. Later she insisted that he must have seen a particular painting in one of the galleries.

"But it's not there. You're thinking of another one," he replied.

"I'm absolutely certain . . ."

"I tell you, it was not there!"

"Well, I'm not blaming you. How could you possibly see them all—or remember them?"

"It's definitely not there! Probably not in Florence at all—not even in Italy!"

Perhaps she felt then her exacting manner was a bit out of place, too pernickety in the winey atmosphere of the red and purple map. For she said more mildly: "Of course, I'd forgotten they're sometimes removed for exhibitions. Naturally there'd be blanks here and there." It was clear he admitted no such thing. But he said no more. Once in a while he looked puzzled and somewhat taken aback. He had forgotten about books—forgotten the way some people still travel if they can manage to push back a suffocating day and start revving up for the night's reading—a revving up which, if you're to get off the ground at all at that hour, takes nerve, speed, and an absolute jet-engined willpower.

Next came Switzerland. Switzerland was tougher for some reason. It wasn't, anyway, a country we'd ever thought very much about. We were unprepared for Switzerland. And the map was more detailed. In fact, though he's no climber himself, our cousin had got hold of a climber's map and the mountains were shown, coiled tight at the peaks, like dark brown spirals of wire ready to spring. But below this the lines grew less taut, gradually loopier, until at last they relaxed into great, gentle swathes of green valley and blue river. No, my sister was not like herself as she stared at this map, silently steeping herself in it as though in some mysterious way, unlike the other maps, it had an extra dimension, a softness and hardness which she was gradually discovering on her own. Here and there she must have sunk pretty deeply into the snow. And what clear lakes did she slowly let herself down into, recklessly leaving clothes, bags, letters, laundry, medicine bottles, hot water bottles, whisky bottles, typewriters, tin-openers, shovels, dusters, pillows, mothballs, pills, bills, art books, travel books, blankets and Bibles—on the banks?

For the first time Robert drew out a small magnifying glass from his pocket and gave it a polish with his handkerchief before letting us look. It was useful on this map especially for finding the source of rivers and spotting the smallest lakes.

"I read somewhere . . ." Janet began. But he was staring through the glass at the peak of a mountain.

"Well, what?" he said.

"I'm thinking of those fantastic blue cracks," she said, frowning a bit. "Have you seen that?"

"Those what?" said her cousin. His hands were flat on the map and he turned his wrist for a second so that he could take a look at his watch.

"Those blue—there's no colour like it anywhere else—those blue cracks in the ice. Did you see that?"

"Cracks? Oh, crevasses you mean?"

"From a distance they're like cracks."

"Yes, crevasses."

"Did you see that?"

"I wasn't climbing, you know."

"So you didn't see this blue?"

"Refraction. No, I was never really high enough."

"Not even through binoculars?"

"No, I didn't have binoculars. There was plenty else to see though."

"Oh well, so you missed that!"

"I can't see everything, can I?"

"No, I suppose not," said Janet, smiling at him.

"I think I've done pretty well."

"You certainly have," she said, continuing to smile, and not her pleasantest smile either.

"What exactly is she talking about?" he said, turning to me.

"She's talking about the colour of ice."

"Yes, I gather that. But I don't see why it should become some sort of issue."

"It's just this man we've been reading—'an unearthly blue' is how he puts it."

"Oh, unearthly!" Janet interrupted contemptuously. "Don't let's get bogged down amongst the adjectives! But I can see it was a blue all right. And anyway let's be thankful it is a blue you *can* find on earth. It seems to give us some chance, doesn't it, of actually seeing it some day?" All this flew over Robert's head like sleet in the wind, but he seemed to feel the cold.

"This was a book of Alpine photos and articles we were looking into not so long ago," I said quickly in case she should start again.

"So you were following me, were you?" said Robert, brightening up.

"No, not *following* you at all," said Janet. "Just reading."

There was silence for a moment and then he turned away and gave his full attention to me again. "I imagine some of those travel books can be a bit misleading without the actual colour. Or were they colour photos?"

"Yes. And they were stunning. I'm not so sure about the descriptions."

"Get it out of your head that we were *following* you!" said Janet.

"Oh, for God's sake!" he exclaimed, turning round angrily.

"Because as you know reading's different," she went on. "Reading isn't climbing or driving or walking or flying or sailing or skiing. And it certainly isn't following! Not leading either. Misleading perhaps. But not following!"

131

Eventually when she'd worried it down to a last wretched rag of a word she calmed down and we all had coffee. She became more than usually polite to her cousin and listened to the rest of what he had to tell like someone sitting still in a darkened room waiting for the bang of the stick announcing the next slide. All the same she's always had the ability to see what's described as though it were there before her—throwing her head back at towers, peaks and skyscrapers, staring plumb down through the carpet into creeks and bottomless lochs. She doesn't waste much. Every scrap is examined and given full value. And some of them are no more than scraps, there's no doubt about that. For all his experience, Robert isn't exactly an Othello when it comes to describing his adventures. You'd say my sister was the better traveller, despite the fact that she hasn't yet set foot in plane or ship.

Later in the evening he described this waterfall. I've no idea when or where he saw it or why, but it was a spectacular sight. Yet it wasn't he who made it spectacular though he gave us its height and its relative volume compared to other waterfalls and its position among trees and rocks. Yes, he gave it its position all right. But Janet gave it something else. She stared with eyes that took in the whole awful glassy sweep of it. But no, she wasn't looking at this waterfall, she was inside it. She was leaning on that green slide, her fingers prised apart, her face transformed with the catastrophic shock as it crashed upon her. And she was still staring through the deluge when there came a knock overhead. Not a spectacular knocking—it never is that—not the thump, thump with the clumping great stick at the side of the bed familiar in accounts of tyrannical invalids. This was a reasonable knocking, quiet, but not apologetic either. The firm, gentle knocking of someone who has taken it for granted for months and years past and who is going to take it for granted for months and years to come that this knock will be heard and answered *whatever happens*. That is to say, whether her daughter is standing inside a waterfall or out of it.

Janet heard the knock but she didn't respond at once. It isn't easy to emerge from a cataract into the thin suburban air. She had to burst from the depths and, like a sea-creature, hurl herself out on to land. But at last she made it. She left the room quickly and we heard her running upstairs. Almost as soon as she'd gone my brother came down with a book in his hand and a thumb in the book to keep the place. He has a horror of getting involved in anything going on upstairs or downstairs, but particularly upstairs, which hasn't anything to do with his work. So he's restless and on bad nights roams from room to room, giving the impression that he may even be forced to sit and work on the stairs until the disturbance is over. This was a bad night. He didn't sit down. He stood, his thumb still in the book, waiting without speaking. After a while, as my sister still did not come down, he put his head back and rolling it round towards the table, exclaimed: "Ah—another map!" The position of his head, tilted back, forced him to droop his eyes, to look sideways down his long nose.

Our cousin was obviously annoyed by what he felt was patronising in this attitude. But you could see he was determined to be patient with this family. So he merely said: "I've quite a collection now. Yes, I think I've got just about everything you could ask for in maps. Everything but a relief map and a globe," he added with a smile.

"Relief map!" exclaimed Paul. He put the back of his free hand against his mouth and gave a burst of laughter.

"I said everything *but,*" answered Robert, this time really annoyed and showing it by the spreading redness on his forehead.

"Relief!" cried Paul again, rolling his head to and fro against the wall. I thought he was going to worry the word, worry it to death as my sister had done. But he let it go. Soon after we heard her coming downstairs and almost before she'd reached the bottom Paul barged up past her and we heard the suppressed bang of his door at the top. How will he get these half-bangs out of his system, semi-slams that have to cut out just before they reach the crash?

Our cousin stayed away for quite a long time after that. Then late the next autumn, long after everyone had forgotten about holidays, he returned. A windy night had been forecast, but he arrived before there was any sign of it. We had a quiet supper, no one talking much, not even Robert, for he likes to save what he has to say till later when we can give it our whole attention. He ate well, the meal was long-drawn-out and it was nearly nine before we were finished. Usually this is the moment when he unfolds his latest map and spreads it out on the cleared table. But this time he unfolded it and laid it out on the floor. It was made of thick, hard paper, still with the new creases ridged across it, and he smoothed it with his big, white hands, crackling it down flat on the carpet. As he did this we sensed the first rustlings of the night begin outside. It was nothing yet—scarcely a movement, or only as though the wind were gently turning the leaves over, one by one, and once in a while lifting some scrap of paper from the street and discreetly laying it down a few inches further on.

It was a map of the world. I've no idea why he should bring the world on this particular night, when it was Spain he had last visited. Maybe he'd lost his Spanish map. Or maybe Spain wasn't enough for him this time of the year. Anyway it was the world all right and rather cheap it looked too, lying directly under the ceiling light like some crude abstract painting in pink, green and yellow, surrounded by a hard sea-blue. Although he still had his finger on Spain he kept his eye on the rest of the world, and after a bit when he got really tired of Spain his finger moved off it and he began to trace devious routes round other countries. It was bound to be a rougher journey than usual, seeing the map was laid out on the floor. We may be proud but there's no time to be house-proud, and every now and then, or let's say every two thousand miles or so, his moving finger would feel some gritty part of the carpet, or maybe as he drew his nail across the Atlantic Ocean it would subside into a ragged patch—a real Sargasso Sea of weedy threads. Once his nail notched on a halfpenny and with an exclamation of impatience he flipped up the map and spun the coin away till it struck the wainscoting on the other side of the room, then smoothed the map down again with a careful hand.

There was now more than a restlessness outside. The wind was really getting up and through the uncurtained window I could see the tops of the trees across the road swing riotously every now and then against the street-lamps, and then as suddenly grow still. My sister was kneeling on the floor the way people kneel to look at maps—I mean those who are really keen—her ankles close together, arms folded round her body so that nothing loose about her clothes should dangle down to disturb the brazen pink and yellow face of the paper. She made herself neat and tight. Even her chin was tucked in, but her eyes travelled the world slowly, absorbedly, as though she were in love with it. Round the coast-lines she went, slowing down to follow rivers inland and bending closer for their source, then back again to the coast, holding closely to it through thick and thin, never mind the treacherously splintered inlets or those parts where it was necessary to navigate hundreds of miles of water dotted with quaky islands. She moved at an explorer's pace, steady, dogged, missing nothing, wide-eyed yet cautious—whole-heartedly dedicated to adventure. Long ago she had given up listening to her cousin, who was now explaining how he had nearly lost his camera in a waiting-room of the Paris airport, and by the time he was standing gesticulating on the tarmac beside the waiting plane she was working round the coast of Greenland, steering through gigantic chunks of ice. A lonely route, but she was determined on it. Our cousin, who had stopped for a moment in his story to follow the direction of her eyes, remarked that when he flew to America—and he certainly intended to go there soon, if not at the firm's expense then under his own steam—the route, depending on the winds, might not necessarily be the most direct one but possibly over the southern part of Greenland, or at any rate near enough to see it. "Though these flights can sometimes be disappointing," he added. Whatever route Janet was taking she was not disappointed. Nor satisfied. She had a fierce absorption in her travels which was painful to watch. It made me wish that he had brought a globe if he had to discuss the world, something that would spin gently at a touch or could be held between the hands like a child's head. Anything but this uncompromising square of paper sealed to the floor. Yet, after all, it was not fixed and before long our cousin grew tired of speaking to the air and he put his hand on the map to draw it aside and fold it up again.

It was as though he had touched a spring in the person kneeling beside him. With one, abrupt twist of her body she instantly turned, stretched herself out and lay flat on her back, her head on the map and her arms folded across her chest. The change from reverent kneeling to stubborn lying was all accomplished in a couple of seconds. Although I was taken aback I wasn't apprehensive. There was no question of a faint and she certainly wasn't ill. She looked, as she lay there, like one of those figures on a tomb—some overlooked noblewoman stubbornly determined on survival, even if it was to be only a survival in stone.

"What's the matter?" said Robert.

For answer she closed her eyes tight. A thick strand of hair which had come loose was curled about the South American continent, her collar ruffling along its western coast like a great wave.

"What's the matter with her?" he said again impatiently, this time turning to me.

"Nothing's the matter," I said.

"Isn't she interested in maps?"

"Oh yes, of course." Because it seemed odd that we should be talking over her as if she were deaf, I moved through the open door into the adjoining kitchen. He followed me uneasily.

"What is it then? Is she annoyed at something? I suppose the map of the world bores her?"

"She's objecting to it."

"The world?"

"No. The map."

"It's a funny thing," he said, looking annoyed himself.

"What is?"

"If she's going to start objecting to the world. She's taken most other countries."

"That isn't the world. It's a map."

"Well, what about it? Doesn't she like maps after all?"

"The difference has just struck her. This time it's really pushed her over!"

"What's the matter with this place tonight?" he exclaimed. "If it wasn't a convenient night you could have said so. The difference? The difference between what?"

"How should I know? Between paper and prairie, maybe."

"You're out of your wits!"

"Or the difference, if you like, between paper and desert, or paper and blue ice, paper and palm-trees. Between paper and people! That's the worst. Paper and people really is the worst!"

"Oh, if I'd *known* it was to be this sort of night!" he groaned.

"What sort? The wind? I don't mind that wind. I love it."

"The trouble with this family is it's always lacked proportion. Does there have to be this obsession with every single thing you pick up? And to get worked up over words!"

"Oh we take the words seriously all right. Books! Did you know she's starting on Russian now? She's got the records, the dictionary, the pamphlets and grammars. Everything. Last time it was German. Who knows? It may be Swedish next."

"All right. That's fine. What else do you want me to say?"

"We're waiting for all those books and maps to change. The dictionary made flesh. What kind of juice can you squeeze from

136

print? Paper's skin-thin. Paper's got no fat at all. It's flesh and blood we need—sun and salt and marble and hot sand!"

He looked frightened, then sympathetic, and at last exasperated. He said nothing but peered through the door into the other room. After a bit he said: "Of course I know you have a quiet enough life of it here . . ." Janet was still lying there, giving an impression of this quietness—no doubt about that—but it was an alarming quietness all the same, a quietness that dared anyone to disturb it—stubborn and forbidding. It must have been pretty chilly lying there though, for by this time draughts from all sides were stirring the corners of the map. Who would have thought that in the space of an hour or so and from its first, soft dust-siftings, the wind could have reached this uproar? Between two gusts he repeated: ". . . a quiet enough life, but I always imagined that was the way you liked it . . ." Heavens, how the wind began to tear the trees, taking great crackling handfuls of twigs from the upper branches! "At any rate," he said, "I haven't heard either of you two girls . . ." He had to lift his voice to repeat: ". . . never heard either of you complain!" above the sudden, roaring, rending lament outside. I pulled up the window and as I snibbed out the complaining wind I heard the knocking begin upstairs. Or perhaps it hadn't just begun—perhaps it had been going on for some time. We both automatically moved back into the other room and looked expectantly towards Janet. She had risen on to her elbow and was staring intently out of the window. You'd think from the look of her that the summons had come from outside, from such a distance that she had to strain and stare. If she'd been recording sounds from the ends of the earth she couldn't have listened harder. Yet the knocking was very clear now and persistent. She lay down again with her head on the map.

"Why don't *you* go up?" I said to my cousin.

"Me? She seldom sets eyes on me!"

"All the more reason."

"But she might want something."

"Then you could give it to her."

He stood looking towards the ceiling, then said cautiously: "Well, I suppose I could." He waited another moment to see if either of us would make a move. But there wasn't a flicker. I may have smiled but it was not a smile which could keep him lingering long. He went upstairs.

"You'll have to get up," I said to my sister. "What can you do for yourself lying there? Get up on your feet! From now on things will be different. I promise you. We're really going to move around!" At this her hands moved slightly along the carpet as though she were testing out this promise in her fingertips for a start. And I went on: "We're going to move around—and I mean travel—travel the world. There must be ways. Money never defeated anybody who really . . . Can't someone come in and take over? If not for both of them, then surely someone else will offer . . ." My voice trailed off at the crucial points. How I despised it for losing all bite on this last word. Yet the idea of anyone offering to put up the man of the house for days, let alone weeks, was about as imaginable as expecting the decent front doors to open up willingly to a battering-ram.

Comfortings and cajolings went out of my head. I abruptly exclaimed: "He's going to want that map when he comes down!" Her head moved slightly, rolling across God knows what depth of ocean. "He's coming now! Isn't it time you were on your feet?" But she lay there, sinking deeper into the fabulous underwater world lying, still unmapped, beneath the other. Robert entered the room.

"Yes, that was all right," he said briskly, not looking at either of us, but staring about the room. He had his coat over his arm. "She was very glad to see me. I must go up oftener. No, it was nothing. Just the company. I think she just wanted a bit of company—and she was very pleased to see me. I must go oftener." His glance as it skated swiftly over us made it clear that he would be only too glad another time to go where he was wanted. It had been a bad evening with relations—coming right out of the blue— the kind he'd heard other people tell about but had never yet experienced himself. "It's high time I was off," he said, putting on his coat. He drew on both his gloves and walking over to my sister he bent down, took one corner of the map between finger and thumb and very deftly, smoothly, as though practising sleight of hand, he slid it, with his gloved fingers, out from under her head. Her head rolled a bit again but more roughly, as though jarred on some gravelly sea-bed. He did remove one glove to fold the map—smoothing it very carefully and slowly along the correct creases. "I've always contended and I always will: women can do everything men can do—except fold maps the right way," he said, shoving it in his pocket with a slight smile. It didn't fit there properly and he had to pull it out. Again he shoved it down and pulled it out, and finally he had to lay it on a chair behind him while he buttoned his coat and rearranged his pockets. Even then he was a long time getting off. At last I accompanied him to the door which he reached without looking back.

"Well, I can't imagine what the next map could be, unless it's a star-map," I said. I knew there would be a long gap between this visit and the next. He paused with his hand on the knob of the front door. "Don't think I'm not worried myself," he said. "I knew she was upset from the word go. But I wouldn't let her lie there much longer. When people like that flop it takes more to get them on their feet again."

"People like what?"

"I mean so stiff and straight," he said.

"But if it *is* a map of the universe," I said, "she knows about stars too. She really has read it up. She knowns her way about the sky."

"Look, I daresay she needs a break," he said. "I daresay you both need a break."

"A break? Oh yes—a holiday. I really do mean that about the stars. I'm not joking. She can point out whole star continents."

He had the door open now and we were standing on the edge of the garden which every now and then swirled like a whirlpool— gravel, leaves, pale flowers on stalks—all circling and then all still again. But there was also a strong draught blowing from inside the house, for Paul, who works with his window open in all weathers, had come out of his room in the last few minutes and was standing at the top of the stairs. My cousin gave a nod and a wave and as he stepped out, the door left my fingers and slammed shut in a sudden gust from inside. An almighty slamming! The kick and slam and crash of pent-up fury could hardly have made it more. I had to wrench it open and shout after him. But the roaring night swept up the apology and tossed it about. I doubt if a word reached him. He was striding off at a terrific pace.

At the top of the stairs Paul stood, laughing angrily, and behind me my sister was slowly raising herself on her elbow from the carpet. Above her on the table lay the folded map which Robert had left. In all the time we've known him he's never before left any part of himself behind. When he goes he removes himself utterly. If he doesn't actually shake the dust from his feet—not a scrap, ash, crumb of him ever remains. But there it was.

"Oh, how he deserved that!" Janet exclaimed. "Oh, how I hope he heard that crash you sent after him!"

"You're wrong. It was the wind."

"What was that he called me? Stiff and what—?"

"Straight. You're hardly that tonight."

"I've had enough! Him and his damned maps!"

"It's there above you then." She looked up at it and was about to lower herself down again on her elbow as I exclaimed: "You'd never lie down again!"

"Take it away then. Can't someone go after him? What'll we do with it till he comes back?"

"What do you want me to do with it? Go out and scatter it to the wind? Don't for pity's sake lie down! Do you want me to wrap you up in it—or what?"

She sat up slowly and stared at me, arms round her knees. "How severe you sound. Are you angry?"

"I'm angry all right."

"With him?"

"No, with us."

"With me, you mean of course."

"No. With us. The lot of us in this box. Book-ridden, bedridden, beer-battered, bogged-down lot!"

"It's a box all right! Oh, if I could breathe in it! Why should he bring his maps to us?"

"Well, it's here now and it'll have to stay. He'll not be back in a hurry."

"Take it away. Put it on the shelf in the bedroom cupboard—under the blankets. It'll be safe there."

"And silent. You want it muffled?"

"I can't take another word about it. I'm finished. Oh, he's exhausted me—him and his world! You'd better go up and see if everything's all right. Finished! Say I'll come later if she needs me. I'm stiff too. Better go up then."

"In a while." I found nails for the job in the kitchen, came back and shook open the folded map in one jerk. Like a sail it flipped out stiffly, sending paper napkins skiffing along the sideboard and shaking the withered petals out of a jug of chrysanthemums.

"What now?" she cried.

"It's going up," I said. "Up here on the wall."

"But it's the last thing . . . !"

"I want it up. So do you. It's better than a window."

"Oh, but just look at it! What do you mean—so do I? That pink and green! You're joking. What does it look like with the pictures ?"

"Awful. Maybe they'll have to come down."

"You can't mean to keep it there ?"

"I'm keeping it here. I'm going to nail it in."

"Till he comes back ?"

"No, till we get out. I don't much care which country it is. The last nail comes out when we're on our way. Which will it be first ? France ?"

I started to hammer the first tack in—maybe with more force than was necessary, for I struck it hard several times and at the fifth dunt I heard a door fly open at the top of the stairs. Paul again, shouting this time. I started on the second nail. Maybe it was a tougher piece of wall. It needed more and harder blows before the top edge of the map was fixed. Then I strated on the bottom right-hand corner—really swinging it. I felt strong enough to hammer the house down. When the third nail was well and truly sunk I started on the last. I'd got two blows in before I heard the first bang from above—a real, powerful dunt it was—on the floor of her room. I hammered my nail again, and from above came an identical bang as though it were determined to have exactly the same force, the same weight and timing as the one below. Again I pounded and again it was echoed above, stroke for stroke, will for will—steady, strong, competitive. The last nail was far in now, but I went on. It developed into a steady rhythm, like the rhythm maintained by two workmen hammering on a metal post—one stroke below, one dunt above, and a second's silence; one stroke below, another above, and the wait again. I could have gone on all night if necessary, but suddenly I found I was hammering alone. No answering bang came from above. For a few minutes more I went on, to make absolutely sure, but more and more quickly and lightly. For now the hammer weighed next to nothing and nothing divided us from the outer air, as though the pull of gravity inside the house had grown dramatically less. Then I flung the hammer triumphantly down behind me on the carpet. There was dead silence—silence above, silence at the top of the stair. My sister was silent and white, staring at me from the floor.

"All right," I said. "You can go up now. That job's done

141

anyway. The map's up."

She still sat, listening and staring, never taking her eyes off mine. Then slowly, very cautiously she got up, stared from the map to me, from the map to the ceiling, and back to the map again. She really focused on it now. There was life in her eyes.

"And what shall I say?" she said.

"It's all right. Don't worry. The map's up. We've got it up now, and there it stays."

"But what shall I *say*?" she asked again. "What'll I say about your hammering?"

"*My* hammering? Weren't there two lots—below and above. Ask her what *hers* was for!"

But again she said: "Listen, what'll I say about that hammering?"

All the same, she was stiffening up now. The nerve was coming back.

"Tell her about the world," I said.

"Just like that?"

"Yes, tell her about it. Tell her you mean to look at it one of these days. No, no—as soon as possible. If it's not possible, you'll go anyway. What else would you say?"

"Yes, what else?" she muttered. She wasn't looking anywhere but at the map now, as though, given another chance, she might this time make the journey round the Southern Hemisphere. She might have been regretting even the few minutes longer spent on the carpet, when she could have been on her way. One more look into the centre of Australia to test the dust and space, and a moment to recover herself along the shores of the Pacific Ocean— then she turned to the door and I watched her go upstairs. This time she set each foot down determinedly, unhurriedly. It was the explorer's tread again—the patient, plodding pace of someone who had trained a hope for years, who now had the mind's eye focused so dead straight on the map that, at first hint of opposition, she could reel off—if only to sustain her till she got there—every sea, river, lake; every city, port and mountain village that came to mind. She would make her point. If need be she could pinpoint, bringing forward more and more detailed maps to her aid. She went steadily on past her brother's open door, on and up into her mother's bedroom.

SPACE

"IT's SHAPING well. I congratulate you!" exclaimed Mullen.

He was standing in front of a large, rectangular piece of water-colour paper which was pinned to cardboard and propped against the base of a chestnut tree. On the white paper were two interlinked shapes—a small oval, outlined in pale green and discreetly spotted with darker colour like an egg, and in front of it, in brown outline, a rectangular shape crossed with regular bands like a cage whose bars, on closer glance, were seen to resemble the thin, gnarled trunks of trees. A small, grey spiral, tightly wound, occupied the right-hand corner.

The two men were standing on the edge of a grove of trees. In the shadowy hollow behind them a group of young men and women were sitting working on pieces of white paper which were rather smaller than that which the men were studying. The only sound was the splashing of their brushes in a dozen jampots of water which stood beside them on the ground and sparkled whenever the leaves parted to let in the sunlight. The moment should have been idyllic.

"It is not shaping. It is finished," answered the other man bravely, and a shade wearily.

He now folded his arms and walked some distance back from the painting and stared at it sternly but appraisingly. There was a silence, and the chestnut tree threw shadows of leaves and branches tactfully across the paper so that for a few seconds it was filled to the four corners with quivering dark blue scrolls and a network of fine lines. When these were erased Mullen said, smiling easily: "In that case, I must beg your pardon. I was

143

simply judging by man-in-the-street standards. Of course, it was the large spaces of untouched paper—these white patches, which led to the mistake." Some muscle in the side of his neck seemed to stiffen, and he added softly: "—if it was a mistake."

"A very common one," answered the painter. "The white forms have a meaning as well as the coloured shapes. Would you rather I had filled them in with white paint?"

"My dear fellow, I see you mean to make a fool of me. In my line of business I've always preferred to watch a man giving himself too much to do, rather than too little. But I see painting is a pleasanter job than I had imagined!"

Mullen bent over to give a burst of laughter, then let himself down gingerly into the long grass, his cheeks still crimson with the effort of doubling himself up over nothing. It was a sultry day. His laughter came back with a hollow sound from the circle of trees behind him, and the groups of serious students looked up with startled faces from their drawing-boards. For Mullen it had been a wasted half-hour, and he expected nothing more from the rest of the morning. At the best of times he preferred to see his landscape over the steering-wheel of a fast-moving car, and for company he liked men, and particularly women, to be more than mere outlines. He disliked the kind of lunch which he anticipated would be simply a share in some other person's paper bag, and he liked his jokes as he liked his meat—lavish and full-blooded. There were no white spaces in his mind.

Mullen and Fisher had been at school together, but since then had seen nothing of one another until the chance meeting that morning. As he had gone up slowly over the brow of a hill in his car, Mullen had caught sight of a head which he recognized, rising from the field in front. With its unfamiliar background of sky and branches, he could not at first place it. When he did, he stopped with a jerk and climbed out of the car, breathing heavily with sentimental astonishment and enthusiasm. As the whole of Fisher had come into view out of the hollow, he had slackened his pace considerably, and he was strongly tempted to turn and make for the car again when he saw that the man, far from being alone, was surrounded by demure bunches of young women in smocks on tiny stools, and groups of long-haired young men in check shirts, bright socks and sandals, tip-toeing backwards and forwards from easels. It was a bad moment. Fisher, he knew, had dabbled in the old days, but here he was—a serious teacher of painting, out with his pupils. All were staring before them clairvoyantly at rocks and bushes, and now and then they withheld their brushes to listen to Fisher, as they might pause to hear the words of an oracle speaking for them out of the air.

Mullen had pushed himself forward with an effort, for he could see there was no use backslapping his way into this crowd. In a few minutes, however, the two men had described and explained the events of years. Fisher, from his own account, was an unusually successful painter who had now more private pupils than he could manage. He painted all the time, inside and outside and whether he was teaching or not. At this point he had indicated the painting against the tree.

"May I ask if you are actually making use of any of those things in front of you?" Mullen now asked, feeling slightly more relaxed in his sitting position. "Where, for instance, is the link-up between that tree over there and what you've put down on your paper?"

Having eased himself with this question, he did not listen to Fisher's answer, for he knew there could be no satisfactory one as far as he was concerned. Now and then the painter's voice came through to him, irritably repeating: ". . . based on them . . . merely based on the forms of the natural world . . ." and Mullen continued to stare up at his face with a look of concentration so intense that, prolonged much longer, it could only become downright insulting.

Mullen prided himself on keeping in touch with what was going on outside the business world, because he liked to be thought a man of wide interests, having a circle of varied and colourful friends. He liked bold contrasts to be seen in his house, occasionally in his clothes, and in the kind of entertainment he provided. The jam factory which he owned dominated the countryside for miles around, and advertised itself in the city by a series of posters showing, in the foreground, a jam which was rich, red and globular; and a white, streamlined factory in the background. The chutneys and sauces which he manufactured on a smaller scale made posters which would have been less colourful but for the addition of a fruity sunset behind the factory and a richer green in the fields, to prevent brown from dominating the picture. Contrasts—yes, on the whole he welcomed them. But this morning his nerves were on edge. He got to his feet, looking about for comfort, and found none.

"What about taking a little stroll and seeing some of *my* work?" he remarked, stealthily moving back a step and blocking the view of a young woman who was basing her shapes on a gorse bush beyond him. "You can get a view of the factory from the top of that hill, and the fields will be just below us. You show me your stuff, I show you mine. Fair enough, isn't it? You tell me the boys and girls will be moving back to their chalet, or whatever they call it, in half an hour—so what about it? They'll never miss you in the time."

The painter lingered for a while around his pupils, frowning slightly to dispel any notion that he might not be wanted, then moved slowly off with Mullen up the slope—the latter staring with particular annoyance at the jam-jars as he passed them. But they had not gone far when the painter stopped abruptly, exclaiming: "Just a minute! What about my painting? I shouldn't like anything to happen to that, if you don't mind. I've put the best part of three days work into it—and I may as well tell you, it's the most interesting thing I've done yet. Could we stow it in your car for the time being?'

For answer, Mullen airily waved him to go on, and went back himself to pick up the picture. Inside the car he helped himself swiftly and liberally to something stronger than the biscuits and tea he had anticipated. He also found a packet of cigarettes and a large bag of the best caramels, and as he made up on Fisher and saw the direction in which he was staring, his geniality returned and pride warmed his heart. In a few minutes they would be looking down on to his kingdom. But Mullen was not going to show himself an ungenerous victor. In the meantime, he asked Fisher about his exhibitions and his commissions, he enquired about the prices and titles of his pictures, and the painter, still occasionally murmuring over his shapes and spaces, walked on with the companion of his schooldays, until they reached the ridge of the hill and stared down into the long valley below.

There in the full midday sunshine lay the fields, stretching far out on either side in a rich pattern of greens, and tufted with rows of dark fruit bushes. Narrow, brown lanes and low hedges, geometrically straight as those of a formal garden, cut through this ground, and its boundaries—separating it from the unkempt

146

fields and hedges of the surrounding countryside—were marked by high walls where scores of fruit-trees were spread symmetrically against the warm stone. Orchards grew on the opposite slope. No one was about, and below them was silence, warmth, and an absolute stillness, as though the things which were growing down there, having been fed and watered that morning, supported for comfort on canes and trellises, and cut back to allow them ample sun and air—were now breathing out their pleasure through leaves, stems and fruits, in a faint, warm steam.

It seemed to Mullen that there was also a sweetness rising up from the green lanes below, which he alone could smell and even taste on his lips. Even from this distance he could see where raspberries and heavy, black knots of currants were hanging, ready for picking, and where great mats of strawberries were ripening under nets. The taste on his lips was now almost sweet enough to lick—the taste of Mullen's Full Fruit Standard Preserve—a famous jam which had taken years to bring to perfection. On the opposite ridge was the factory where it was made—a long, white building, glinting with glass and polished stone, and surrounded by flower-gardens, tennis courts and miniature sports pavilions. Every detail of this scene—orchards, fields, factory and garden—had been worked out to the last inch of ground, and was set down serenely in the surrounding country-side, like a magnificent modern palace and its park, cut out of a wilderness.

Mullen, now standing with his head modestly averted from his own work and seeming to look only at the rest of the drab land-scape, which was Fisher's concern, felt a pang of pity for the fellow. Was not this the creative work—this carefully worked bit of land where, week after week throughout the summer, every plant and tree would bend to a deeper curve under its weight of fruit—this, or the various empty spaces emerging, no doubt, week after week throughout the summer, on Fisher's squares of white water-colour paper ? He felt at once generous, scornful and compassionate. In a moment he would have laid his hand heavily on Fisher's shoulder and begun to speak about the old days and the swift passing of time. But dark clouds had been slowly blowing up behind them: beyond the factory the sky had taken on a stormy, yellow tinge, and a few minutes later they were making for the nearest clump of bushes through a stinging downpour of rain.

As they crouched together, irritably intimate, with their backs against the prickly gorse bushes, the idea of comforting or confiding in anybody, least of all Fisher, began to fade from Mullen's mind. After ten minutes he realised that there was nothing he now wanted but to reach his car and be off with the greatest possible speed, at the same time breaking any ties which might accidentally have formed between him and the old school friend against whose bony shoulders he now unwillingly pressed himself. For a few minutes the rain was heavier than ever—stotting up from roots and stones, and making the soft earth bubble at their feet as though innumerable springs were hidden underneath. Then it as suddenly ceased and the sky cleared. They began to go back quickly the way they had come, and this time Mullen made no attempt to draw Fisher out about his painting. The painter was silent on the subject of jam.

In spite of being near his own factory and fields, with his car just at hand, Mullen was oppressed with the feeling that he had fallen into some vacant region of the world that afternoon—a vacuum where for an hour or so he had floated and bounced, his heavy body no more than an empty bladder in air. Space—of course, it was that—he had felt it ever since seeing Fisher's picture. Holes, gaps and silences—these affected him in the very pit of his stomach and now gave him a sinking sensation of emptiness which he knew it would take hours and hours of good food and company to fill. The particular place which they were approaching again had been very efficiently flattened out for him by Fisher. The man had obviously stripped the fat and flesh off everything that his eye had rested on. He had made the trees seem mere skeletons of themselves, he had squeezed all the colour and juice out of the grass, and would have emptied the sky of birds, sun and stars, only given the time. Even the light falling here was cold. Long ago the girls had vanished with the boys. The car, alone among them all, stood out as a concrete thing, its shining, bulbous body filling half the road above them. Muttering about water for the engine, Mullen hurried towards it, leaving Fisher behind in the deserted grove, staring into space.

As he approached the car, Mullen abruptly slackened his pace, sweating with dismay at the sight which met his eyes. He had forgotten to put the painting inside the car; it was still propped where he had left it against the back mudguard. But that was not

148

what made his eyes bulge and the palms of his hands grow damp. The picture had changed; yet change was too mild a word—the thing could scarcely be said to be there at all. Rain had washed most of it away as successfully as the damp sponges had removed the less significant brush strokes of Fisher's pupils. It was just possible, very dimly, to make out the shapes, but they were no longer linked. The white spaces had expanded enormously. Whichever way he tried to look at it, Mullen kept seeing one thing with horrible clearness. A painting, valued by Fisher at pounds, had virtually vanished and had been replaced by a piece of curiously stained paper which it was left for him—Mullen—to dispose of or explain. Breathing heavily, he picked it up and climbed into the car, and anyone who knew him would have been surprised by the tender caution with which he preserved the peace of the countryside, as he shut the door behind him.

Some time later, Mullen got out again and began to walk slowly over towards Fisher. But a change had come over him in the last few minutes. He looked like a man who had been forced to make an important decision while cooking some delicacy over a red-hot stove. His face was a congested purple, puffy round the eyes, and these eyes appeared to have shrunk back into the folds as though the spirit had hidden itself in flesh for a moment's respite. Nevertheless his look was determined, and when he came up to Fisher his face split into a smile of terrifying amiability.

"What's wrong?" exclaimed Fisher, startled in spite of himself. "Can't you get her to start up?"

Mullen came closer, and now his eyes bulged again to the surface with the effort to be gay.

"Nothing's wrong," he said, "I'm going to spring a little surprise on you—that's all. You said it was for sale, didn't you? Well, all you've got to do is to name your price, and the thing's done. I'm buying it."

"Buying what?" replied Fisher, staring now, with his mouth open.

Mullen's amiability seemed to crack up with fearful suddenness. "What else is there to buy around here?" he yelled. His smile returned at its fiercest, and he went on: "Look, Fisher—you don't mind, do you—I'm in a hurry; the fact is I've wasted too much time already and I'm due in town in exactly fifteen minutes. I'll have to step on it if I'm to get there in twenty. So, if it's all the same to you—"

"You're not telling me—" began Fisher.

Mullen's face was now contorted in an expression of shocking aggressiveness. "I'm telling you," he whispered ominously. "Look here. Remember me? Am I the sort to shilly-shally over things? And maybe you'd better know that I don't spend much time nowadays explaining myself to other people!" Mullen paused and unclenched his fists: he made an effort to control an emotion which threatened to explode him on the spot.

"You may not have thought so, but it quite took my fancy," he said, speaking more calmly, and swallowing down some round lump of profanity in his throat. "Something about it—the white spaces, perhaps—it intrigues me. You don't get it? Well, why should you? I'm a perverse creature—not quite as simple as I make myself out to be, am I? And I'm fond of puzzles—always have been. So now we'll just leave it at that. All you have to do is to name your price, and I'll be off."

There was a long silence, and Fisher studied Mullen intently, as though trying to fit him into some absolutely new picture which was forming in his mind. Then he said slowly: "All right; I'll think about it. Where *is* the picture? I've hardly studied it myself yet. Fetch it, and we can talk it over."

Mullen seemed to stagger in his amazement at these words. He threw up his arms with a groan; he implored heaven to give him patience—only a little patience and strength to go through with something which might soon be the death of him. But when his arms came down to his sides again, he was calm. He said kindly: "There is no need to fetch it—I'm telling you, there is just nothing there to discuss." His eyes were luminous for a moment because he spoke the truth. "I simply did it up very carefully in brown paper and string, and put it behind the back seat for safety."

The suede wallet which Mullen now held in his hand was as soft and velvety as the thick and padded paw of some well-trained animal, and, as to an animal lover, its touch made up to him a little for the brittle inhumanity of human beings—their bony handshakes, their silences, and the coldness of their eyes—unable to focus affectionately even on the friends of childhood.

"How much do you want for it?" he asked sternly.

"I'm asking twenty guineas," Fisher replied at once. His

uncertainty had gone. Both men looked at one another with simple hatred, and Mullen did not flinch at the words. He even allowed himself to murmur consolingly, through clenched teeth, as he counted over the notes to Fisher: "How do you fellows manage to live at all?"

They were his last words to the painter. He believed that one minute more of Fisher's company, one other word exchanged between them, might bring on some serious illness—a heart attack perhaps, or a sudden collapse from severe nervous exhaustion. He began to walk quickly towards the car. But Fisher kept up with him, step by step. Even when Mullen had slammed the door and was starting up the engine, Fisher put his head through the top of the window before it could be screwed up, with an expression on his face like that of an outraged, young mother, forbidden to see her own child. His lips moved, but the sound was lost in the noise of the engine. He was compelled to withdraw his head swiftly to prevent decapitation, and the car shot off and disappeared in a matter of seconds over the brow of the hill.

Mullen drove on furiously through the countryside, causing stolid cows to lift their heads from the grass, and the sheep to skip aside like spring lambs. Old men sitting in doorways and young men leaning on spades in the fields shook their heads at him as he went past. But he did not slacken speed until the chimneys of the town appeared in the distance, and the occasional farmhouses on the outskirts merged into rows of country villas—wedged more and more closely together until they finally solidified into the grey streets of the city centre.

As the houses closed in, Mullen, for the first time that day, began to feel safe, and the fearful hollow inside him began to fill up as though he had already started on his solid meal. The stomach in him might easily enough be filled. Yet there was something else demanding a satisfaction which was harder to get. He had not only made room at the back of his car for thirty by twenty inches of the best blank paper, but he had emptied the contents of his wallet to pay for it. Out of this transaction—what had he got but two aching voids in the chest? The one on the right, beneath the inside pocket of his jacket, was due for a quick cure. But the other, somewhere in the region of the heart where his pride dwelt, was a space of widening dimensions, more difficult to close. Speed, food and company could do little for it. Even the

151

memory of past triumphs scarcely filled it for more than a moment. The only way out was simply to hope that the one cure, in the natural course of events, would bring about the cure of the other. Taking a chance on this, Mullen accelerated in the direction of his bank.

THE EYELASH

"I FEEL rather disgusted," said a dark-haired girl in a brilliant green dress—one of a party of four having supper in the corner of a narrow, crowded restaurant. "I've nearly finished eating and now I see there is an eyelash on the edge of my plate!"

The young man beside her leaned over and examined the plate. "There's a chance, isn't there, that it might be your own?" he said. "In fact more than a chance. It's by far the most likely thing."

"I don't see that," said the girl. "Look where it is—stuck right up on the rim. It must have been there for a long time. Anyway, all lashes are much the same, aren't they?"

"Are they? But surely you're wrong. Or why would one person feel the need to put on mascara and not another. There are obviously lighter lashes and darker ones; though dark ones are the ideal, of course. What colour would you say this one was, Olive? If it's very dark there's a good chance it belongs to you."

"Oh, don't speak about it! I tell you I'm disgusted; I don't want to spend the rest of the meal examining it. Of course it must be the cook's eyelash or perhaps the waiter's."

"It's a peculiar thing," said the young man, "that anything belonging to oneself should seem so much less disgusting than anything belonging to somebody else. After all, every eyelash has more or less the same function. Yet if you could prove this was your own, you would feel relieved at once. You might even rather admire it."

The other young man was now leaning across the table, but the girl on his right—a blonde with doleful eyes and sparkling eyelids —leant further back in her chair and looked about the room with

153

a heavy sigh.

"Olive is lucky it's only an eyelash," said this young man. "Now a hair is different, a hair is really disgusting. It can be any length and any colour, straight or curled, animal or human. There is something loathsomely ambiguous about a hair."

"I admit the fact that it can come in so many varieties gives it a peculiar unpleasantness," his friend went on. "All the same what I was saying applies there too. If she were to find one of her own hairs it wouldn't appear loathsome in the least. Tell me this now. When you find a strange hair anywhere, do you at once connect it with some imagined person? From one hair do you see in a flash a complete human being with all the details?"

"I see nothing," said the girl in green, though the question had not been addressed to her. "I'm always so disgusted I see absolutely nothing. My imagination doesn't work at all. I'm paralysed with disgust!"

"Oh please! Haven't we finished with hairs and eyelashes on plates? I'm talking about a hair you would find, say, on a cushion in a strange room. There would be nothing out of the ordinary about finding that, would there?"

"All the same, I should never think of actually picking it up," said the girl.

The young man turned away impatiently and again addressed himself to his friend on the opposite side. "What I wanted to know was simply if, seeing a certain hair, you immediately thought, let us say, of a girl with straight brown hair, rather plain perhaps, rather silent—or on the other hand with a single wavy hair do you conjure up a fair, curly-haired girl, very gay, very friendly—blue-eyed perhaps?"

The blonde who had been tipping her chair back at an alarming angle let it down suddenly and began to giggle. But the young man who had been addressed stared before him with a serious, almost a stern expression. He had taken off his horn-rimmed glasses and now he laid them on the table between himself and the girl and watched sharply until she had removed her elbow from their vicinity.

"I must admit I haven't got that sort of temperament," he said. "I seldom take these great jumps from one thing to another. When I look at any object I'm content to contemplate it as it is. If it's a hair, for example, I would be able to describe exactly what

154

that hair was like—its length and colour, the curve it took in the air. But I would say nothing, never even venture a guess, as to the sort of person it belonged to. That wouldn't interest me, I must say."

"The things that go on behind the scenes in some of these kitchens!" the girl in green was muttering. "I believe if one could get a look, just a glimpse through one of those swing doors, one would never eat out again. And that goes for even the best of them!"

"Don't worry," said the young man. "It never occurred to me that I was taking you to the best. It does happen to be the newest however, and that's the only reason I suggested it."

"And I know that it's very expensive too," said the girl. "The newest and most expensive, I've no doubt about that. It's just that these things can go on anywhere. It doesn't seem to make any difference how much you pay."

"What things go on? You mean cooks pulling out their lashes and hairs and throwing them into the soup just for spite? You do admit, don't you, that a falling eyelash is just about the most purely accidental thing that could happen to anyone? Cooks aren't surgeons, after all. They can't wear eyeshields and even their caps don't come down over their ears. They may wield knives but they're not exactly engaged in an operation. Granted there should be hygiene, but you can hardly ask for the hygiene of the operating theatre."

The girl laughed. "I certainly know better than to ask for anything like that, not after some of the things I've heard. I happen to know that a friend of mine was recently eating the most expensive meal of his life when one of those swing doors swung back a few inches further than it was meant to go and he caught sight of a chef standing over a cooking-pan picking his teeth with a fork."

The young man's expression had changed to one of exaggerated politeness. He sat absolutely still and it seemed that he was concentrating on giving every scrap of his attention to the experiences of this unknown friend. But the young man with the glasses who had been leaning forward impatiently during the last few minutes fixing the couple with an insistent and reproachful stare, now managed to snatch this moment of silence for himself.

"I suppose you've put your finger on the difference between

155

us," he said, removing the salt and pepper from their stand and setting them against one another in the middle of the tablecloth. "I can well believe that from one hair, or for that matter anything belonging to a person, you might try to conjure up a complete picture of that person. I can even imagine a touch of the clairvoyant about you like those people who handle a watch or a brooch for a couple of minutes and then describe exactly the owner, or relate whole chunks of his life-history. With me it's different. It's the thing in itself that matters. I could give you a clinically exact description of every detail of the actual thing."

" 'Clinical' again!" exclaimed the girl. "It seems I'm not to escape the word. When I said picking his teeth with a fork I didn't mean that he simply put it on one side afterwards or plunged it into a sink of boiling water. No, when he'd made a good job of his teeth he simply used it again for stirring the pot or whatever it was he had on the stove."

"Do you often stir things with a fork, then?" asked the young man at her side. He had not let up in his expression of icy concern for her friend.

"I suppose you're now trying to tell me that what my friend described was not a correct description of what he saw."

"Not at all. I'm simply asking a question about cooking. Are things often stirred with a fork rather than a spoon?"

"Certain things are," replied the girl with a cool willingness to enlighten. "Things that have to be kept light, I imagine. Some egg dishes perhaps, or things with a creamy consistency that have to be whipped as well as stirred."

The other young man had put back the pepper and salt in the cruet. He had put on his glasses again and was sitting with folded arms, his face rather flushed.

"You two—can't you give it a break?" he said. "What is it now? Recipes? A few minutes ago you were making this terrible fuss over a hair."

"It was not a hair," said the girl in green. "If you remember, it was an eyelash. And I made no fuss about it at all—simply remarked on it being there. I'd enjoyed all the rest of the evening and it simply came as a slight disappointment, for some reason."

" 'Disgust' was the word you used," said the young man beside her. "And, do you know, I think the disgust or the disappointment or whatever it was came a long, long time before that. Now I should say the evening disappointed you from the first go-off. Your disappointment, if it wasn't actual disgust, was beginning to show to great advantage when I called for you. You sulked ferociously during the last interval because all the rest of us had enjoyed the play . . ."

"Oh, but I say—wait a minute!" said the other man, still flushed but smiling tolerantly. "I doubt if 'enjoyment' is quite how I would describe . . ."

". . . peculiarly rude to the taxi-man," went on the other, ignoring him, "and when we stopped here you had long ago decided that you were going to hate the place, the food, the decorations and the people. I believe, in fact, that you had been looking frantically for this eyelash the whole evening—and now at last you've found it, haven't you?"

The young man was now fiery-faced. The girl had become rather pale but all she said was: "Have you finished with your analysis?"

"Quite finished."

"Then we can go."

They both rose at once. There was something acrobatic about this movement, for with one hand the young man removed his chair from under him and swung it lightly back, replacing it again exactly as it had been, only after a slight pause as though waiting for a certain beat of music—and with the other hand whisked several pound notes from his waistcoat pocket; while the girl managed to leave the table in a half-pirouette, balancing on the fingertips of one hand and swinging her jacket off the back of her chair and swirling it across her shoulders with the other arm. Then with both hands raised and head back, smiling coldly to some distant gallery, she flicked a smooth tail of dark hair from under the collar of her coat. Both wore the detached and utterly absorbed expression of persons engaged in tortuous feats too difficult to explain except to the initiated. A waiter who had been standing by the wall now started towards them, shambling a little as befitting the next performer coming on after a streamlined act.

"Hey . . . !" called the other young man who had been left sitting at the table. "What about us? We're not ready yet! Maud here hasn't finished her coffee!"

But the couple were lifting their hands in an extravagant farewell. They were passing tables—the man with his fiery face and the pale girl—from which people glanced up momentarily and flinched, still munching, from the inexplicable wave of heat and ice passing over them.

The blonde girl who had heard her own name spoken for the first time in two hours brightened up a little. She stretched out her hand and placed it on the two crumpled napkins lying in the middle of the table, and examined from a distance her silvery-lilac finger-nails.

"Well, what was all that about?" she said, languidly drooping her neck towards the empty chairs.

"I have, quite simply, absolutely no idea whatsoever," said the young man, still staring over her shoulder at the door.

"Because I don't believe in letting one person spoil the whole evening," said the girl, and added: "as she did over that eyelash."

The young man made no reply.

"Do you suppose he was right . . . ?" she went on.

"About what?"

"About fair girls being gay and friendly?" Her own lashes were navy blue and very long. In spite of them she seemed to be seeing the young man with a deadly and increasing accuracy.

"I have, quite simply, absolutely no idea whatsoever," said the young man.

A VISIT TO THE ZOO

THE shocking title, stinging us instantly to attention, was read out one afternoon amongst the usual fortnightly choice of essay subjects: *A Visit to the Zoo*. We were in the highest class of boys and due to leave school in a few months. After a stunned silence these words were greeted with incredulous whistlings, loud and prolonged hoots, sickened groans and a great shuffling and stamping from the back seats where young men with brilliantined hair and narrow shoes were sitting, casually hacking great slivers from the underside of their desks with outsized penknives. Our English master, who was new to the job and unsure of himself, quickly withdrew the subject, explaining that it had got mixed in with a set from some lower form. But the damage was done and it was a long time before the class settled down. A sense of outrage hung menacingly around, ready to ignite explosively with the chalk and dust in the dried-out air at the first hint of further offence. Gradually, however, still muttering savage threats, we sank heavily to the business of writing, after making our reluctant choice between *The Advantages and Disadvantages of a Political Career* and *The Dangers and Benefits of the Space Age*—giving only a scornful glance at *Whirlpool* which had been thrown in as the sop to those who had more imagination than knowledge. Yet throughout the whole hour from its blank beginning to the frenzied bout of last-minute writing, I felt the impact of that subject which had been withdrawn. It was indeed the one topic which for a long time I had been at pains to avoid, but here it was now forcing itself up unexpectedly like something painfully green and fresh amongst all those stony opinions which I was doggedly setting

159

down on paper.

Almost three years before a young woman had come to live with my family for several weeks. I knew nothing about her except that she was a cousin of my mother's, that she was convalescing from a serious illness and that she expected to be left quite free all day to go out and in as she pleased. Two or three bottles of brilliant-coloured tonics, placed there by my mother, appeared on the bathroom shelf amongst our normal collection of dingy brown ones, throwing stained-glass wedges of light into the bath on sunny days but remaining corked throughout her visit. Nor did she appear to follow up any of the suggestions being offered on all sides as to the best method of "taking her out of herself". For it turned out that the one and only cure she had chosen for herself was to go often and alone to the zoo which was on the other side of the city.

I was on holiday—the only young person in the house and it seemed obvious that, sooner or later, she would ask me to accompany her. At first I was both surprised and thankful that she did not; then I grew angry. Later, however, as I watched her going off day after day by herself, I believed that by not taking it for granted that I would have to be asked she had given me a certain value apart from the family and had somehow included me in the adult world where people could be free and separate from one another if they wished to be, with no reasons given. In this way I gradually, silently came closer to her, and indeed believed that I could share the emotions which kept her all day and in all weathers restlessly on the move.

Then one day while casually drawing on her gloves she flatly enquired with an indifferent glance directed beyond me into the hall mirror: "And are you coming out today?" We walked together to the centre of the city, moving silently and apart, going our separate ways with our own thoughts until we came to the junction of roads where a policeman directed three great streams of traffic. This place where there was hardly a person to be seen but only a steady whirl of glittering cars had for me an unreal and precarious brilliance that afternoon. Even the policeman seemed to take on the authority and abandon of some white-gloved clown who can draw a crazy collection of vehicles after him with a wave of the hand or keep them circling dizzily until he has decided at what corner he will point his finger. I followed with my eyes the direction of that hand down one broad street as far as the eye could see to where it narrowed and a faint green of trees could be seen. They were still the dusty city trees, sparsely planted, and the zoo was still a long way beyond them, but that day, for the first time, I saw this greenness with a painful shock of pleasure.

Now, day after day, we went to the zoo. Sometimes it was wet and we would be almost alone there, and on the stormiest days gusts of rain fell against the metal roofs of the monkey-houses like handfuls of sharp nails and even the enclosed pools were raked into miniature waves on which old crusts, orange peel and dusty feathers rocked desolately together. Sometimes it was so hot that after we had made a tour of the lower houses we climbed no higher but sat for a long time on a bench beside three empty cages which stood on their own in the shade of the only group of trees in that part of the garden. These cages had no labels; there was no way of knowing whether the animals there had died or been moved to some other part or whether the place was being prepared for new arrivals. In the heat we sat and stared at the dusty straw and the empty troughs wondering what the inmates had looked like, and my eyes would climb up and down the wire netting behind the bars as my imagination moved from ostriches and giraffes down to some almost invisible rodent hiding in the straw.

"I wonder how old you are," she said one afternoon as we were sitting in the half-empty tea-house. It was unlike any other restaurant. Half of the roof was glass and on hot days there was an almost tropical atmosphere about the place. All round the walls grew tubs of tall, waxy green plants whose leaves were always damp from the quantities of steam which rose from the tea-urns at one end of the room. The concrete floor was sandy and children would pad silently back and forth carrying flashing glasses of lemonade which they drank holding them above the table, the straws tilted at an angle—thus keeping their chins high enough to see what was going on out of the windows. The smell of elephants penetrated to this place and above the high bushes one could catch an occasional glimpse of the two rows of children rocking by, perched back to back on an ornamental tray which swung like a hammock at every step. Long ago, in another age, I also had swung there. Now I was sitting silently at table opposite a young woman who had been watching me intently for some time while I finished my tea.

"I'm fifteen," I replied, abruptly pushing my plate away from me.

"Yes, I know that," she said, "but I'm wondering how old you are in other ways. I mean," she went on, leaning her elbows on the table, "what do you know about people—about men and women? Do you know, for instance, that they can illumine the most dense, the most boring objects or places or people for one another, and then, by one word or even one look, turn the whole world to iron?"

I looked up quickly. But she was smiling slightly as though to take back a little of the impenetrable hardness, the numbing coldness she had put into that last word, at the same time looking aside again through the hedges, to imply that it was not after all a real question which required an answer but simply a statement of fact which needed only mutual recognition. I had not taken my eyes off her, but now she appeared, in the space of a few seconds, to be quite changed. She was a person who had at last spoken directly to me, who had broken through the restless, drifting indifference of the last few days with something unequivocal as a shout or a fierce gesture of the hands, and I tried to hold her there at the point where this momentary and precarious contact had been made by taking a more careful note of her appearance.

Her hair was straight and dark, with a faint bronzing of lighter colour at the back of her head where it was intricately plaited and twisted up into a heavy coil like a great unripened blackberry. In front it was brushed well back from a smooth, narrow brow which, while absorbed in some thought, she would often touch, tapping her fingers gently between the eyebrows, then drawing them firmly up over her brow and carefully round the temple down to the cheekbone, as though she found deep lines there corresponding with certain ineradicable grievances in her own heart. She had fine dark eyes but most of the time she seemed to look at things with a peculiarly blank and fixed stare as though she would not bother to see objects unless they presented themselves within a very limited field of vision which for her was usually straight ahead. One had the impression that only at this particular spot were human beings clear or even human before disappearing into the amorphous background from which they had emerged. She seldom followed them with her eyes. Occasionally she would drop her head and tuck her chin down into the folds of a broad scarf of blue silk which she wore even on warm days and drew up over her head if it was wet or windy. In this position, and without moving her head, she would stare up and down her person from toes to bosom with the same blank indifference with which she might look down at a flat and uninteresting landscape. I remembered all these things clearly now. I also knew in a flash that the extra bottles in the bathroom—the tonics, the laxatives, the vitamin pills—were all nonsense; my mother's insistence on gritty brown bread, her references to deeper sleep, extra milk and fresh air—meaningless. All these were no more a likely cure for love than a bandage over the finger for some internal injury.

From that afternoon all the childishness of the zoo disappeared for me, and as the days went by its whole character changed; its cruelty and beauty, its strident colours and harsh cries gradually took the place of all those mild and comic impressions I had experienced there as a child. Now something savage and sad brooded far back in the darkness of the cages we passed. When I stopped to listen I would hear sounds I had not been aware of before—strange rustlings and whistlings from hidden birds, those unidentified croakings and hoots belonging rather to midnight than to noon; and sometimes there came a howl, heart-freezing, yet so distant that it seemed to come, not from the trim confines of the garden, but through the black arctic air and across miles and miles of snow-covered plain.

Everything that had been associated with earlier visits faded out. The animals themselves had changed. Now it was horrible to remember that I had ever expected them to clown for my entertainment—painful even to stare too long at the yawnings and scratchings, the sudden blows and caresses, or to meet the brooding, yellow eyes which stared back, unblinking, at grimacing human faces. Even the seals, flopping off the hot boulders, or rocking from side to side on their flippers ready for a fish to come hurtling through the air, looked mournfully out of place. No longer hypnotised by the velvety backwards and forwards padding of the lioness, I waited only for the slow, swinging turn she would make at each end of the narrow cell, and heard, with a sinking of the stomach, the soft swish of her great shoulder as over and over again with sickening regularity it brushed the same spot on the wall.

As the days went by and our outings never varied I began to

wonder if the likeness of the man she loved might not, after all, be found in one of these animals at which we stared so long and gloomily; depending on my ever-changing feelings towards him I would find him on certain days amongst the monkeys, on others amongst the brilliant and talkative birds, and occasionally, when the thought of him began to bore me, I found him in a tank of brown, wrinkle-headed fish, gaping coldly at us like some jaded business man sealed inside the plate-glass of his office. One day I caught a spark of interest in her eyes for the first time as she looked after a well-dressed man who was strolling by himself round a pond of black and green ducks—a spark instantly extinguished when he turned his head; but from that moment I quickly removed this man of hers, whoever he was, from any likeness to certain of the monkey race—those tousled ones, shamelessly unbuttoned, who wore frayed fur round wrists and neck or, worse, patches of bare, scarlet skin on their backs. There were other elegant species to which he might still belong: monkeys with silky chestnut hair parted in the middle and falling smoothly over cleanshaven cheeks, whose fingers were long and delicate, rosy-pink on the inside. But the most likely place for him was still amongst the stylish birds; even if he was fat and formal it was possible to find him amongst the penguins who could stand for great lengths of time, tilted backwards, presenting plump, snowy shirtfronts to the admiring crowds.

One afternoon I was peering into a cage which had seemed empty, but hearing a rustling in the inner passage I had put my head against the cold bars with both hands grasping them on either side. For a long time I stared but nothing appeared except a mouse which darted across and disappeared into a pile of straw. A chill disappointment had been growing in me for the whole of that day and now it was a raging discontent. Long ago I had lost the early liberties and privileges of this zoo and now, coming back again, had found nothing to put in their place. It was becoming clear to me that I was not to be allotted any of the responsibilities of being a real companion to this woman who stood behind me at this moment. She might speak flippantly about herself, but she did not bother with any comments I might make. She asked questions without expecting an answer; and sometimes after sitting silently for a long time she would give a deep sigh which she cancelled out immediately by a loud burst of laughter, at the same time turning her head away as though any reaction which might come from me was the last thing she could endure. The holidays were nearly over. That particular afternoon the zoo was almost deserted and inside me and around me was emptiness, a feeling that everything was already falling from my grasp. I hung on grimly to the bars as I spoke:

"Why don't you do something about it? Go after him, if that's how you feel—or find somebody else! Anything's better than wandering about day after day! Why did you choose us anyway? We're no use to you and you know it. You even show it—yes, that's true—you don't even bother to hide it—you've shown it all along!"

I shouted these last words in such a desperate voice that somewhere nearby but out of sight, the steady raking of a gravel path which had been going on for some time in the background ceased for a few seconds. Indeed at that moment everything seemed dead silent over the whole zoo.

She stepped forward quickly and put her hand round mine which was still holding the bar—grasping it so hard that the fingers were crushed about the iron in an instant's bone-cracking pain. The ache of iron was in my wrist, in my arm; cold iron was moving towards my chest when she dropped her hand. Mine remained on the bar until slowly, with the greatest caution, I withdrew it and held it up before me, still painfully curled and shaking slightly from its rigid grip. Slowly I stretched it out, finger by finger, and finally brought it close and peered into the palm which still held a blurred white bar-mark. No sooner had I seen this mark than I clenched my hand again as though concealing a painfully won prize and thrust it deep down into the pocket of my raincoat. We walked on without a word.

A few yards away was a signpost bristling with half-a-dozen white-painted arms pointing in all directions and on which were inscribed: Giraffe, Monkeys, Wolves, Gents, Reptiles, Elephant. Cautiously taking the middle path between the Reptiles and the Wolves I arrived at a small pavilion hidden behind bushes and here I sat down wearily on the short flight of wooden steps which led up to it. There was nobody about. I sat perhaps for ten minutes wondering if I would always be tired now, if perhaps this heaviness in the limbs and the slight giddiness which I felt as I bent to tie up a shoe-lace were the characteristic signs of maturity, and though I welcomed these, I wanted nothing better than to return for a few moments to my normal state. It was a relief to turn my eyes, hot with staring at fantastic birds, to the few dusty sparrows hopping about near my feet amongst leaves and stones which concealed only the common spiders and beetles which I could have found any day in my own back-garden. There was no mystery here and no glory. Not far away a gardener, clipping back a high hedge, kept the distant howlings at bay.

I had imagined that when I went back to the main path I should find her sitting on some nearby bench, or perhaps walking slowly on ahead, waiting for me to catch up. But when I at last emerged I saw her far off in the distance, already at the entrance gates. She turned once and waved—a friendly but casual gesture which slowed me down immediately, so clearly did it indicate that our afternoon together was at an end. I decided there and then that from that day I would leave nothing to chance. She would see that it was no dumb schoolboy she had on her hands. I would break ruthlessly through silences. If need be, in the days ahead, I could shift the whole scene of action to some entirely new and less disturbing territory.

But there were to be no more days. The next afternoon was hot and thundery; I was outside the front door of the house, casually turning over the pages of a newspaper which lay on the steps and occasionally flicking away the flies which zigzagged erratically across the avenues of black print. Although seemingly absorbed, I was only awaiting the one cool look from her which was the usual signal that she was ready to go if I wished to join her. I waited a long time, and at last she came out. But the look was not casual. Instead, I saw with terror that her expression was kind. She paused, looked down at my paper in silence for a moment as though something of interest had caught her eye. Then she said, pointing, still with her head bent:

"They're absolutely wrong about that because I happen to know the town myself. A fishing river indeed! With paper mills along the banks! I suppose they'll be making out it's a holiday resort with freshwater bathing next. I'll see it later. Save it for me till I get back."

She turned away and went quickly down the path to the gate. Usually she let it bang carelessly, not looking to see whether it was shut or not, but this time I heard her lift up the latch, then let it down carefully into its slot behind her, as though to emphasise that though such barriers between human beings might be absurd there was nothing to be done about them, so one might just as well learn to manipulate the various keys and latches and the cunning little iron bolts which had so thoughtfully been provided.

A week or so later she was gone; the summer holidays were over and I was back at school. The duster flouncing out angrily across a density of figures on the blackboard released great clouds of spinning white chalk, silently exploding nebulae through which we stared in the direction of the window and out over the dark chimneys of the town. But all was grey dust now, dust in the air we breathed, dust in the air outside. All illumination had come to an end.

A LOADED BAG

Two young men and a girl sat at a table outside a café in Venice one hot August morning staring down through the balustrade into the Canal. They were silent, simply watching that part of the water which was directly beneath them. It was a particularly busy quarter near a landing-stage where large boats from the Adriatic put in, and here the water was full of all sorts of objects which floated slowly by—bottles and corks, lemons hollowed out like plastic teacups, socks, sticks, flowers, shoes, and a minute, drowned kitten, cream-coloured, with a trailing collar of seaweed about its neck. Bobbing past with all the rest was a grey, bulging cloth bag tied tightly at the opening.

"What do you imagine is in that bag?" asked the older of the two men.

For some time now he had been sitting well forward, his long legs pushed up against the balustrade, his head moving slightly from side to side following the course of each item as it slid beneath him. The other two sat further back, their eyes half-closed against the sunglare. At first they ignored the question, but the man was insistent.

"What do you imagine is in that bag?"

"No thanks," said the other man, now opening his eyes wide. "The question's loaded!"

"Loaded? Not at all. The bag's loaded. I simply ask what's in it."

"No thanks again. I'm simply being invited to say the most disgusting thing I can think of. I'm not on."

"Well, for heaven's sake! What on earth's this outburst in

aid of?"

"Of course you'd make out it was that, even if I'd never raised my voice. If you're posing as a psychiatrist why can't you do it subtly?"

"In fact, I'm absolutely flabbergasted. A simple question!"

"Not simple at all. You want me to think of the unspeakable and then say it."

"Well, well!" exclaimed the other, leaning back from his scrutiny of the water. "I ask politely for an opinion . . .!"

"That's it. This constant probing and questioning and asking of opinions. Why do you take it for granted you'll get an answer?"

"I agree," said the girl, turning her back to the water. "Here we are in the most beautiful city in the world . . ."

"One of, anyway," murmured the young man.

"And you want in your leering way to destroy it, all for the sake of that cloth bag there." There was a moment's silence.

"Are either of you too hot by any chance?" said the tall young man. "Because if you are we can move. We can go straight back to the hotel if you're tired."

"I'm not too hot," said the girl. "But I *am* terribly tired. I'm terribly tired of you. You may pride yourself you miss nothing, but you give absolutely the same attention to everything you see. They're all equal value, aren't they—mosaic doves on golden backgrounds or those tatty pigeons, pearls or droppings, that obscene little bag down there . . .?"

"Oh, *is* it obscene?" said the young man.

"That bag," the girl went on, "or a jewel-studded purse. It's the same."

"A voyeur," said the other man. "I'd say he's something of a voyeur."

"Well of course," said his friend, "I *do* use my eyes. Anyone who looks too long and hard ends up labelled indecent by somebody. Supposing on top of that he was also an artist."

"Oh, *are* you one?" said the other. "Then you've certainly managed to keep it dark all these years."

"No, I said 'supposing'. I'm simply carrying the argument a step further."

The girl now sat well away from the balustrade, leaning over the table and studying the others in the café. There were many tourists, some students from the nearby university and a middle-aged Italian in an elegantly-tailored suit writing a letter. It was near midday and very hot, but every now and then a slight breeze came from the water and separated the big green leaves above the tables. Amongst the holiday-makers were a few postcard-writers—slow, at this hour, and rather grim over their task. The letter-writer, however, had a gentler expression and each time his pen approached the paper, after long pause for thought, he gave a smile which was quick and sweet and which faded gradually as he came to the end of a sentence. Unlike the others he wrote for love not duty, and when at last he sealed the letter and got up to go his air was serious as though virtue had drained out of him to make the envelope in his hand a full packet of sweetness. The postcard-writers were reluctant to see him go. He had given some heart and dignity to their labours.

"Yes, I think I'll go back and write my letter," said the girl, following the man with her eyes. "There's that cool spot near the hotel where I can stay till lunch."

"Oh, these endless, endless family letters!" exclaimed the long-legged man. "And who is it to this time?"

"This time it's to my father," said the girl, "and amongst other things he happens to be the person who's handing out the money for my trip. Incidentally you come in for some of the side benefits yourself."

"I suppose I do. Side benefits! It's a peculiar phrase when you come to think of it. But I know it means food. You, or rather your father, do occasionally pay for the odd meal . . ."

"And last night's was one of the oddest," said the other man quickly by way of switching the conversation. "Do you suppose those baby octopus were really Siamese twins or was it just an arm or two had got stuck during the cooking?"

The girl refused to be drawn. Her wicker chair was now tipped far back, her hands pressed down on either side as though she were in the first stage of detaching herself from the table. On her left hand she wore a thin copper ring which the older man had given her. It was open at the back, adjustable to any size and she changed it about from index to middle finger, occasionally on to the other hand and even momentarily, in times of exasperation, to her thumb. She took care to avoid her engagement finger as though it were mutilated.

"Don't, for any sake, go further back," said the ring-giver. "Or else your head will be right in that band of sun." It was actually striking the back of her head already, making it shine like a long curve of dented, yellow metal. They had seen a lot of gold lately—in halos, melons, bells, bowls, plates and coins—but this was one of the best.

"No, that's all right. Because I'm off," she said, bringing the chair down and gathering up papers and sunglasses from the table.

"Then I'll come with you," said the younger man. The girl said nothing and the other didn't move except to turn his eyes again to the water which was now carrying along on its surface a bouquet of withered flowers, a rusty pot-lid and a double fleet of blade-like waves from a passing boat. While still in sight of the tables the girl walked briskly, her eyes straight ahead. But as soon as they had gone round the steps of a curving bridge she slowed down. Seen in this setting amongst the crowd there was a certain gawkiness about her. She held her fine head rather awkwardly, poking forward a bit, as though she felt the pressure of each new sight and the responsibility of giving every stone its proper value. The two men had been in Venice before, but this was her first time. She was transported and sometimes swamped, ecstatic and indifferent by turns. The town she had come from was in parts as ugly as hell, and though she had never noticed this before she had, in the last few days, begun to suspect it.

"Well, perhaps you understand him best," she said at last when they were well away from the café. "You can explain why he's always got to tell one exactly what's inside the dark corners, the dirty little bags."

"Wait a minute," said the young man. "Let's straighten this out. Because when you come to think of it, he didn't tell us. He asked. And what's more, it was we who supplied him with the information."

"I certainly did not. How could I? A bloated bag tied tight at the neck!"

"Well, we supplied the nastiness, shall I say? All right then. Sorry! Of course I mean, *I* did!"

The girl having slowed down almost to a stop walked on again at this exclamation. She said in a casual voice: "Yes, I remember now. It *was* you. Anyway you suggested he'd something horrible in mind."

"And you, I believe, didn't waste much time in backing me up. You might have been waiting for just that chance all morning. You really waded in!"

"Are you suggesting . . . ?" She swerved on some steps to let a handcart piled with slabs of shining white ice come down. It was manipulated by a boy whose face she had seen modelled in fragments of green, brown and pink mosaic that morning. "Oh, I can't take that! So you mean it's really *us*. We're the ones who find and look for horrors! Smells and rubbish is our province then? Not the palaces and bells. And not the lions either—just poor, drowned kittens. Is that it? We're really the lowest form of tourist, then, so low that beauty galls us, makes us jeer and point!"

He laughed at this outburst, but glancing sideways saw that she looked rather wretched. He took her arm and they wandered not in the direction of the hotel at all, but through a winding street overlooked by windows where whole families were sunning themselves and old ladies looked out, fluttering small black fans and chatting down to others looking up from windows below. The noise towards noon was terrific. Business men in elegant, cream suits carrying briefcases went by, weaving deftly between clattering handcarts loaded with melons, slabs of meat, T.V. sets, chairs, cages and huge bunches of plain and painted candles. Two earringed, white-dressed babies went past in their high prams, pushed by gesticulating mothers, and at every corner tourists squatted, taking shots of inaccessible ornament, or lay on their backs and on their stomachs amidst a constant whirring and clicking. Sometimes they sat with the camera between their legs or stood on tiptoe lifting it high above their heads or walked, swinging it from elbow and shoulder, or let it grow like a protuberant third eye from the navel. The man and the girl now turned from this street into a lane of shadow between high walls where purple flowers hung almost to the ground, and going quickly past a painter who was busy scooping up lavish dollops of honey and purple from his palette they emerged into a quiet square. This was in stunning contrast to where they had walked a few minutes before—empty, except for two slow-moving girls who crossed it carrying baskets, and a black-scarved old woman shuffling down step by step from the curtained doorway of a church. In the centre of the square where the paving-stones sloped down a circle of thin, grey cats sat motionless beside a fountain. Here the couple

172

seated themselves, facing the church and trying to penetrate to the coolness beyond the curtain, occasionally catching glimpses, far back, of the crusty gold and white altars where candles flickered. They heard the remote and icy tinkling of bells.

"Don't worry," said the young man. "Relax. We're not as bad as all that, even if we *are* knocked over now and then and have to start kicking up a fuss."

"I'm not kicking up any fuss," said the girl. "And who or what is supposed to be knocking me over ?"

"Listen," he said. "It takes people differently. Some sail in and out again, rapturous but unscathed. It's perfect love all right, but fortunately they also look forward to getting home again, and once back forget all about it and get on with the job. Good. But there are others . . . this woman, for instance—this is fact, by the way, not fiction—who came here for the first time with a female cousin when she was nearly fifty—very sensible she was, absolutely no nonsense and with her head screwed on. It took *her* in a strange way !"

"Oh, did it indeed ? Of course we've all got our heads screwed on somehow. No doubt you meant to say hers was screwed on the *right* way. Never mind. She eloped with a gondolier of course ?"

"No. But for a while she acted as though possessed by the very devil. In a constant rage. At first glance of the place—and what a glance that must have been, for I can assure you her eyesight was first rate and it was early morning in June—at first glance she retired to her room in a huff. When she emerged she could find nothing right. There were the smells and the heat. There were the starving cats. There was the noise at night . . ."

"I know," said the girl. "Every half-hour a splintering crash as though someone had dropped a load of iron bars mixed with glass."

"There were the Italians," went on the young man, "—lazy, graceful and amorous. There were people moving about, hideously, on their knees in certain churches and grotesque old women stroking the shiny toes of Christ with bony hands. We can safely bet that amongst other things there would be an obscene little bag or two twitching in the water. O, what a stupendous struggle she put up! For a start she had somehow to shut her eyes to that light and the magnificent colour at every turn. And she managed to do this by wearing a very peculiar pair of dark glasses—bought,

173

you'd imagine, expressly for that purpose—glasses which, believe it or not, could almost reduce gold to ashes and did turn rose to mud. Fortunately they also hid the expression of her eyes. And what expression was that? Again, no one will ever know."

The girl, who was wearing dark glasses herself, but the best, the kind that scarcely alter a tone or colour, removed them carefully, smiling. "Go on. It's hard on the eyes without them. Ageing too. But never mind."

"There were the Galleries, of course," said the young man, "—palaces of paintings which she didn't try to avoid though she'd never been a great picture-lover herself. She walked through in a stoical daze, seeing paintings on one side, and on the other—out of the corner of her eye—the dazzling Piazza below where waiters were quickly putting up the little tables and chairs again after one of those rare and sudden downpours."

"How do you know all this? She told you herself, did she?"

"Maybe she did. But wait a bit. She's still walking along and now that she's turned a corner in the Gallery the windows are framing the blues and golds and white marble of the Basilica—angels, flags, flutes, horses, birds, wings, crowns, halos and suns, and on her other side, framed along vast stretches of wall, are other, deeper blues, and golds, flags, angels, wings, robes, crowns, flowers and suns. She is still walking stoically and steadily, keeping her balance in the heat, and finally she reaches those rooms where a few Northern painters are gradually beginning to creep in—none from as far north as her own country, but a good halfway there. Now from behind the serene virgin other creatures emerge. A mongrel dog with its tongue lolling out peers from behind a tree and a strange lizard scuttles back to its hole. The wings are thicker, the flesh heavier. A darker sky rolls up. And gradually, going deeper and deeper, a whole world of jokes, songs, grotesque mouthings, whisperings, ticklings, lickings can be seen. Until she finally meets a few of St. Anthony's Temptations. The landscape is pretty stony here, but some of the stones turn out to be gigantic eggs which have cracked open to reveal squirming shapes. There are elephantine ears spewing worms, mouths from which the legs of frogs protrude. Here are breasts which leer and grinning bottoms. All this seemed to quieten her a bit—took her mind off her own troubles. Not that she welcomed horrors—no—but here was someone who'd given them maximum voice. It steadied her

174

up, somehow, seemed to justify her fault-finding and temper, and made up for some of the inexplicable anguish she experienced when she allowed the city to make its full impact on her. For when she compared it . . . well, we've not looked at that yet, have we ? I mean her own home town. When she compared it to that!"

"Why did she need to compare Venice with anything ? Such a contrast would be meaningless anyway."

"Poor thing, she'd probably been brought up to make such comparisons and to profit by them."

"Anyway, it was probably no better and no worse than your own town, for instance."

"No better, anyway. It had the look of being built with immense care, love even, bad brick on bad brick, and all with a patient, cunning misarrangement that showed the years and years of practice behind it. People make a mistake if they equate ugliness only with carelessness or hate. No, there were halls and towers here too. It even had its bells which at certain hours could peal out nearly recognizable hymn tunes. There had been one or two fine buildings of course, but the word 'progressive' was getting around so they came down, and quickly too. From an aeroplane the place must have looked rather like a crossword puzzle—long, black, yellow and white streets of new cement and brick cut by the sooty red of older streets and squares, and dotted all over it, like highly-polished red and yellow crosses, were the churches—dozens of them. Now she'd never in her life had a word to say against this place, had never complained about any other city as far as I know. Until she set foot in Venice. Then she complained. Oh, how bitterly, bitterly!"

"Poor thing—because her life seemed suddenly short ? Because there was hardly any time left ?"

"Well, hardly time left for Italy, anyway. They were due to return in a few days."

"Wait a minute. I've got some impression of her town. I want to know about the woman now. What did she look like ?"

"But I was to mention this. There's only one thing that matters to us. She has this dark red hair. Heavy, rather striking."

"How was it done ?"

"Oh, I can't tell you that. Anyway it was long enough. It would make a striking pile-up on her head."

"A striking pile-up ? Well, I suppose I can arrange it myself if I want to. Go on."

"No. I'm to get on to their last few days. And she didn't make them any more agreeable for her cousin, I can tell you that—this relation of hers who had nothing but praise for everything she set eyes on. Until finally they decided to spend most of their time apart, meeting only at the end of the day. Sometimes the cousin might see her in the distance, going slowly along one of those narrow streets between the tiny, perfectly designed shop-windows, or she would catch sight of her in the middle of a crowded pavement café. And once, without warning, she came face to face with her at a corner. It felt strange, she said, to meet her eyes and get for the first time for many days a detached but friendly enough smile as she went past. It was like the greeting of a stranger which indeed during the day was what she was—a silent woman walking about slowly on her own, sometimes turning, stopping, going back to look, going on again, and using her eyes as though she'd at long last found their exact function. In the evening when they'd join up again she could still use her tongue sharply enough, but the cousin felt that tongue and eyes had got strangely disconnected.

"Then came the last day, on the evening of which they were due to leave. Can you imagine her in the midst of all the confusion of packing on a broiling afternoon, yet managing to look as efficient as on the day she'd packed the stuff up in Britain? You can visualise the kind of thing—folding blouse-sleeves the proper non-crease way, whatever that is, even though they were on their way back to the ironing-board, squeezing the bottles of sun-lotion, stomach-powder and aspirin inside the toes of shoes—then pressing the whole thing down with the palms of her hands to get it nice and flat before the lid goes down. Finally the whole thing is closed and snapped shut. At this point there was such a long and absolute silence in the room that the cousin turned round to see what had happened. She found her standing there, motionless, staring down at the case with a strange expression in her eyes and with her hands grasping her head in an attitude which the cousin described as being like someone frozen in the act of tearing her hair. She remained in this rigid emotion for a few moments then dropped her hands, covered her mouth with them as though to stifle a shocking cry, and crossed quickly over to the window.

" 'Oh, what *have* you lost?' exclaimed the cousin. 'For heaven's sake tell me! Whatever it is, there's still time to look and ask!'

'There's nothing lost. Nothing," replied the woman at the window.

'What's happened? Is it something you've just remembered?'

'No. Nothing. I have been ten days here—that's all. And this is the last. I'm torn to bits by it all. I won't speak about it.'

'Yes, talk. Go on. So it's been a fiasco, has it? Why? Why should it turn out like this? Have you felt ill? No, you would have told me if you had. Then have you really hated this holiday so much?'

After a silence the other answered in a strong voice: 'I've loved this place! Every single step and stone of it I've loved. Oh, the hatefulness of words! Did you hear—"step and stone"? That's pure travel-folder. Never before for any place or person ... No, not that either. So there's nothing more to say. Just this, though. From the first day—the thought of going back! The very thought of it! Back *there!*'

The vehemence on the last word appalled her cousin, but she recovered herself to say quietly: 'You mean *home*'—pressing down on the word as though still confident of its power to cure everything. But it didn't work.

'I'm going out now,' said her companion, turning abruptly from the window.

'Remember there's not much time.'

'Time enough. I'm out to get my hair thinned!'

'Yes, yes, of course,' her cousin answered faintly, though never pausing for an instant, 'and you'll feel a lot better for it. If only you'd had that done before. We're not—either of us—used to this heat ... and your poor head!'

'I *adore* the heat!' were the other's last words before she rushed out.

"So she spent her last hours in the city having her red hair trimmed, did she?" said the girl.

"No, she had it cut."

"Trimmed?"

"Cut off. Her long hair cut short."

"Off! Oh, no! Do you mean it was some ghastly mistake of language? I can't bear that for the end. It's got to end better than that."

"I can only tell you what happened."

177

"Surely she could have stopped him in time. The man's scissors would open slowly, wouldn't they? He wasn't a maniac?"

"My dear girl, she *asked* for her hair to be cut off. No doubt her Italian would be dismal, but she had her little book. There was no difficulty in getting what she wanted. If you ask me it would be the barber who'd hesitate, if he wasn't actually affronted at what she was asking him to do. Possibly he would ask her to repeat it—and very slowly too—after which he himself would demonstrate with anguished swoops of the scissors what exactly was about to happen to her hair. Imagine how he would flay himself over it—anything to get this implacable English woman to feel the drama of the thing, even, if the worst came to the worst, to get some spot of fun for both of them out of it!"

"And it was all no use?"

"The only certain thing is that she was perfectly satisfied with the results. Her cousin, anyway, saw no regret in her."

"And they had only a short time before they left? They were flying back?"

"That night."

"Tell me about the cousin."

"I know nothing about their meeting after the haircut. The story's blank there. A blank of shock, perhaps. For me, anyway, there seems to be only silence, with drawers opening and shutting and a totting up of bills."

"Hadn't they already packed?"

"Oh, but this is last minute stuff. Things under chairs. Odds and ends they'd dropped earlier in the day when it was too hot to bend for them. And then this woman suddenly produces her hank of hair and twists it up into a tight coil."

"Well, thank God she had it safe, anyway. Don't call it 'hank'. It was never that. Did she lay it carefully on top—probably inside an old nylon stocking?"

"No. The cases were finally shut. While they were waiting for someone to take out the heavy luggage they gathered together the usual light stuff—handbags, string bags, maybe an Italian basket or two crammed full of odds and ends. Then the woman with the new haircut picked up this bag which she'd brought from home— maybe it had had stockings in it or handkerchiefs—a small white silk bag with drawstrings. And she put the hank of hair inside and drew it tight again. It looked odd in her hand. It looked out of place. All the rest of their stuff was comprehensible, but the bag was nothing but pure unknown emotion and it made her cousin nervous.

" 'Tuck it in here—in there, if you like,' she kept saying. 'Or I'll open the case and you can shove it in somewhere.' But no. A man came for their stuff and they followed him down. It was only a short distance from the hotel to the Canal where the motor-boat was waiting—round the corner of the square, across a bridge over a narrow waterway and they'd be there. But on the other side of this bridge the woman paused for a moment and looked at the water, her silk bag in her hand.

" 'Oh, *please*!' exclaimed the other in an anguished voice. She was scarcely aware she'd said this, or why. It was simply the painful embarrassment which overwhelms certain people when some tightly-packed but inexplicable emotion is about to break suddenly loose. Her friend had flung the bag into the water. No, 'flung' is far too violent. She laid it on the water."

"She gave it."

"Yes. Gave is better. It was taken from her and carried slowly, slowly away."

The man and the girl were both silent for a time, their heads bent under the white of noon. A cat stepped out of the nearby group, making for the shade at the far side—and one by one six thin, grey cats followed, slowly padding along in line, their thinner black shadows beneath them. Only one was left to watch, jealous-eyed, as the group reassembled in the shade. The square was empty.

"Was it a penance to the place, do you imagine?" said the girl. "Or a love-gift? A sacrifice to the gods? It wasn't, anyway, just a gesture of good riddance to bad rubbish?"

The man shrugged. "We can only watch her doing it. And some of the other tourists would probably watch it too as it floated calmly along, and people sitting at tables further down, if it ever got that far, would look into the water and discuss the little bladdery bag bobbing past. They might quarrel over what exactly was inside it."

The girl turned her head to look at him, but he had his newspaper up now, shielding his eyes. "But they would never guess," said the girl, still with her eyes on his face.

"Probably not," said the young man. "And yet they would draw

179

every conceivable thing out of that bag, according to their moods, their experience, according to whether, at that moment, they were unhappy or not. Flowers, guts, locks or hanks of hair, rags, pearls, bones—they could take what they wanted." The girl was putting a white silk scarf over her head for the sun was fierce.

"And did she ever come back?" she asked.

"No. But she'd made her peace with this place."

"And with her own town also?"

"Let's hope so. For that's where she lived and where she died not so many years later."

The girl got up. "I'm going back now. Don't stay too long in the sun."

"But I'm coming with you. This was only a diversion. We were on our way to the hotel. Remember?"

"No, I mean I'm going back to the tables to see if he's still there."

"Very probably not. All the way back there in the sun for nothing. Don't go!"

"We'll be seeing you soon."

"No, wait. What's drawing you back?"

"There are lots of things I want to say now . . ."

"Which can't wait an hour?"

"Just things that came into my head, for instance, as you were talking about this woman. Maybe that story of yours has sparked something off."

"Oh, good. Good."

"Made me feel freer. I must explain myself to someone."

"Oh good. But not to me? I'm here waiting. I can sit all day if you like, just listening or talking."

The girl smiled and again said: "We'll be seeing you soon."

She walked off, very slowly at first. But this, he knew, was only to save his feelings. For soon she had started to hurry, and as she went down the dark-walled lane leading to the square she was walking so quickly that her head in its white scarf was only visible for a flash under the line of light falling from a high wall-grille, before it disappeared like a bubble spinning on a black stream.

The young man, leaning forward and intent for those few minutes, now sat back with a sigh, his arms folded. He was now quite alone in the square. The last grey cat which had been bunched up, its head bent, listening to a secret sifting in the dust,

180

straightened out as though sensing his prolonged stare and started
to amble over towards the circle in the shade; and all over the city
the man imagined the universal, slow shift to shadow—animals
and persons moving to join groups under trees and awnings, in
courtyards and shuttered bedrooms. He got up and began to cross
the square in the opposite direction to the cat, until a sudden clang
of great bells made him stop short and stare up into the sky as if
it was the sun which had blazed and burst the silence. But far
behind him the cat was still moving forward, looking neither to
right nor left. It had been born to bells. Its father and grandfather
had been born to bells. It padded slowly, steadily on towards the
shadow.

A COLLECTION OF BONES

JENKINSON kept the wishbones he found in chickens and other birds hooked up on nails and along various ledges and shelves in the kitchen. They were all sizes and all ages. Some, fringed with withered and stinking brown skin, dated from years back and looked as though they might have been dug up out of some ancient mass chicken grave; there were others smooth and yellow as fragments of ivory and always one or two brand new ones still stuck with tasty pieces of white flesh. Yet Jenkinson would have it believed there was no particular meaning to his collection—he referred to them as bones, never as wishbones. From the cool way he dealt with unwelcome questions he might have been an anatomist keeping the secrets of his trade from ignorant minds. But whatever people might be talking about, the atmosphere of these unspoken, silent wishes hanging around in the kitchen gradually penetrated into the conversation—it hung in the air faint but unmistakable as the smell of old chicken skin. Occcasionally someone would try to humour Jenkinson out of his obsession.

"Look here Jenkinson, aren't you ever going to use those wishbones?"

"Use?" he'd say. "How do you mean—'use'?"

"Well, I mean what exactly are you keeping them for—they're wishbones, aren't they?"

"Yes, of course they're bones. It's a collection like any other collection, isn't it? It might have been stamps or seaweed or old spoons. But it happens to be bones I have here, if it's all the same to you."

"Look, Jenkinson, they're wishbones! People only hang on to

182

wishbones for a particular purpose."

"Oh, I don't know anything about these people and their purposes. What do you say they keep them for?"

"For wishing with!" the other would yell in a burst of confusion and exasperation at Jenkinson, at himself, at the little hoops of bone sprouting from every corner. For a moment Jenkinson would look incredulous, then smile slowly, rubbing his chin in contemptuous amusement. He would say nothing. Nothing more would be said about bones of any description.

Sometimes Jenkinson would lift up his head and study the round, red faces of his four children, his wife, and his wife's mother with amazement. They seemed to him to be without a care in the world. He himself was tall, round-shouldered and very thin, with long nervous arms and twitching fingers. His black eyes were set rather closely together in their deep sockets, giving him a suspicious and at times a somewhat miserly appearance. But it was only wishes he was miserly with—wishes which he had hoarded and kept to himself throughout the years. They had piled up more thickly however, in the shape of bones, from the time when he had begun to leave his business—a thriving hardware shop—more and more in the capable hands of his wife and his married son. About this one thing he showed he had a will of iron for his wife was certainly not the sort of woman who would ordinarily tolerate old bits and scraps around the place. It seemed possible that at one time or other there must have been a catastrophic row in which bones human and inhuman had been broken. Nevertheless the family remained united and the collection went on growing.

A close study of the Jenkinson's kitchen would have given most people the feeling that this family had eaten nothing but fowls since the time they had moved in. Yet their eating habits were no different from the average family. They had the usual steaks, stews, fries and hash, a chicken every fortnight or so, a turkey at Christmas and for the occasional celebration. But on the chicken days there was an unmistakable tension at table. Oddly enough Jenkinson did not carve himself and never insisted on this. His wife carved and as she wielded the knife and flicked pieces on to the seven plates Jenkinson's eyes would dart suspiciously from dish to dish. If he found the precious bone himself he would pick it up and put it on one side, but his face would remain expressionless. Occasionally he would look wearily resigned and even slightly

183

grim as he handled the object as though the weight of adding yet another to his pile of unused and yellowing desires was beginning to be more than he could stand. If, on the other hand, as the meal went on no bone had yet been found he managed to induce by his stares and twitching fingers a sensation of choking round the table. The girl and the three boys—ranging from seven to seventeen, would gulp down the boneless pudding lackadaisically and make for the door, gasping in the heavy air of disappointment and suspicion. In his grinding impatience Jenkinson would wait on until everybody had left the room, and while his wife escorted her mother to her chair he would go through to the kitchen and peer and poke through the scraps on the dishes till he found what he wanted. If by that time the bones had actually reached the rubbish-bin he left them alone. He drew the line at scrabbling for wishes amongst egg-shells and potato peelings and the woolly black wads of dust from the vacuum cleaner.

Long ago when his collection was quite small and still had a whiteness and a gleam to it Jenkinson had suffered an immense shock when informed by some kill-joy that these bones had no potency unless their snapping was shared by some other person. Up till that time he had kept himself going when all else failed with a vision of himself on some dark night working his way out from under the stuffy quilt of the double bed—stamped with garlands resembling funeral wreaths—kicking his way silently through the horrible conglomeration of old shoes which seemed to work their way out from under the bed at night, like rooting animals of the dark—out into the faintly snoring passage and down the stairs. There, alone in the kitchen over a fragile heap of gleaming bones, he would snap off his wishes one by one with his own bare hands. There was a terrifying, unimpeded bareness about the whole scene which he had known all along in his heart of hearts was too good to be true. When he was enlightened about his bones, realising that human beings had caught up with him again and might actually try to take a hand in the business, the zest for collecting became even more fanatical. Only over his dead body would he let those nearest to him snap his bones. For nowadays he could imagine no wish which might come from him, however secretly, which would not automatically be annihilated by its dead opposite flying from his wife. He thought of their wishes as fierce birds, swift as stones or bullets, bursting from the window together into

184

the outer air only to dash one another to bits before falling to the ground. As for his children—they were not the wishing kind. He could not imagine them standing still long enough to hook a finger round a dried-up chicken-bone when they already had enough in their pockets to make their particular wish come true by simply taking a quick walk round to the most expensive store in town. He had then taken a long look round the small circle of his friends and found not a man, woman or child whom he would care to see laying a single finger on his hoard.

This was how things stood and how they would likely have gone on if it had not been for a chance meeting Jenkinson had from his own kitchen with a window-cleaner who had been working on the office windows next to their own. The Jenkinsons lived three storeys up and a narrow balcony with iron railings joined the two windows. It was eleven o'clock in the morning. Jenkinson had been standing at the sink staring out and the window-cleaner was squatting on the balcony with a couple of cloths slung over his shoulder smoking a mid-morning cigarette. He had just got to his feet and before starting in again had swung himself sideways to take a quick look into the neighbouring window. He was not put off by the morose figure standing inside, but the fine bone drapery around the sink and along the shelves obviously shook him. He pressed his face close to the glass and steadied himself with his hand on the inside sill of the window which was open at the bottom.

Now Jenkinson knew when his bones were being scrutinized and was always as much on the defensive as though every one of them had been hand-carved by himself. So he advanced with a menacing squaring of the shoulders and they stared eye to eye on each side of the glass.

But the window-cleaner was not to be intimidated. He bent his head to the opening and said: "That little lot there must add up to quite a fair number of fowls, if you don't mind my saying so. Do you never eat anything but chickens around here?"

"We eat the same as everyone eats—the normal diet—same as you eat yourself," said Jenkinson threateningly. But he had pushed the window up as far as it would go and the window-cleaner was now sitting on the outside sill with no glass between them. He had taken a cloth from his shoulder and was folding it contemplatively into a square. Either directly or through glass he had seen a lot of things in his day and he did not believe that it paid to hurry people out of their secrets. He was in no hurry himself. He lit another cigarette and examined the tip intently. Then he pointed it along the shelves.

"Your idea to string them all up, then?" he asked. Jenkinson glowered and bunched his shoulders.

"Because if it was you've shown more sense than some," said the other man soothingly. He had now put one leg over the sill. "I mean why shouldn't you save them all for a rainy day and, blow the whole lot together. Get your money's worth out of it! Not that stingy, cheese-paring, one here one there sort of style some people go for. Blow 'em all sky-high! Lord—what a blasted bright lucky crack-up there's going to be one day!"

"Crack-up?" repeated Jenkinson warily, keeping his eyes fixed on the man's face.

"That's right," said the other. "One after the other—snap, snap, snap—and the wishes whooshing off like rockets! Boy— what a blast-off!"

"It takes two," said Jenkinson dourly.

The other put his head inside and took a good look round the kitchen, listening for sounds from other rooms—then said, lowering his voice: "You're telling me it takes two! Haven't they got it all arranged now so there's hardly a thing left you can do on your own? It's like that every way you turn these days—blocked all along the line!" He cocked his thumb sideways. "Isn't she willing to take a snap at them?"

"I never asked her," said Jenkinson.

"How about the family?"

"They get what they want," said Jenkinson. "They don't need bones."

The window-cleaner nodded slowly and brooded for a while. "How about you and me finishing them off?" he said at last.

"Finishing them off?" repeated Jenkinson looking round him with dull eyes. He was still thinking of his family.

"Sure," said the other. "We could bust the whole lot at one go. I'm telling you those wishbones are going to go stale on you if you keep them strung up there much longer."

"*Wish*bones," exclaimed Jenkinson; but the scorn was half-hearted. This outsider was here either to wreck the old order of things or to deliver him forever from his bony shackles. Nevertheless for a long moment he was silent. The window-cleaner waited, leaning his head back against the side of the window and from his lips, triumphantly, a tilted blue smoke-ring rose quivering up into the air and seemed for a moment to encircle a distant bird moving slowly up from the horizon. Jenkinson said out of the unplumbed, grudging depths within him: "Right. You can come in."

"I won't come in; thanks all the same," said the window-cleaner, quietly stubbing out his cigarette. A polite formality had established itself between them in the last minutes as between two persons on the point of a grave decision. Jenkinson was glad. He was glad that the man was not going to sling his legs over the sill, but continued to sit there, half in and half out of the place—an inhuman, uncommitted creature straddled between the stews and steams of domesticity on one side and the giddy drop of space above and below him on the other. This made it easier for Jenkinson who had begun to gather up the bones from around the place—picking them off their hooks and knobs and putting them into a large pudding-basin. The oldest ones made a dry rustling sound as they were brushed from the high ledges where they had lain for years. But none of them got broken. At last he came over to the window holding the bowl in both hands.

"Is that the lot?" said the window-cleaner sharply, leaning in as far as he could go. He had all his wits about him now as though balancing himself for some particularly tricky job. Jenkinson poked about with his finger amongst the bones to indicate that there were enough.

"But is that the lot?" asked the man again more sharply, at the same time giving him a long, penetrating stare. Jenkinson was unnerved. He walked slowly towards a cupboard, opened it and plunged his hand down into a pair of old Wellington boots and brought out half-a-dozen more bones which he took over and dropped reluctantly one by one into the bowl.

"That's more like it," said the other man. "Are you ready then?"

Jenkinson gave him a look. He had been ready for years. Long before this young man was born he had been ready. Slowly he picked out a bone and held it up.

"Not that way!" cried the window-cleaner irritably. "Do you want to mess up the whole thing? Like this." He inserted his little finger into the hoop and motioned Jenkinson to take the other side.

When the first bone snapped Jenkinson started as though he had been shot and at the second as though some vital part had given way inside him. For a long time he went on twitching, starting and jerking but when they had got a quarter way through the bowl he had settled down a bit except that now and then he winced and his lips moved slowly as he bent over the dwindling bones. The window-cleaner allowed no time to elapse between the snapping. He was in a hurry now, but his face remained impassive as systematically he flung bits of broken bone over his shoulder down into the backyards below. They worked in silence. Jenkinson's wishes were forced from him under fearful concentration and they hung so heavily over him that the air within the four walls of the kitchen seemed to grow every minute more dense. The window-cleaner's wishes flew casually from him into the air. They were obviously light things which he forgot as soon as they left his mind. Sometimes a gust of wind bore the frail hoops up, and once peering over the ledge Jenkinson saw that the sooty branches of a tree in the yard below had burst into a peculiar one-sided blossom from the white bones which had got stuck there. His own bits he had dropped carefully behind him into the ash-bucket. At last the pudding-basin was empty. "That's you now!" cried the window-cleaner gleefully drawing his foot back over the ledge and crouching on the outside sill. He appeared to be suspended between earth and sky without a care in the world, without a tie. There was nothing more for him to say. He began to move sideways, still stooping, the cloths flapping from his shoulder. And he was out of sight.

Jenkinson never saw him again and never wished to see him. The window-cleaner had done his job thoroughly. He had delivered him from a pile of bones which had been going sour on him and at the same time killed in him any desire ever to make such a collection again. As for Jenkinson himself it would have been odd if some sort of change had not showed itself in a man who had got through a great basinful of wishes which had taken him a lifetime to think up. Some people might have expected a little luck to show on him—even if it was simply a fishy shine that would make him faintly visible in the dark. Even those with no superstition in their make-up might have expected him to brace himself in some all-out effort to ensure that at least one or two of these wishes came true, even if he had to work himself to the bone for it. But nothing of the kind happened.

Almost overnight Jenkinson had given up all idea of luck or anything else. He became a loose, dangling sort of a fellow with an aimless gape to the jaw and a peculiar limpness which extended through all his joints from his flaccid fingers right down into his shambling feet. Family meals were no ordeal now. In fact the lessening of tension around the house and the complete absence of his former spites and suspicions would have made him an almost amiable chap to be with if only he could have brought himself to show the slightest spark of interest in anyone or anything. As it was most people found it almost impossible to make contact with a man who in fact looked and acted as though every single bone in his body, big or little, had been cleanly and systematically snapped in two.

A WOMAN OF SUBSTANCE

At the end of a day, Miss Reed, who was fifty-nine and had lived alone over the past few years, would occasionally cry out aloud to strangers, in the course of shopping or waiting for the bus, that she was going home now for a nice, peaceful evening by the fire. The challenge and emotion which she put into these words had a startling effect on certain people who had expected them to be accompanied by a more peaceful expression. By her stares and glaring smiles she seemed waiting to be contradicted or even intercepted on the way home, and people were usually relieved when they saw her well on her way there. Yet, having fired off her challenge, Miss Reed would become as mild and silent again as though she had never even opened her mouth.

The evenings which she spent, however, were not usually so calm, but rather restless and taken up, for the most part, with looking for things which she had missed during the day. She would spend a long time rummaging vaguely about inside her handbag or down the side of her armchair, scooping up pencils and coins which had been lost months before. There was a satisfaction in saving things before they joined those others which had been missing for years and could be heard jingling about in the lining deep down in the bottom of the chair. Sometimes she simply sat still and searched about in her mind for names or faces or words from the past which she needed again if she was to enjoy some particular memory to the full, in the same way as she rummaged about in the toffee-tin to find the two or three whose special flavour could ensure her the most satisfactory half-hour. Yet it was at these times that she found it difficult to avoid one fact about herself which had an odd taste—odd and sour and un-accountable amongst all the rest—namely, that after spending her youth and middle years in the company of close friends and relations, she had one day found herself suddenly and absolutely on her own. All the same, she treated any chance remark or question about this as a great indelicacy on the part of the questioner—something she might still prevent by turning her head sharply aside, smiling as at some flippant remark, or simply pretending not to hear at all. In this way she felt she had averted some danger which had come too close, and might in the end threaten her whole existence.

She was, moreover, aware that certain changes which she felt in herself from one week to another would make it difficult for her to give a straightforward account of herself to any other person. There were some mornings, for instance, when her limbs felt so heavy that, as she slowly started to dress, she began to think of herself as a person with a thick body—almost a fat woman. At these times she put nothing on which would restrict her flesh, and she dressed in thick, soft clothes as though making the most of a fatness which had simply not been there the day before and might well disappear tomorrow. Even her hats varied with her sensations of lightness or weight. With the thick clothes she wore a plushy felt hat and a fat-petalled brown flower lolling across the brim. Under this, the skin of her face looked as soft and mild as dough from which every line had been rolled, and her expression was serene. On the other hand there were times, coming much more frequently and more unwelcome, when she felt herself to be an absolute lightweight, as though she could float in the air as easily as she could walk. It was then a kind of duty for her to leave off the padded comfort of her heavy clothes and get into things more suited to her lightened condition. Everything about her then became unfixed and flighty, from an insubstantial hat of wavy straw and thin, loose-fitting coat, to the pair of open-strapped summer shoes which would not have looked out of place in a dance hall.

On these days her mind would float vaguely over the events of the day before, settling on nothing for more than a second, or sometimes bringing up some unwanted object from the past which had no relevance to anything else in her present existence. What-ever it was—an advertisement for some out-of-date toothpaste flaking off a brick wall, an oddly designed box of chocolates, or sometimes a whole landscape of houses and figures—it would remain as though suspended in the air before her until she deliberately banished it by fixing her eyes on something close to her which, by simply stretching out, she could touch with her hand. Her room was full of square-set objects which had rescued her, at some time or other, from these other things.

Miss Reed had come to this town several years ago to live with her widowed sister, and the sister having died within a year of her arrival, she had stayed on in the two large rooms which were left to her. She was high up and could look right along the main road which led down towards the sea at one end, and into the centre of the crowded town at the other. There was a green park opposite, and she liked to feel she could see country, city and seaside simply by drawing back the curtains as far as they would go on either side of her bow windows. Nevertheless, she could never feel that she was anything but a visitor to this town—a holiday guest who had been stranded there by accident and was simply waiting for the chance to get home again. She still walked about the town slowly—a belated sightseer, sometimes puzzled and sometimes pleased by what she saw, but never unconcerned and certainly never at her ease. People would turn to look at her as she strolled about in the evening, endlessly straightening her hat or smoothing her collar and sometimes speaking to herself.

"Well!" she would exclaim loudly, stopping dead to gaze at a monument in the middle of a square, or the view at the end of a narrow lane which she had passed a hundred times before. "I do like that—that's really very good! Yes, I must say I think it's very fine indeed!" And she would smile round at anyone who was standing near as though congratulating him on having a town so interesting to a visitor like herself. Sometimes she would stand for a long time on the edge of the pavement, rummaging in her handbag so that she could listen to two people talking, as she might have stood in a foreign country, waiting to catch familiar words and phrases, and even staring round pointedly when she had at last caught the theme of the conversation. In this way it seemed to her that she had entered innumerable discussions—about other people's families, their housekeeping and shopkeeping, and the complex deals they made in other cities. It was a story of continual buying, lending and losing, but one which, after all, did not surprise her so much. She was already familiar with the immense loss and waste which went with every day. Scarcely an hour passed but she read or heard not only of wallets or jewels which were lost, but of people who lost their jobs without warning or whose best friends became enemies overnight; aeroplanes vanished into thin air over mountain ranges and ships went down at sea. For herself, she had only to put down a parcel and turn her eyes from it for a second—it was gone. If she left her seat in park or café, to get a closer look at something, the place was taken before she could turn round again. Sometimes, in the time it took for her to walk to a litter-basket and back, a complete row of new faces would take the place of the former set on the park bench. Nowadays, when the voices of the pavement ceased she was left with the feeling that under the tide of traffic and pedestrians a heavier, blacker current flowed into which objects and persons could simply sink silently and not be seen again.

It was her fifth year in the city. She had now been so much on her own that if, while she was walking about the town, a stranger should stop to ask her the way, or somebody accidentally wedged against her make a remark on the weather, her response was immediate and ardent as though she were about to make a remarkable new friend; and if any man, young or old, made way for her, picked up her glove or offered her his seat in the bus, the flush of surprise would show on her throat a long time afterwards, while, with her gloved hand, she would attempt to hide a smile which was startling and shameless in its pleasure. She had moments of excess when her thanks were repeated over and over again and her confidence given away too lavishly; there were times when she laughed too suddenly and loud, or stared so avidly that she raised angry looks from the mothers of prim children; moments when, with her big, flowery head nodding, she leant sideways with a coquettishness which could be terrifying to all but the most hardened. Sensitive people avoided her because she looked too exposed, and as time went on Miss Reed came to rely more and more on the contacts she made with energetic people who had only just time to listen to her for a minute or two, and no time at all to study her and find out what kind of person she really was. In her turn, she began to avoid all those who walked by themselves, talked to themselves or stared at her from a distance with sympathetic eyes. These days she preferred to sit down

193

beside those people who showed by the way they gripped the handles of their umbrellas or folded their newspapers when they had finished reading, that they had a good grasp of life—even, perhaps, an actual love of it, which could include her without, however, taking much notice of her.

It was all the more important to discover such people on the days when she woke up without her weight, for although it was not always an unpleasant sensation, it meant that she must find a seat in the park more quickly and be very wary of her choice of company. On these days when she went outside, whether she was standing or sitting, she rummaged endlessly in her handbag and in her pockets as though to find there the one heavy thing which would weigh her down—something which, if only she could lay her hands on it, would prevent her from ever again experiencing the panic which came over her when she began to feel that her feet were not properly attached to the ground. When she was not rummaging her hands moved about her person, fastening and unfastening the buttons of her coat or vaguely ruffling round her collar to find some hidden hook. There was always some way of resisting the sensations which made her feel airborne. Occasionally she would stoop quickly and secretly touch the toe of her shoe, tapping it with her nail like a bird testing a shell with its beak, or her fingers, fumbling about her head, would at last discover her hatpin and settle quietly for a long time upon the small, hard bead which seemed to anchor not only her hat to her head, but her whole being to the earth.

Miss Reed did not often make the mistake of going out on windy days. Usually she had some warning of it early in the day and so would stay in her room, keeping her eyes from the tumult of the air outside her window where all sorts of unattached objects might rise suddenly without warning, or float past as though on the crests of waves. On the worst days she had seen not only leaves and feathers, but whole newspapers lifted and twisted high in the air. This autumn afternoon, however, she had no warning of the rising wind until she was well inside the park, and even then it was only a slight swirling of the dust beneath the benches and an agitation in the tops of the highest trees—something which might be expected on any afternoon at that time of the year. Nevertheless, Miss Reed at once began to look about her for a sheltered seat and more particularly for a person who might provide a bulwark against the disturbance in the air and the rising panic in her own breast. She saw this person at once, recognised her instinctively as a person against whom wind and waves could beat without effect, and made towards her without for a moment taking her eyes off her.

The woman was sitting by herself on a seat under a group of young rowan trees. She had on a stiff, crimson mackintosh and a pointed cap of the same stuff tied under her chin and a pair of Wellington boots coming halfway up her legs, so that the effect was of a person encased from head to foot in some metallic substance which crackled and hissed with every movement. She was knitting energetically at a red woollen garment which was crawling slowly down over her knees to the ground and had to be snatched back every few minutes. In spite of this sudden, darting movement as she caught the stuff, the woman gave the impression of immense calm, and each time as she bent forward her eyes took in the entire circle of the park in one sharp, authoritative glance. Now and then a few leaves from the tree behind were shaken over her and slid, unnoticed, down the sleeves of her coat, as though down two cones of polished metal. She took no notice as Miss Reed approached, for her eyes were focused only on the complications of her knitting and on the far distance. What was happening in between seemed to have little interest for her, though occasionally she stared with disapproval at a paper bag which had got stuck on a nearby railing. She was staring at this as Miss Reed sat down and Miss Reed automatically stared too.

But there were worse things to be seen than a paper bag pierced by a railing. The wind was suddenly stronger, and for a few minutes there seemed to be pandemonium in the park. The air was whirling with things which a moment before had been on the solid ground or held tightly in the hands, and from all around came a harsh ripping sound as of private things being ruthlessly torn apart. Under the trees people were running and spinning with arms lifted to their hats and their uncoiling scarves, and close to Miss Reed's feet a letter went past, newly unfolded and boldly written, so that she could actually make out a word or two before it was lifted up again and pressed between the roots of a tree. Nobody followed it, and Miss Reed, who seldom received a letter from one year's end to the next, shuddered at what seemed the worst exposure of all. Out of the corner of her eye she could still see it, white as the palm of an opened hand, and spread out for anyone to read. Now the wind was plucking great wads of paper from the overflowing litter-baskets attached to the bigger trees of the park, and from the cone-shaped mounds of new-mown grass the tops were blown as though they had been green mountains dissolving under some catastrophic storm. Then, as suddenly as it had arisen, the commotion died down. The people who had been running about dropped their arms and went back to their seats again, as at the abrupt ending of music, and now that the whistling and the ripping in the trees had stopped it was possible to hear the steady roar of traffic beyond the gates, and louder than ever, close at her ear, Miss Reed heard the swift hissing of the knitter's elbows brushing past her armoured hips and the crackle as she bent and tugged the wool up over her knees. For a moment she rested her hands in her lap and took a good look round her, pursing her lips and sniffing once or twice before she could bring herself to speak.

"It's not much of a park, to my mind," she said to Miss Reed, yet still staring ahead of her. "At any rate, nothing like the sort of park I was used to before I came here. You may have noticed, there are hardly ever any gardeners about, or when they do come it must be just a case of standing about leaning on spades, because you've only to take a good look under the trees—and I don't just mean the ones at the far end, but even there at the main gate—you've only to look, I say, to see an absolute wilderness of weeds. The fact is, the whole place is going to seed and in a few years' time I just wouldn't like to say what it will look like." She took up her knitting again to count the stitches and Miss Reed watched her two sharp finger-ends walking rapidly up the length of the needle.

"Then there's another thing," she went on when she had come to the end of the row. "I'm referring to white flowers. Personally, I'm not a lover of any kind of white flower, but that's neither here nor there. All I'm saying now is—and most people I've spoken to agree with me—white flowers are just not suitable for a public park. Now, if you take any notice of these sort of things at all, you'll have seen that they use white here more than any other colour—and at all seasons, mind you. And that's just where I quarrel with them—for, rightly speaking, white *isn't* a colour at all. And people have a right to a blaze of colour in a public park!"

She spoke the last words fiercely and her cheeks flushed. "I was very much amused by an article I once saw in a gardening magazine," she went on, grimly smiling into the distance. "It was persuading people to plant white flowers in their gardens, and if I tell you the reason it gave, you'd laugh too. Well, it was partly the smell, but that wasn't the main thing. No, the reason given was that you'd be able to see these same white flowers at night!" She threw back her head in its creaking helmet hat and laughed loudly. "So if you really want to appreciate this park you'd better come and sit here after dark!" Abruptly she bent over her knitting again and was silent.

Miss Reed had, in recent months, become abnormally receptive to words which were actually addressed to herself. They became immediately impressive in a way which no others, merely overheard, could possibly be. So powerful did they become, indeed, that objects or persons spoken about could change out of all recognition in accordance with another's opinion. Now, as though the change had come about in the lens of her own eye, the focus of the park had altered in a way which made certain parts stand out well to the fore and left the rest blurred. All that was formal and safely limited faded gradually out; all that was clear and solid underwent a subtle change. A certain frailness now showed in the plants and trees as though they were not, after all, so well rooted in the ground, or as though a frosty withering had taken place in the last few minutes. Uneasily she noticed it was true that most of the flowers were white, standing separate and delicate all along the dark wall which divided the park from the main road. Even the light had decreased, so that it was not, after all, so difficult to imagine what it would be like to be sitting here in the park at night. The woman in the red mackintosh was speaking again, lifting her elbows wide above the needles which were now moving with a sound like the sharp ticking of a little clock.

"This other park I mentioned—where I used to live—mind you, they worked there! There was one bed shaped like a star, an eight-sided star, I remember it was—started at Coronation time and kept up ever since. It fairly blazed from spring right on into the autumn—red and blue at the centre and the tips were white and sharp as though they'd been cut out with nail-scissors." On the paper pattern which she took from her pocket she now drew a star for Miss Reed to see with the point of her knitting

197

needle.

"You could see it for miles!" she exclaimed triumphantly, holding the pattern out at arm's length. "One of my friends had a top flat looking over this park and from her window you could see the whole thing had been done with a ruler—you'd say there wasn't an eighth of an inch in it one way or the other. I believe from an aeroplane it was quite a sight—a sort of landmark, I daresay." She ran the needle under her thumbnail, relaxing enough to sigh; then remarked briskly: "I haven't been off the ground myself. What about you?"

Miss Reed, straightening up eagerly to answer this question and at the same time shaking her head, gave the impression that though this was an experience so far from her that she found it difficult to imagine, it was one which, nevertheless, she was sorry to have missed. Yet the truth was—she recognised it with a shudder—being 'off the ground' was a state which was gradually beginning to have a special meaning for her. What better way to describe the sensations—at once strangely pleasurable, yet nightmarish—of being completely untethered from familiar objects, so that on certain days, before she even put her feet to the ground from the bed, she must first concentrate with her eyes and imagination on the actual weight of her flesh, on the miracle, for instance, that her round, topheavy head could be supported by her neck for the whole of the day ahead; or she would force herself to feel the weight of her legs, thick as they were, by laboriously shifting them about under the bedclothes before swinging them heavily, and with a theatrical groan, over the side of the bed. If she did not make these preliminary moves, how easy it was for her now simply to slip out into mid-air and to drift from then onwards for the rest of the day. Now, with an effort, she pulled her thoughts from this and concentrated on the woman beside her who was speaking again, lifting the knitting from her chest where it had been creeping, like a slowly heaving billow of scarlet, down towards her lap.

"Twelve cousins in this town alone," she was saying. "But that's to say nothing of the American ones, and I'll never lay eyes on them, of course. And when it comes to Christmas, I don't grudge it. It's your own flesh and blood that counts then, and believe me, I'm not referring to Christmas cards or even calendars. There's not a single one of them that hasn't had something in

198

brown paper and string from me regularly these past ten years—and that means keeping a check on the babies. I make my own woolly balls, of course—dozens and dozens of them I've made in my time, and they're not quite so easy as some people might imagine. I don't know what you think, but I've no notion of my friends at all at Christmas time, and mind you, there's a few of *them* too. No, it's flesh and blood that counts, whether you've seen them or not. Flesh and blood—is that the way you look at it too?"

At the mention of flesh and blood Miss Reed's heart began to pound abnormally fast, and she began to wonder if this time she had chosen the wrong person for herself. The atmosphere between them, which should have been comfortably cloudy, thick with friendly indifference, was thinning rapidly. Already the questions and answers were beginning to pierce it. There was something intimate, yet hostile, in the air.

"And who have you?" asked the woman, smoothing the piece of knitting on her knee and stabbing it, row by row, with the point of her needle. But Miss Reed now looked blank, looked even remarkably stupid as though, in the last few seconds, the skin of her face had literally thickened and almost erased the lines and hollows of expression. Only over the nervous pulse of her temple had the skin remained atrociously thin. It was she who now bent over the knitting and studied it for a long time in silence. The woman had laid her needle down on the seat between them and was now sitting quite still and upright, gazing down on Miss Reed's hat where, amongst the brown velvet flowers, she could quite plainly see not only the silver wrapping from a bar of chocolate wound about one of the stalks, but also the printed purple paper which had been expertly fashioned into a flower-head and boldly pinned amongst the others on the front of the brim. For several minutes she stared and stared like an affronted botanist finding an artificial flower amongst some choice specimens until her attention was withdrawn by a movement from Miss Reed who was looking at something in the knitting.

"Yes, there it is!" she was saying, pointing to a small hole a few inches down. "I think I've found what you were looking for!"

The woman in red took up the knitting again. "Now what exactly are you referring to?" she asked, holding it up formidably high till it quivered like a banner between them and the light. Through the close, scarlet meshes Miss Reed saw the park glow dark and red as a desert where trees and figures stood out black, vibrating dangerously as though before an impending storm. Yet, in spite of her nervousness, she remained stubborn.

"That is where you lost the stitch, isn't it?" she persisted, putting a finger out to point again.

At that the other let the knitting fall back into her lap, smiling grimly. She seemed for a time to find some difficulty in bringing herself to speak again, but simply nodded round about her, gathering support from the air. Then she said: "Do you know this? I suppose I've been knitting garments since I was ten or eleven years old, and I don't believe I've ever, no, never in all that time, dropped, far less actually lost, a stitch. If you'd looked more closely you'd have seen your hole, as you called it, was simply the beginning of the lace pattern. In other words, it's a deliberate hole—and there's another—and there! When it's finished, the holes, as you would call them, will link up as an ivy-leaf border." She did not pick up the knitting again, but sat darting glances about her, now sharing her amusement with a nearby holly bush and the empty seats which were opposite. Miss Reed remained silent.

"Well, who have you?" the woman repeated, more sternly this time. It was Miss Reed's turn to be amused. For some reason, now that she was faced with it, now that there was absolutely no escape from this question, she began to shake with silent laughter—laughter which tore through all the precarious plans she had made to defend herself, like the wind tearing through the ill-kept park. It was only with an enormous effort that she was able to stop herself by doubling up and folding her arms very tightly across her chest. Even then, she could scarcely get the words out between gasps. But, in spite of it all, her companion heard what she said. She showed that she had heard by pursing her lips and nodding slowly several times.

The answer, at any rate, seemed to satisfy her, for she asked no more, but only remarked, when she had rolled her knitting up tightly again and put it into her bag, and tied the hood more firmly under her chin: "Well, I daresay you sometimes feel lonely, living all by yourself. Do you notice those black clouds coming over? Maybe the forecast's been right for just this once. I'm not waiting to find out, anyway." She nodded to Miss Reed and moved off heavily in the direction of the gates, the holly leaves scraping her mackintosh harshly as she brushed by.

Miss Reed followed the woman with her eyes, very still now, with her face slowly changing and tightening. She was frowning intently over what had just been said to her, like someone slowly translating a remark in a foreign tongue, and now the tightness round her lips gave her a grim, almost a witchlike appearance. She realised with something like hatred for this woman who had just gone, that she was now forced to take up this word 'lonely' which had been casually given to her, and examine it. It was a word which, if looked at long enough, could be made to describe certain sights and sounds which were a common part of every day. But, above all, when long-drawn-out and repeated until it had become unfamiliar again, the word was simply an echo of the horns of ships which she sometimes heard very early in the morning or in the middle of a foggy night—sounds melancholy and questioning, which took her past the familiar warehouses of the harbour, past the last rock and the last light, further out than she had ever meant to go, and left her, still floating far out at sea, long after full daylight had come.

It was five o'clock. Around the main gates there was a continual movement of people who had just come into the park after an early tea and those who were leaving to go home to supper. Miss Reed had noticed now, with the beginning of panic, that every person and every object which she had imagined to exist quite separately on its own, was, in reality, attached firmly to something else. Men and women were going past looped together, not only by arms and fingers, but by the looks of affection or of hostility which they turned on one another. Dogs were attached to their owners by leads, and where there were no leads a word could bring them back, as though they had felt the familiar tug on their necks. The tired mothers were attached strongly to the earth by the heads of sleeping babies which, as the day wore on, drooped damp and heavy as fruit over their shoulders. Inside the phone-boxes at the gates, people gesticulated and smiled and emerged no longer alone, but joined to one another by endless lines of crossing wires which, in their imagination, filled the whole of the sky over the city. Under the ground it was the same. For if the eye travelled down the trunks of trees, right down to the earth and under it—there the roots were unimaginably long and tough and all entangled with the roots of other trees and plants which, above

G*   201

ground, had seemed to stand at a great distance from one another.

Seeing suddenly this world vibrating before her eyes with its contacts, its magnificent attachments, Miss Reed felt dizzy and light as a balloon which skiffs the ground and could, at a touch, be sent sailing far above the groups on the ground. She got up and began to walk quickly through the park, not in her usual way, skirting the centre, but going carelessly into the thick of it, past low-hanging trees and crowded benches, past prams and barrows, ruthlessly dividing up the close knots of friends and families, parting the couples who had stood too long together, and walking blindly into circles of children whose hard balls rolled against her ankles. Yet from all of them she wanted to receive some harder blow than this—something which would show her, without any doubt, how solid and sharp they were, so that she would have to push and prod with all her strength to get through them. Only like this could she ever show herself as a woman with weight and bulk enough to be a serious impediment in their way, an interruption to the most intimate talk.

Instead Miss Reed found that her surroundings were swiftly, becoming more elusive than they had ever been before. Things near at hand were wavering as though half-submerged in water. In the distance, the white flowers were all afloat and trees quivered as though rooted at the edge of a stream in flood. She had not interrupted any conversations—the talk flowed round monotonously as it had always done. Behind her the couples had already come together again, and the children, barging past her, scarcely brushed the sleeves of her coat. She stood quite still now and began to look into her huge, black handbag, holding it up very close to her eyes and staring down apprehensively, as into the mouth of a cave. When her eyes had searched long enough she raised them and looked far off into the distance, but her hand explored the dark place and with everything it touched, her eyes, still staring out over the railings, became first excited, then anxious and at last despondent as her fingers scrabbled amongst the familiar dusty stuff and found nothing of weight. At last she snapped the bag shut, and her hand, climbing uncertainly up over the buttons of her coat, plucked at the brooch on her collar, circled the brim of her hat, and came to rest finally with one finger lightly pressing the hat-pin. But even before she touched it she knew that its special power had gone.

202

Her hand dropped at once and she began to walk on; more and more quickly she went until she was right off the path and moving over the grass towards a group of trees. These were not the common ones of the park. Each had a label fixed to the bark at eye level and circles of iron hoops protected the base of their trunks. Miss Reed, still moving swiftly towards them, gave the impression at first glance of somebody intent on reading these labels. Her neck was thrust forward as she neared the trees, and she appeared to rise slightly on the tips of her toes to reach the place more quickly.

But now a few onlookers had got to their feet; some of them were shouting and half a dozen people began to run towards her. Miss Reed's body was tilted forward at a precarious angle. She did not stop when she reached the tree, but tripped on the iron hoops and fell heavily against the trunk with her forehead rammed hard beneath the label. Only for an instant it lay there, but in that time she looked terribly intent, like someone with an ear pressed against a telegraph pole, listening to the murmuring inside. When her head fell back her hands still stroked lightly down the trunk as though loath to let go of it.

The crowd around her was now huge, and although she was lying on her back staring mainly at the sky, she was aware of everything that went on. Yet there was not a part of her body that she could move. From her head right down to her feet, which unaccountably had been removed from her shoes, she was as hard and heavy as iron; and with every breath she could feel herself pressed more and more heavily down into the ground. She had the feeling too that now everybody wanted to touch her and to look at her. Those in front were angrily holding back the children on the fringe of the circle who were scrambling to push in. They stood around her, swaying heavily to and fro from the pressure behind, and Miss Reed could feel the thumping of the grass under her body and the air about her quick and warm with the breath of excited people.

There was another sound which she heard only when she was free of the thudding ground and swinging in mid-air. For two men had now hoisted her up and were carrying her towards the nearest bench. But the sounds they made were extraordinary—out of all proportion to what they were doing and the distance they were going. Incredulously Miss Reed heard the panting and the groaning and the laborious sighs which made a noise like a roaring wind, close to her ears—and she shut her eyes triumphantly to hear it better. She had made no mistake this time in feeling a change in herself. These men had drawn her up out of the ground only with the greatest difficulty, as though she had been rooted there, and now they were grunting and staggering under their load. When they had laid her on the bench she opened her eyes and saw faces, purple with exertion, turning away from her.

"Unconscious," murmured one, wiping the back of his neck with a handkerchief. "It makes them a dead weight to handle."

Meanwhile Miss Reed grew more and more conscious of everything around her, but, above all, she could not take her eyes from the park official who had pushed his way through the group and was now standing beside her, holding her open handbag in his hand. She watched him intently as he felt inside, and in spite of the painful weight of her head, she raised it for a moment off the bench to see him better. For now it seemed to her that on this familiar movement of his searching hand, all her chances of survival as a flesh and blood creature would depend, and with growing panic in her eyes she studied his face for the first sign of disappointment. But he had not rummaged or fumbled. He seemed satisfied with what he had found there, and he read her name out aloud from an old envelope he held in his hand. In his official voice, trained over the years to reach the wild boys whacking at bushes in the distance, he announced her to the whole park, so that even people passing a long way from the group heard and turned to look. Those around Miss Reed no longer pushed, but stood back a little, murmuring her name like guests who had just been introduced. But to Miss Reed, who had put her head back again and now lay absolutely still, the mixture of pain and pleasure which she felt was so overwhelming that it was as though she had been renamed, in the last few minutes, before some solemn assembly. Her eyes were shut again, but the official who had noticed the look in them earlier said: "You'll be all right now, lady. Nothing to worry about at all. Here they're coming in at last!"

The three men in white coats had wrapped her up tightly, and before the crowd could move in again she was on the stretcher and moving swiftly between the earth and the sky towards the gates. This time, however, the sensation was not one of floating, and there came suddenly into her mind a phrase which years ago had been applied to her, but which, amongst the floating, rocking conditions of her present life, had never been heard again nor been remembered by her—not even on those days when she could actually feel the weight of her own body. She remembered it now —and from their faces, careful and severe, she knew that these trained men had it in mind also. They realised who they were carrying—a person who was to be handled with the greatest possible care and skill, somebody of formidable weight to be reckoned with—in short, an unwieldy, cumbersome, woman of substance.

TRAVELLER

IN THE evening, around six o'clock, the man who had been sitting since noon on the stair landing outside the Gregson's door, left the building. Nobody in the family actually saw him go, but the youngest son remarked on hearing footsteps go down some time before, and the mother and daughter and the woman neighbour who had come in for tea all ran to the window. He was there all right, padding along easily in the middle of the road, with the large suitcase swinging lightly in his hand. He held it slightly tilted as though it were some sort of musical instrument—heavier at one end than the other—and as he went past he kept turning his head to look along the sharp blades of sunlight falling between the dark houses on one side. Guilt and anger exploded at the sight.

"Look at him!" cried Martha Gregson, a widow and mother of two grown sons and a schoolgirl daughter. "He's simply wasted all the stuff in that case! In fact the most likely thing is he'll dump it somewhere when he's out of sight. That's it. He'll throw the case in the river. And that's exactly where he's going!"

There was a sense of outrage amongst the women at the naked and unashamed change in the man. You would think now that the stuff in the case had been precious stuff, stuff they had coveted themselves, to hear them talk. Or even stuff that should have actually belonged to them by rights. And then the man was ugly. If only he had been good to look at, or even a thin and hungry wolf of a man, he would have been forgiven. But his thighs were fat, and under his eyes were heavy, dark purple pouches. They craned far out of the window as he disappeared round the corner.

Hours ago Martha had gone to the door and found the man with

206

his case already open at her feet. It was the usual assortment of stuff—coarse pink and green combs, tooth-brushes, penknives and cheap scissors, a few tins, bottles and scarves; there was a hideous doll's head which screwed off to disclose long, tapestry needles, sharp as daggers. The woman smiled sourly as she looked down and shook her head. "No thanks," she said, giving an equal weight and distinctness to both words. The man had been leaning with one arm against the edge of the door and now he shifted his gaze to that side. "Oh well—" was all he said. He looked as though he could not be bothered removing his arm, so there was nothing for him to do but study his hand which he now spread out in order to see round every part of the podgy fingers and the bitten, grey nails. Still the woman waited to be pestered or persuaded or maybe insulted or assaulted. The man yawned, and took his time over it. All near and visible objects were swallowed up in this yawn. The stone stairs beyond gaped dark and hollow with the boredom of the moment. The case gaped, its ugly contents spilling over. The man's eyes, swivelling from his nails to the hall where the woman stood, were glassy as though she no longer existed as far as he was concerned. It was this look which made her stand a few minutes longer trying to correct the focus and adjust the hard line of the threshold between them.

"Well, all right then," she said. "I don't want anything at all." Again she made the last two words distinct and separate. And she shut the door deliberately, being careful neither to slam it nor to close it too gently.

Twenty minutes later she opened the door to put out a milk bottle and found the man sitting a few feet away in a corner of the landing outside. She suppressed a gasp, placed the bottle beside him and quickly decided what she would say when he looked up. He did not look up and she went inside again. There was a lot to be done in the back of the house, but when anything brought her into the hall she was almost certain, judging from the dead silence, that the man had gone.

Meanwhile the man outside had removed a packet from his raincoat pocket and was unwrapping a wad of beef sandwiches, a hard-boiled egg and a slice of yellow cake. He ate slowly and intently, occasionally flicking crumbs from between the buttons of his coat and staring closely at each piece of food until it came too near his mouth to be properly visible. And as he chewed the glassy expression gradually left his eyes. At a quarter to one the eldest son of the house who worked with an electrical firm not many blocks away came back for his lunch.

"Well, who is the fat man?" he asked as he drew in his chair to the table. He had only half-an-hour or so to eat in. "Who's the fat man and what have you got him sitting there for?"

"Oh no!" The woman's face was contorted. She flung down a dishcloth full of knives and spoons and rushed to the main door. This time it was opened for only a few seconds and then properly slammed.

"What did you say?" her son asked when she came back.

"I didn't need to *say* anything. That tramp won't be there long!"

"No, he's not a tramp," said the young man, carefully tipping up the last spoonful of soup from his plate.

"Oh, is that so?" said the woman. "Then what *is* a tramp?"

"A tramp has nothing to sell. That chap out there has a whole caseful of stuff. Besides, look how he's dressed! Better than I am myself. He's no tramp. He's a traveller."

"But he's *sitting down!*"

"I suppose even travellers have to sit down sometimes."

"Only tramps sit in corners with crumbs and spit around them."

"There was no spit," said her son. "Not when I saw him."

The dishes clashed in the sink and the woman glared. So it seemed that her son had allied himself to tramps now. Even now there was a sprawling, grinning look about him. Easy enough to imagine him, given the slightest encouragement, throwing everything up and sinking back into a corner with his legs out. He still had the look on his face when he left her at a quarter to two.

Very few people went up and down the stair at that time of the day. The man had finished eating long ago, and now with nothing better to do he opened up his case and raked through the contents in a desultory sort of way. He would plunge his hand in, pulling out a wad of stuff at random and letting it fall again as though carelessly weighing it, or as though the stuff were not made up of various bits and pieces but was some kind of substance that could be drawn out, fingered over and dropped again like dough. This sort of handling was not suited to some of the hard and bouncy objects. The head of needles rolled from the side of the case and leapt several stairs down to the turn of the banisters where it lolled for a second or two, its eyes staring accusingly. The man watched it go without interest and made no effort to see exactly where it had landed. But after a few minutes some satisfaction showed on his face at the idea of the case unpacking itself with a minimum of help from himself. The stuff had been wedged snug and tight inside for long enough.

While it was still early in the afternoon some of the younger children on the stair came back from school. An eight-year-old girl whose family lived below the Gregsons came in first and picked up the head which was lying a few steps above her own landing. Its yellow hair, which was not unlike her own, fascinated her. But its eyes were terribly hard, and it was no surprise when she unscrewed the neck and found the sharp needles inside. Then she looked up and saw the man with the things strewed around him, and went on up to join him. By this time he had managed to make himself fairly comfortable. He had folded his raincoat under him and undone both his shoelaces. He had looked ready to sleep, but when the little girl appeared he braced up and rummaged about in the case until he found a small, flower-bordered mirror. "How about that?" he asked. The girl squatted down excitedly. She knew by the rummaging hands and the way the stuff was spilled around that this was a free-for-all. There was a feeling of careless, bursting plenty about the scene, too good to last. She put the mirror quickly aside and began to go through the things herself— not rummaging, but picking about with a sharp, birdlike eagerness. Down below a door banged and the girl sprang to her feet. "Up here!" she called, leaning over.

"Come on!" she shouted again to the slow boy who was coming up, trailing a small sister behind him. Following after, more cautiously, came an older girl carrying a schoolcase. Now the voice at the top sounded angry that they should still be dragging their feet up, step by step, when just above them was this lavish stuff spilled out ready for the taking. Anxious and contemptuous, she looked down at them—at the same time waving them on with fierce and generous gestures of her hands which were already full of objects to tempt them, should they dare to slacken pace.

But soon they were squatting round the case. One of the frail combs had already snapped and the yellow-haired girl held it up in disgust to display the gap. She picked up another—a stronger one which raked harshly against her scalp but was still intact when she drew it out. This one she put into the pocket of her blazer. There was no need to ask if she could have it. The man had seemed to enjoy the snapping in a mild sort of way, just as he had seemed indifferent to the crunch of the mirror under his heel when he shifted his foot. The boy was more discriminating than the others, picking up objects, studying them critically and laying them carefully aside until he came on what he wanted. The oldest girl was an unashamed rummager, and the smallest child sat on the step below them, scrubbing it with a yellow toothbrush and making small, circular patches of paler grey on the stone.

The youngest son of the house who worked in an Insurance office came home in the middle of the afternoon. And he was smiling to himself. His mother stared at him hard as he came into the kitchen. In fact she never took her eyes off him, not even while she cracked an egg against the side of a bowl.

"Well, you've got quite a party going on out there," he said. "When did he arrive?"

"I can't believe it!" cried the woman, digging her thumbs into the cracked shell and letting the egg fall into the bowl, still staring at him. But she believed him all right.

"Go and see for yourself," said the boy. "You might get some of the pickings."

"Pickings?"

"Yes. He's handing stuff out. Brushes and bottles and tin-openers. Go and have a look before it's all bashed about."

But she could no more look out than fly to the moon. She could scarcely even bring herself to imagine the awful wastage going on there outside her door—the things flung about anyhow, to be simply picked up for nothing by anyone who happened to be around. Such a disregard of objects made her sick, she said, as well as the sloppiness, the untidiness of it all.

"Wait till some of the men find him," she said. "What else had he in that case?"

"Isn't it his own stuff to do what he likes with?" said her son.

The woman made a sound of contempt. Then she asked again: "What else had he?"

"Oh . . . handcream—Janet's smeared in it up to the elbows—shoe-brushes, coat-hangers, scarves. There were a few pens and pencils. And a shoe!" he laughed suddenly.

"A shoe?"

210

"Yes, his own shoe. I hope somebody doesn't nab that—or he'll be here all night."

"Oh, I see." His mother pondered on this item with satisfaction. "So he's taken his boots off now, has he? Do you know, your brother wouldn't have it the man was a tramp—wouldn't hear a word of it. Oh no, not a tramp at all, but a gentleman with a suitcase! Wait till he sees him with his boots off and wait till he sees what he's doing with the stuff in that case! It'll be a different story then. Removing his boots! Have you ever heard of a tramp who *didn't* remove his boots sooner or later?"

"It's not boots," said the young man. "He's wearing shoes. Not unlike my own, as a matter of fact. And I should say they would cost a bit too." As he spoke he ran his eyes down his tie, down the length of his narrow trousers to his slim, shining shoes. "And I didn't say both shoes. He had only one off when I saw him."

The woman now glared at her youngest son. It was beyond the wildest stretch of imagination to see him as a tramp, but that wasn't to say he might not become a waster of goods—the kind of person who scattered valuable stuff around for the sheer love of it —who wasn't beyond breaking and bashing and spilling. Not a tramp, of course, but a vandal. She watched all his moves until he went out again, and then she watched the door and tried to visualise what was beyond it.

By five o'clock the room seemed overcrowded, though there were only four persons in it. The schoolgirl daughter was home and a neighbour from above had looked in to show them an advertisement for a new kind of stuff which removed old paint from woodwork as easily as it had gone on in the first place. Neither she nor the others in the room had any intention of removing paint from any part of the building.

"What are you going to do about him?" said the neighbour after a bit, the scrap of paper with the advertisement floating, unheeded, to the floor.

"Why ask me?" said the other woman. "Why ask me more than anyone else?"

"Well, it's just how he's placed himself, isn't it?" said the neighbour. "Right outside your door."

"That's true," said the schoolgirl. "Where he's sitting—you could say he actually belongs to us." She had not lingered on the stair with the younger crowd, though tempted by certain shampoo

211

sachets scattered about.

"I haven't had time to take very much notice, I'm afraid," said Martha who had got to her feet and was rearranging all the things in front of her on the table, as though making a move in some game with a squared-off board.

"You could always phone," said the other woman. She did not say where.

"My oldest boy will soon deal with him," said Martha. She made no mention of the fact that he had already identified himself with vagrants of all kinds—might already be on the road himself for all she knew.

"That's right enough, he really *is* ours," said the daughter again with some satisfaction, and taking a cracking bite out of an apple.

But evidently the man had not felt he belonged to any of them—neither the stair nor the town, and not long after the two young men came home again, he made off, leaving behind him some teeth from the broken comb, a circle of crumbs and a paper bag. The children had picked the rest of the place quite clear. It seemed that he wanted nothing more to do with the stuff still left to him. They could tell that when they looked down from the window and saw him swinging the half-empty case, tilted like an instrument. He was going to the river.

"He's going to dump it," said Martha Gregson again. She never moved from the window, and some time later he appeared again.

"Well, does *that* answer your question?" she said, pointing down triumphantly. The others gathered round. Nobody could remember having asked a question, so she got no immediate answer.

"Does *that* answer your question?" she repeated angrily. The man was passing directly below them now. His hands were free. He looked too fat, too warm, too tired to be called a free man. Yet the women felt that he had escaped. He walked slowly with a rolling gait, gently stroking the air with his two big arms like a bather intent only on keeping himself afloat.

"I can think of lots of questions I might *ask*, but I can't see there's been any answered in the last few minutes," said the eldest son. "Which one exactly were you thinking of?"

"We were discussing a tramp and a traveller," said his mother.

"That's right. I remember. And we discovered they have a lot in common. For example, they both of them walk and sit on the

212

job."

"That may be, but as you said yourself, they don't both go in for selling things. Tramps have nothing to sell. Didn't you say that?"

"I did."

"*Now* is he a tramp?" Martha darted her head towards the man who was moving slowly out of sight. Long, blue shadows now barred the way behind him.

"Why should he be?"

"Can't you see he's got rid of his stuff? Dumped it, or given it all away! He's a regular tramp now all right. Taking his boots off!"

"Shoes," murmured a voice.

"All right, he has nothing to sell. So he could be anything," said the older son. "A tramp, a traveller without a case. He could be a tourist if he wanted to."

"Oh, just let him *be*," said the schoolgirl. She was tired of the man, seeing he had never really belonged to them at all.

The woman slammed the window down.

213

CAMERA

"RELAX . . . relax!" Paxton hissed. There was a whirring and a soft clicking from his cine-camera and then a lighter, sharper click of impatience from his own lips. It could have made a splendid picture—their elderly visitor moving in the full blaze of the sun along a path striped with deep blue shadows past a border of magnificent red and purple tulips. But there was a stiffness about the man, an awareness of the camera that seemed to ruin the whole effect.

"Just be natural," called Paxton's wife in a more kindly voice from the doorway of the house. "Don't bother about us. Just try to be perfectly easy and natural!"

But by this time he had actually tripped over one of the broader bars of shadow while staring stage-struck at his own feet. The heavy book he was carrying hit two tall tulips, scattering the petals of one and breaking the neck of the other so that it leant dismally sideways against the heads of its neighbours. The whole scene was hopelessly unnatural. Mr. Fendell, as a moving object for the camera, was not a success.

The Paxtons were still at the experimenting stage. They had already discovered that simple, slow-moving objects were not as easy to come by as some people might imagine. No new thing had moved around their place for some time now, and there was a limit to the number of times they could take one another hanging out clothes, washing down the car or jerking weeds out of the front garden with exaggerated enthusiasm. The children instead of bouncing big, brightly-coloured balls around the flowerbeds had taken to games in which they crouched for hours absolutely still except for slight movements of the fingers and lips. So it turned out that Fendell, an elderly friend of the family, though uninvited, was welcomed when he moved slowly into view across the static landscape.

The welcome, however, did not include anything but the shortest possible exchange of news and opinions. Paxton had never put a high value on ordinary conversation, and lately there had been no need to bother about it at all. He was able now to remove himself to some distance from any moving group or object and the steady whirring of his camera was a far more satisfactory means of communication than any he had tried before. It was utterly mechanical, one-sided and remote. It ended when and where he wanted it to end with a devastatingly final and cruel click. It was also fantastically expensive. Perhaps it was this that made Mr Fendell, an austere man, so self-conscious in everything he did. As he went through his motions he seemed to hear the cash clicking away down the drain and the banknotes shuttling through in a never-ending film of enormous extravagance. Like some bungling amateur actor he felt that his own gestures were simply not worth the money.

Now for about the tenth time since his arrival that morning he tottered down the garden path baring his teeth in a smile of appalling embarrassment as he went past the camera.

"No, no—don't smile!" shouted Paxton. "What we want is something perfectly natural. Just be yourself! Never mind me!" The trouble was that their guest had certain preconceived notions about what was natural and what wasn't. He seemed to have got it into his head, for example, that one of the most natural activities for a human being was to play with children. But even during their short bursts of activity between static games, something desperate in his approach to play affected the two of them. Balls dropped listlessly from their hands and rolled slowly, slowly away into the bushes. The wheels of their tricycles automatically slowed down and then stopped spinning altogether. Everything would become immobile and silent except for the menacing whir and click a few yards away; while Fendell, left bending unnaturally, almost abjectly over the children, made up a group which would have been poor even as a still and was completely hopeless as a movie. Then there was plant-life. Human beings, Fendell seemed to infer, were always natural when involved

215

with plants. As though he had not already done enough damage, he bent over the flowerbed and began timidly but deftly to snap through the tulip stalks. The bed was half bare and he was holding a good-sized bouquet before Paxton's wife broke through her paralysis and came running over with a shriek to stop him. Everything he did was exaggerated. When asked simply to pause at the front door and look up with a natural show of interest at the ornamentation above it, he pointed with a shaking finger at the roof. This awkward gesture made the whole building appear doomed, as though crumbling to its very foundations; and his little trick of waving casually over the wall to people who weren't there was positively eerie.

Nevertheless he was kept going the whole day. Although not allowed to pick any more flowers, he weeded, raked the garden path and went back and forth from the greenhouse carrying heavy pots of flowering shrubs. He beckoned to the glowering children, pointed to passing planes, and occasionally with a despairing gesture which swept the whole sky from horizon to horizon, he would follow the flight of birds as though begging to be set free from solid earth. He had his dramatic moments but on the whole he was a severe strain on the Paxtons' patience. They had done everything they could think of to make him film-worthy. There was even a special early lunch laid on for him in the garden so that Paxton could shoot him sitting by himself at a small table under a tree—thus getting the benefit of the branches swaying in the background and in the foreground Fendell's hands nervously sawing away at a slice of steak.

But the spring wind, as well as bringing splendid movement into the picture, had brought a blue tinge to Fendell's cheeks. His look of cringing discomfort had certainly spoiled the entire lay-out, and even Mrs Paxton's smiling entrance on the scene carrying a plate of homemade ice-cream did nothing to bring the thing back to life. By four o'clock, having painted part of the Paxtons' new fence and given one or two touches of comic relief to the film with the spots of lime-green paint on his trousers, he was directed to the garden seat in the arbour where he poured out tea for himself, lifting cup after cup to his lips with the palsied precision of a fainting man. At four-twenty he was on his feet loading a wheelbarrow with hedge clippings and steering it slowly along past the newly-painted fence because the circles and lines of the scarlet barrow made an unusually good composition set against the vertical green bars of wood.

It was growing late and long shadows were climbing the walls of the house. The wind had gone down and in the garden everything was very still except for the two men—the one bending, circling, picking ceaselessly like some mechanical toy with a tight-wound key in its back; the other fixed in his one gesture—holding the little box close to his eyes and occasionally backing away or moving forward rigidly along one straight line. There was time for only a few more shots.

"What about one on the steps?" Paxton shouted suddenly. "One more before we go in. A very simple one—you could just come down slowly for a last look at the garden. That's right—go right up to the door and then come down looking round you in a perfectly natural way!"

Without a word the older man mounted the front door steps, turned at the top and, not pausing for an instant, began to come down again staring about him with a look of hectic, terrifying interest. On the third step something new seemed to occur to him. He gasped, threw up one hand as though commanding silence, then slowly, making a perfect spinning turn, he keeled over heavily towards the earth and lay—his head on the grass edge of the path, his legs up on the steps in a splendidly relaxed position, like a man who has been told to keep his feet up as much as possible for the sake of his health. Paxton's camera went on whirring and clicking for several moments. Then he came over and looked down at Fendell, and a twitch of annoyance crossed his face. He bent and went through the conventional movements of feeling the old boy's chest, but he could tell by just looking at him that his heart had stopped. He went past him up the steps and into the house where his wife was just bringing the meal through to the dining-room.

"Isn't Mr Fendell coming in for his supper?" she said.

"He's lying out there on the grass," said Paxton shortly.

Moodily he began to edge the sausages from the serving-dish onto two plates. The other empty plate he placed on the bottom ledge of the small trolley-table beside him.

"Did he manage to relax in the end?" his wife went on. Paxton topped half a sausage with a cap of tomato and paused for a moment before putting it in his mouth.

"Oh yes, he relaxed all right!" The twitch of disapproval, of irritation passed over his face again. "The trouble about old Fendell, as I suppose you've noticed, is simply that he *overdoes* everything—every single thing's exaggerated! I'd say, in fact, that he went utterly beyond the limit in everything. That's what makes him look so unnatural even when he *is* relaxed."

"I suppose so," said his wife without much interest. She stretched over and touched the bowl of tulips in the middle of the table. She had done the best she could for them but Fendell had broken the stalks so awkwardly—long ones and short ones together—that they stuck out at all angles.

"Yes, it's amazing, isn't it," she said with a resigned sigh, "how he's managed to make even the *flowers* look freakish?"

A Collection of Bones

c. 2800 ? (+)

27
3
206
230

40
7
280
2800